UNLIKELY PARTNERS

As if Cal conjured her up out of his imagination, Lily came bustling back out of the house with a burlap bag in her hand. She held it out to Toby.

"This should be enough for tonight and for breakfast in the morning. I'll cook you both a proper meal as soon as you get back."

Toby accepted her offering. "I'll keep an eye on young Wade for you, ma'am."

"I appreciate that, Mr. Thacker," Lily said. "I worry about him out there by himself. He means well, but he's too young to carry so much responsibility on his shoulders."

She shot Cal a knowing look, which closely echoed the one Toby had on his face. He'd heard enough on the subject of young Wade for one day. On the other hand, he wasn't about to let them know that their comments had scored a direct hit.

"Well, Toby, enjoy yourself." Then he tipped his hat toward Lily, knowing the gesture was more likely to make her mad than impress her with his good manners. "You can just give a holler when dinner is ready."

He could hear her sputtering with indignation as he walked toward the barn. For the first time all day, he felt like smiling.

Dear Romance Readers,

In July of 1999, we launched the Ballad line with four new series, and each month we present both new and continuing stories set everywhere from medieval England to the American West—the kind of passionate, romantic stories you love best, written by the most gifted authors. At the back of each book, we tell you when you can find subsequent books in the series that have captured your heart.

Premiering this month is **Light a Single Candle**, the first in the dramatic new trilogy *The MacInness Legacy*. Written by sisters Julie and Sandy Moffett, the series is about three long-separated sisters who discover their heritage includes witchcraft. Talented newcomer Pat Pritchard is next, with the first in a pair of books about two men whose lives are changed by a game of poker. Meet the first of the delectable *Gamblers* in **Luck of the Draw.**

Reader favorite Kathryn Fox returns with another of her *Men of Honor* in **The Seduction** in which an intrepid young reporter looking for scandal in gold-rush territory finds passion instead. Finally, beloved author Jo Ann Ferguson introduces a heartwarming new series called *Haven*. In **Twice Blessed**, when an orphan train stops in this small Indiana town, a shopkeeper becomes an instant "mother"—but when she meets a widowed father new to town, she dreams of becoming a wife.

There's romance, passion, adventure to spare. Why not read them all? Enjoy!

Kate Duffy
Editorial Director

The Gamblers

LUCK OF
THE DRAW

Pat Pritchard

ZEBRA BOOKS
Kensington Publishing Corp.
http://www.kensingtonbooks.com

ZEBRA BOOKS are published by

Kensington Publishing Corp.
850 Third Avenue
New York, NY 10022

All Kensington titles, imprints, and distributed lines are
available at special quantity discounts for bulk purchases for
sales promotion, premiums, fund-raising, educational or in-
stitutional use.

Special book excerpts or customized printings can also be
created to fit specific needs. For details, write or phone the
office of the Kensington Special Sales Manager: Kensington
Publishing Corp., 850 Third Avenue, New York, NY 10022.
Attn. Special Sales Department. Phone: 1-800-221-2647.

Zebra and the Z logo Reg. U.S. Pat. & TM Off.

First Printing: March 2002
10 9 8 7 6 5 4 3 2 1

Printed in the United States of America

To my good friends Dave and Joanne Gunderson.
Thanks for always being there for me.

One

If nothing else, the pair of ladies in front of him promised to make Cal's evening worthwhile. He didn't smile or acknowledge their presence in any way, but that didn't mean he failed to appreciate their appearance. On the contrary, together they could make his efforts finally pay off in a big way.

He tossed two of their companions down on the table. "I'll take two."

The dealer slid two more cards in his direction. With years of practice, Cal hid his pleasure at seeing that another of the ladies had decided to pay him a visit and had brought along a second ten to match the one he already had. A full house should be enough to capture the sizable pot that was piling up in the center of the table.

It had been a long time since the best cards had seen fit to come his way. He and his friend were just this side of going hungry. Even one good night at the tables could make a difference in their fortunes. But now was not the time to be counting money he hadn't yet won.

From the frown on his face, the cowhand was wondering how far the cards he held would carry him. Finally, with a look of disgust, he tossed his hand face-down on the table and stood up.

"I'm going to quit while I have enough money to

buy me a bottle." He picked up his remaining few chips and headed for the bar.

Cal always admired a man who had the sense to walk away when Lady Luck wasn't with him for the night. He glanced around the table. There weren't as many players now as there had been an hour ago. He fully expected most of the rest to quit sometime soon. The cards weren't being generous tonight.

Only Cal and the dark-eyed youngster sitting across from him had consistently won more than they lost. Eventually, it would come down to the two of them testing their luck to see who the gods were favoring for the night.

Cal raised the bet. Just as he'd expected, of the three remaining players, only the one held onto his cards and met the bet. Then he raised it again himself. Interesting.

Cal looked at the three ladies again. They were definitely women of expensive tastes. To keep them happy, he would have to be willing to spend a fair amount of money.

He reached for his chips. He hesitated long enough to make his one remaining opponent look up. "Raise you a hundred."

For a fraction of a second, the stranger seemed to pale, but then he tossed in his last chips without a word. It was enough to raise the cost of staying in yet again.

Was Lady Luck flirting with them both? Cal was feeling damn good about his cards. Besides, if he doubted the ladies, they could very well take it as an insult and turn on him. He didn't think of himself as superstitious, just cautious. He tossed out his chips, adding a few to keep the game interesting.

His opponent looked disappointed but determined. Cal knew what it felt like to be backed into a corner, where the difference between eating and going hungry was in the turn of a card. Understanding the man didn't translate as sympathy. On the contrary, that little slip in letting his true feelings show through made it that much easier to come away the victor.

The youngster reached inside his jacket pocket and drew out a few bills folded together. He stared at the money for a few seconds and then signaled the dealer to change them for chips. It took ammunition to continue the fight for control of the table. That done, he met Cal's bet and once again raised the bet.

A small crowd was starting to gather around the table as word spread that the two of them were playing a high-stakes game. The men who surrounded the game spoke in hushed voices, well aware that the two players wouldn't appreciate any distractions.

Cal made a point of ignoring his own dwindling stack of chips. If things went on like this for much longer, he could very well end up sleeping in a field somewhere. It wouldn't be the first time, but he'd grown fond of clean sheets and quality hotels.

He tossed in enough chips to meet the bet and then, after only the slightest of hesitations, added a few more for good measure. The crowd was several people deep now, blocking out the noise from the rest of the saloon. The world had narrowed down to the few feet of table between them.

"I seem to be a bit short." The stranger held onto his cards, though. "I assume you'd accept my signed promise for the rest." His voice cracked a bit, causing a few folks to snicker.

Cal ignored both the boy's nervousness and the spectators' bad manners while he considered the risks. The winnings already on the table would hold him and Toby for a good while, even if the man failed to pay off the debt. He nodded and watched the man scribble a note on the back of a paper he'd pulled out of his pocket. He tossed it onto the pile in the middle of the table.

"I call."

Cal spread out his cards on the table, revealing his three lovely ladies and the two tens. The other man neatly laid down his own—three jacks and a pair of nines. With a surprising amount of dignity for one so young, he stood up and offered his hand to Cal.

"It has been a pleasure, sir." Without a backward glance, he walked away, the crowd parting before him as he disappeared into the night.

While the crowd dispersed, Cal took care of the business of scooping up his winnings and having the chips exchanged for cash. He considered it bad luck to count his winnings while still in the saloon, so he tucked the money into his wallet and the paper into his shirt pocket.

He tossed the dealer a tip and bought himself a good cigar and a drink. He knew he should head directly for the stable, where Toby was waiting for him. Instead, he leaned his back against the bar and took a deep draw off the cigar, pleased with himself and the world in general.

Lady Luck was fickle, to be sure, but when she chose you for her partner, life was good.

Cal whistled as he walked along the street, feeling better than fine. He'd stayed at the saloon longer than he meant to, but the cigars had been good and the whiskey even better. Then there was the time he'd spent upstairs with the very talented Mary—or maybe it was Marie, not that her name mattered. All that was important was that she'd plied her trade with a great deal of enthusiasm—a perfect ending to the day.

Toby would be mad that Cal had kept him waiting, but he'd get over it the minute he saw the tidy pile of bills in Cal's wallet. They'd have enough to keep them in hot meals and warm beds for a month or more. He wouldn't like the promissory note. If they were ever going to collect on it, they'd have to stick around for a while, and neither of them was much on staying in one place for long.

But hell, he was feeling generous. Maybe he'd just tear up the note. He wasn't greedy. The boy would have learned a lesson about risking more than he could afford to lose, but it wouldn't cost him as much as it could have.

Cal stopped at the end of the sidewalk to finish off his cigar. He was almost to the stable and didn't want to waste any of the best smoke he'd had in months. Only a fool took fire into a building full of hay and straw.

He looked up at the sky and admired the number of stars he could see. This time of night was always his favorite, when most everyone else had sought out their beds. He would join them soon, but he always took a minute or two to enjoy having the night to himself.

The sound of a muffled footstep disturbed his reverie, alerting him to the fact that he wasn't as alone as he had thought. He waited to see if he heard the sound again, trying to tell which direction it had come from.

When the noise came again, it had company. Three, maybe four, men came charging out from between the buildings, headed straight for him. He went for his gun, but they were on top of him before he could get it clear of the holster. He went down in a flurry of kicks and punches. Although he got in a few solid hits himself, he was no match against the combined strength of several determined men. Who was mad at him this time?

"Get his wallet, damn it!"

His winnings! The bastards were after his hard-won money. He bellowed for help, but knew that it was

unlikely to come in time, if at all. Cal kicked out at
the nearest man, buckling his knee with the force of
the blow. His assailant muttered a few choice curses
before returning the favor with interest.

Toby's going to kill me if I survive this, was Cal's
last thought before a darkness blacker than night
washed over him.

Painless oblivion didn't last for long. He didn't want
to wake up, despite the insistent voice he recognized
as Toby's telling him to. Once he opened his eyes, he'd
know just how much he hurt. Damn, he hated pain,
but Toby wouldn't give up.

Hell, no. He wouldn't want Cal to miss one second
of the agony. It hurt to breathe, warning him that a
few ribs were cracked or worse. Then there was the
hammer pounding on his brain.

"Damn it, Cal, open those eyes of yours. I know
you can hear me."

Cal did his best to comply, coaxing his reluctant
eyes to flicker open. Although the worry on Toby's
face was gratifying, even the dim light of the kerosene
lantern was too bright for comfort. He took a shuddering breath and tried again.

"I take it I'm alive." His effort to smile was less
than successful, due in large part to the fact his lip was
split and swollen.

"Barely." Toby managed to sound both relieved and
mad at the same time.

Some things never changed. His friend spent most
of his time warning Cal that he was on the path to
ruination. He was right, of course, but that didn't mean
that Cal wanted to hear about it all the time. He struggled to sit up. Toby's gentle assistance belied the constant grumbling about Cal's lack of good sense.

Once he was propped up against a pile of hay, Toby

held a canteen up to Cal's mouth. The water stung his lip and tasted of dust and blood. He spit it out and tried again. This time, the cool liquid felt good sliding down his throat.

When he signaled that he'd had enough, Toby rocked back on his heels to get a better look at him. His friend shook his head in disgust. "What the hell did you do to make someone this mad?"

His swollen mouth made it hard to talk, but he knew Toby wouldn't rest until he pried every dismal detail from Cal. "Nothing that I know of." He remembered someone saying something about his wallet.

"Shit! They were after the money." He ignored the pain in his ribs as he tried to reach for his wallet. He knew it was gone before his hand touched the empty pocket. "Sons of bitches stole my winnings."

Toby looked thoroughly disgusted. "You won to-night and stayed late to celebrate." It wasn't a question. "I don't suppose you managed to hide any of it before they got to you."

Cal tried for sympathy. "I don't remember much. They knocked me in the head."

It didn't work. Toby shook his head. "Hell, they're lucky they didn't break their hands on that rock-hard skull of yours. Wouldn't do you much harm either, seeing as how it wasn't good for much to begin with." With little regard for Cal's comfort, he started patting down Cal's pants pockets and then started on his shirt.

When he pulled out a piece of paper, Cal remembered the boy's IOU. At least it was something.

"I took an IOU from a man right after I took his last dollar. That ought to be worth something when we collect on it. At least we won't be stone broke."

"We might as well be." His friend didn't even bother to ask how much the IOU was for but did ask the obvious questions. "Who is he and where does he live?"

Cal didn't bother to answer. Toby already knew.

"You took an IOU from a stranger?" Toby spit on the ground, coming within inches of Cal's legs. "Haven't I taught you better than to mix cards and drink? What the hell good is a piece of paper when you don't know where the man is?"

His head about to explode, Cal tried not to whimper. He'd give his last chip for some sleep, even if it was in a pile of hay instead of the hotel across the street. At last Toby ran out of things to cuss about and stretched out beside him, giving Cal some much-needed quiet.

Not that he was out of the woods yet. Toby knew full well that he'd have tomorrow to work Cal over some more. And the day after that. They were both aware that if he hurt now, it would be worse in the morning. He'd face Toby's anger when the time came, but for now he gave himself over to the blessed release of sleep.

"Hell, if I'd known you were sleeping with your horses, I'd have charged more. I don't much mind seeing to the needs of the animals, but I surely do hate cleaning up after sorry-looking drunks."

The comments were accompanied by raucous laughter. If Cal could have moved fast, he'd have taught the stable owner some manners. He pried open one eye and then the other. When he got a good look at his tormentor, he decided to laugh along with him. The man had arms like tree trunks, meaning he didn't just own the stable. He was the blacksmith as well. Even on his best day, Cal couldn't have taken him on, and this sure as hell wasn't his best day.

His ribs immediately reminded him not to make any sudden moves. Ignoring the stabbing pain, he struggled to his feet. He wondered where Toby had gone, but he wasn't going to worry about anything until he managed to clear the fog out of his head.

"Where's the pump?"

"You can use the one out back. When you're ready for it, I've got some coffee made."

The stuff was probably strong enough to melt iron, but it still sounded like heaven. "I owe you."

"Naw, don't worry about it. I've been in the same shape myself a time or two." The blacksmith was still chuckling as he disappeared into a nearby stall.

Cal took a cautious step and then another one. Everything seemed to be in working order, more or less. Carrying his saddlebags, he wended his way to the back door of the stable. Doing his best to brace his aching side, he reached for the pump handle. Each stroke hurt, but the water was blessedly cool and tasted like heaven to his parched mouth and throat.

Cupping his hands, he splashed the water on his arms and chest and then held his head under the running water. The cool flow did much to ease the pain centered right between his eyes. He almost felt alive again. Using his dirty shirt as a towel, he wiped off the water and yesterday's sweat.

"Feeling better?"

Ignoring Toby for the moment, Cal pulled his last clean shirt out of the saddlebags and tried to put it on. Try as he might, he couldn't manage it without help. Without comment, Toby slipped it up onto Cal's shoulders and then made a move to button it for him.

"I can do that myself." Even that hurt, but he would have died before admitting it. A man had to have some pride. When he was done, he went in search of the blacksmith's coffeepot. He poured himself a cup and then one for Toby. It was a struggle to keep the first few swallows from coming right back up. He waited a minute or two before trying again.

He noticed that Toby was looking like the cat that got the canary. His friend wasn't quite smirking, but it was obvious that he was enjoying himself, and no doubt at Cal's expense. He was probably waiting for Cal to feel more like himself, so that Cal could get the full effect of whatever bad news he was about to impart.

Toby finished off his coffee and held out his cup for some more. While Cal poured, Toby announced, "Heard tell one of them saloon gals lit out last night without any warning. Seems one of her customers was bragging about the amount of money he won in a poker game before coming upstairs to celebrate with her."

Toby got what he wanted. Cal was instantly mad at the world. "Hellfire and damnation. Her name wouldn't be Mary by any chance?"

"It would." Toby's smile gleamed in his dark face.

"And she probably had a man friend who wasn't too particular how he earned his money."

"That's the story, all right. Seems his brothers are still hanging around town, but he's nowhere to be seen. I got a look at a couple of them. One of them is limping and another's sporting a beauty of a black eye."

Cal leaned against the stable wall. "Is that true or are you just telling me that to make me feel better?"

"No, they're sure enough right down the street."

Cal tossed the rest of his coffee on the ground. Feeling energized, he started for the door. "Come on. We'll find the sheriff. If we get the brothers thrown in jail, maybe the thieving bastard will bring our money back."

"The sheriff is easy to find. He's the one with the limp. The deputy has the black eye." No longer able to hold back, Toby's rich, deep laughter rang out.

Not for the first time, Cal wondered why he kept Toby around. Truth was, he could count the number of men he'd trust to cover his back on one hand with several fingers left over. Toby was one of them. Maybe the only one.

"Are you through having fun at my expense? Besides, I'm not the only one who's going to go hungry if we don't find a stake of some kind."

To give his friend credit, Toby did try to stop laughing, just not very successfully. Between chuckles, he did manage to tell Cal, "The blacksmith back there says he'll pay for lunch if we give him a hand cleaning out the stalls."

Cal couldn't believe the irony of it all. Last night, he had all kinds of ideas how he'd be spending today. None of them included shoveling shit just for enough to eat. Hell, who said the universe didn't have a sense of humor?

Thoroughly disgusted with everything, he rolled up his sleeves and picked up a nearby pitchfork. "I don't suppose you could have told me that before I put on my clean shirt."

That set Toby off again, but Cal couldn't blame him. Side by side, they started in on the closest stalls.

It was several hours later when it finally occurred to Cal to take a closer look at the IOU that Toby had put in his packs. He pulled it out and stepped out in the sunshine to get a better look at it. If the signature was legible, maybe someone in town would know where the young rancher could be found.

The day was warm. Dust hung in the air, stirred up by the last in a long line of wagons passing through town. More fools heading west, convinced that life will be better over the next rise. Stupid bastards. He'd been born in California and didn't give a damn if he ever saw the place again.

Of course, he wasn't feeling so damn smart himself right now. If he'd left the saloon when he was supposed

to, there would have been too many witnesses to risk
robbing him right out on the street. Once in the stable,
he and Toby could have held them off. And it was
unlikely that the blacksmith, who lived above the stable, would have let their call for help go unanswered.

All of it was just blind bad luck. And now he was
going to pass some of it along to the hapless fool who
gave him the IOU. Cal unfolded the piece of paper and
began to read.

"What the hell?"

Toby chose that moment to come walking out of the
stable. When he saw what Cal was looking at, he asked,
"What's the matter? Did you take another IOU from
George Washington himself?"

Out of habit, Cal snarled back, "I told you to shut
up about that. That happened once—ten years ago."

Even Toby could tell his heart wasn't in it. "Seriously, Cal, what's wrong?"

"That stupid son of a bitch! What the hell am I
supposed to do with this?" He shoved the paper at
Toby and stalked off. He needed time to cool off before
he punched someone.

Toby was hot on his heels. "I take it you didn't read
this last night."

"Hell no, I didn't read it last night. We were in the
middle of a poker game. Who would have thought he'd
be so damn stupid? I mean, who ever heard of signing
your ranch over to a total stranger?"

"He didn't exactly sign the ranch over to you, you
know. Just his half."

"Same damn thing. Besides, that's not the problem.
We need money now, not when he manages to sell his
herd." He gave a rock a satisfying kick, sending it flying through the air. "Hell, you and I both know that
could take weeks, maybe months. What are we supposed to do until then?"

"Well, the blacksmith seems happy with our work. Maybe we could stay on here."

Cal knew full well that Toby wasn't serious. It still made him mad. "I'm not shoveling out stalls for a living. I'm a gambler, not a stable hand."

"True enough, but you're not likely to get into a game with no money to put down."

Cal glared at his friend. "Quit being the voice of reason. I'm in no mood for it."

"I figured one of us should be reasonable, and it sure isn't you."

Toby walked along beside him for a few minutes, giving Cal the chance to simmer down. After a bit, he spoke up. "Someone's got to know where this Wade McCord's ranch is. Why don't we ride out there and get the lay of the land, so to speak?"

Cal turned back toward the stable as he gave the matter some thought. He had to agree that their choices were few and far between.

There was no way in hell he'd risk another poker game in this town, and truth was, they didn't have enough money or supplies to get to the next one. If the blacksmith could point them in the right direction, it wouldn't hurt to check the place out. Maybe McCord really did have the money. If not, there had to be something worth selling on the ranch—even the ranch itself.

"Let's go talk to the blacksmith."

Lily stood at the window and watched her brother-in-law ride his horse at a full gallop over the creek and out of sight. Sighing, she turned her attention back to the last of the breakfast dishes.

Something was bothering Wade, but she had no idea what it could be. Ever since he'd come back from town, he'd been jumpier than a cat, constantly watching the horizon. She'd asked him more than once if something was wrong, but he either pretended not to hear her or else just walked away without answering.

She would put up with his foul mood one more day, she decided. After that, he'd better shape up. She had problems enough without his adding to them with a rotten attitude.

Meanwhile, she had laundry to finish and bread to bake, neither of which held any appeal for her at the moment. Her back was still aching from weeding the garden yesterday, not that it mattered one bit. The work had to be done regardless of how she felt.

Which brought her back to worrying about Wade. The ranch was a burden to them both—maybe one too large for them to bear. There was a limit to what one woman and an eighteen-year-old boy could do. It had been different when there had been three of them to share the work and the dreams.

The small graveyard over near the creek drew her eye. She knew Thadeus hadn't meant to die. No one ever did, but sometimes he seemed to have lacked just plain good sense. The horse that killed him had already stomped two other riders really badly. But Thad wouldn't have it any other way but to prove himself more of a man than they were.

Now she and Wade were alone, a young widow and an even younger brother-in-law, trying to scrape enough money together to make the next mortgage payment. With luck and hard work, they stood a fair chance of doing so, but if anything else went wrong, the two of them could very well end up homeless and broke.

Instead of just broke.

She thought of the money sitting in the bank. It amounted to a little over half of what they needed. If the herd made it to market safely, they'd have the rest and enough left over to carry them through until next year.

If she were the only one, she would have accepted the offer Upton Boone had made and sold out months ago. But Wade was so intent on filling his older brother's shoes that he wouldn't even consider that they might both be better off without the ranch and its mortgage hanging over them.

Telling herself that nothing would get finished if she didn't get busy, she went outside where Wade had set up the wash tub for her. She picked Wade's shirts out of the pile and began scrubbing them clean. Laundry wasn't her favorite job, but the monotonous routine served to soothe her jangled nerves.

She hummed as she worked, taking comfort from an old hymn. One of her favorite memories from her childhood was her mother singing the same song as she worked around the house, no matter where they were living. Her father had the wanderlust something powerful, but her mother had seemed content to follow him each time he'd felt the need to move on.

Lily was the only one who resented being constantly uprooted. Perhaps her mother's obligation was to do as her husband wished, but it was their children who had suffered in some ways. Lily had sworn to put down roots the first opportunity she had. No children of hers would ever have to wonder how long they'd sleep under the same roof.

She had to admit, though, that after twenty-five years of marriage, her parents had still been deeply in love. She used to try to picture herself and Thad that far along in their marriage, but the image never seemed to be quite right. She'd loved Thad, but maybe not enough. She quickly pushed that traitorous thought aside. He'd been her husband and he'd done his best.

He was different from her father, that was all. She had no right to try to twist him to fit some idea of the perfect husband. Especially now that he was dead.

Which brought her right back to . . .

A movement out on the hillside interrupted her thoughts. She straightened up and shaded her eyes in order to see better. Riders were coming in. A surge of near-panic almost sent her running for the house. Wade was well out of hearing, helping their two hands move the cattle to fresh grazing out beyond the creek. He wouldn't be back until close to dark.

It was easy for a woman alone to feel vulnerable, what with folks always passing through the area on their way to Lord knows where. Most were harmless, wanting nothing more than to water their animals at the creek. But some weren't harmless at all, and it wasn't always easy to tell the difference.

Better to be cautious than sorry. She wiped the soap off her hands with her apron and headed back into the house. One of the first things Thad had taught her about ranch life was how to use a rifle. Now that she was alone so much of the time, she kept one loaded just inside the door.

She wasn't sure if the riders had seen her yet, but it wouldn't take them long to realize that the place appeared deserted. With luck, they would water their horses and keep right on going to wherever they were headed. But if they spotted the washtub with the water still warm, they'd know for sure someone was around.

Hiding behind the curtains seemed like such a cowardly way to handle visitors, but Lily wasn't about to make the mistake of assuming they were friendly. She hovered at the edge of the window, watching until they got close enough that they could see her as well. All she could tell for sure was that one of them was dressed all in black, his clothes far too fancy for any man she knew except Upton Boone.

That didn't sit well with her. Whether it was because she didn't trust fancy men or because she didn't trust

Upton Boone was hard to say. The second rider was a
black man, but he rode at the other man's side as an
equal. On the other hand, he was dressed in the same
kind of clothes that Wade and other hardworking men
wore.

The two were an interesting contrast. Both sat their
horses well, and from where she stood, their mounts
looked well cared for. Finally, she moved back out of
sight and prayed for a peaceful encounter. She'd already locked the doors, but if they were determined to
get in, there was always the window. Her rifle might
slow them down, but she couldn't reload fast enough
to stop them if they timed it right.

And as badly as her hands were shaking, chances
were, she wouldn't do them much harm. They didn't
have to know that. Their final approach to the ranch
house took forever. It came almost as a relief when
one of them called out a greeting.

"You in the house, we're here to see Wade McCord."
The voice was anything but friendly.

A sick feeling settled somewhere deep inside her.
There was little doubt in her mind that the two men
outside her door were responsible in some way for
Wade's bad mood. That didn't mean that it was their
fault, just that they were mixed up in it somehow.

Since they had obviously seen her, there was no reason not to answer. Although she wouldn't exactly lie,
she didn't mind skirting the truth a bit. "He's no longer
here."

"Are you expecting him back soon?"

"No." It could be hours, even though she prayed it
wasn't. "I'd be glad to tell him you stopped by, though,
if he does come back sometime."

She thought she heard a muffled curse or two. The
creak of leather didn't sound as if they were turning
to ride away. It was more like the sound of two men

dismounting after a long day's ride. Now she really was trapped.

A new voice spoke up, obviously the other rider. "Ma'am, we've got no choice but to talk to Mr. Wade. We're right sorry if we're causing you to worry."

She risked a quick peek through the window. Although both of them had gotten off their horses, neither had made any move toward the house. That alone made her feel a little more kindly toward the pair, not that she was about to fling open the door and welcome them inside.

"We'd sure appreciate some water for our horses and maybe some hay. They've had a hard ride."

Though it wasn't exactly a question, Lily treated it as if they were asking permission. "Help yourselves. There's hay in the barn. Turn them loose in the corral if you want."

"Much obliged, ma'am."

She waited until she heard the horses move away before she looked out again. The black man was leading them both away, which left his partner standing right out in front in the noonday sun. The heat alone would be enough to make the man angry, but he was glaring at the house as if he hated the sight of it.

"There's a pump around to the side, mister, if you want a drink of water." That was as hospitable as she was feeling.

He seemed content to help himself to the water. Then he wandered out to help his friend with the horses. Finally, the two of them sat down in the scant shade afforded by the barn. There was little doubt that they meant to see Wade, no matter how long it took.

Time dragged on. It appeared likely that her unwanted guests were going to sit and suffer through the heat of the day while waiting for Wade. Other than an occasional trip to the well, the two of them did little

more than doze in the shade. Although she wasn't foolish enough to think that their calm demeanor meant
they were harmless, they hadn't made a single threatening move toward her.

She soon tired of staring out the window at two men
who weren't doing anything. The day would go faster
if she kept busy. To that end, she got out the ingredients
for bread and the week's baking.

As she started the tedious business of kneading the
dough, she couldn't help but wish that her brother-in-
law had trusted her enough to tell her his problem. At
least then she'd know whether the two men were
friends or enemies. For now, all she could do was
wait—and pray.

Two

Cal squinted as he looked up at the afternoon sky. The day had started out bad and hadn't got one damn bit better. He was never much on staying in one place. Sitting on his ass in a pile of dirt with the temperature only two degrees cooler than hell was not helping his mood.

He doubted the woman in the house was having it any better. From the smoke pouring out of the stovepipe, she must be baking bread for someone. That alone would be enough to convince him that she was trying to cover for Wade McCord. Then there was the half-done laundry, mostly made up of men's clothing.

It was always possible that she had taken to wearing trousers and shirts around the ranch like some other women he'd heard tell of, but he didn't believe it for a minute. They'd only caught a brief glimpse of the woman before she barricaded herself in the house, but it was enough to show the clothes would be far too large for her.

No, Wade McCord was somewhere nearby and would undoubtedly be returning sometime soon.

Toby had been stirring around restlessly for the past half hour. Finally, he spoke up. "I can't sit here all day and do nothing. Think she'd take it poorly if I did some chores?"

Cal shrugged. "You could always ask."

Toby got to his feet and dusted off the seat of his pants. If his were that bad, Cal figured his own clothes must look a damn sight worse. Well, they wouldn't get any better as long as he was wallowing in the dirt, trying to find a comfortable position. He stood up and took off his coat and rolled up the sleeves of his shirt. After stowing the coat with the rest of his gear, he followed Toby into the barn.

His friend had already picked up a shovel and was heading into the closest stall. Cal leaned against the rail and watched. He didn't mind doing work for pay or even a hot meal, but damned if he would break his back doing it for free.

"Who do you figure the woman to be? As I remember him, McCord looked too young to have a wife."

Toby paused in his shoveling and gave him a dirty look. "You never said that he was a boy."

"If he's old enough to play poker for high stakes, he's not a boy. I don't rob children." Not ever. He had few scruples, but that was one of his unbreakable rules. Of course, he rarely was around any children, so he hadn't had to deal with the problem.

Cal pulled out his pocketknife and used it to clean his nails. "It's just that this place doesn't look like it was built all that long ago. If she's his wife, he must be older than I thought."

Toby moved on to the next stall before responding. "For all that it looks pretty new, the whole place still looks a bit run down. Like things aren't getting done like they should."

There was something in Toby's voice that caught his attention. "Listen here, don't you go feeling sorry for McCord. The money he owes me is all we have."

"I'm not sorry for anybody stupid enough to lose all their money in a poker game. That lady over there in the house, though, she might deserve better."

Toby's weakness always had been his conscience. It probably had to do with that religious streak his mother had drilled into him. "She isn't our problem, Toby. The money is."

Then, knowing it would provoke his friend, he added, "And how do we know she's a lady?"

Sure enough, Toby came boiling out of the stall and got right in Cal's face. "You don't have any call to think that poorly about a woman you haven't even met. Besides, we both know that the kind of woman you mess with is the reason we're in this fix right now."

Cal held up his hands and backed away. "Sorry, Toby. You're right, of course. No doubt she's beyond reproach."

Once again, Toby spit right at Cal's boots, a sign he was thoroughly disgusted with him. "I know you don't have much experience with decent women. . . ."

"None at all, actually," Cal allowed. "And I plan to keep it that way."

"You listen to me," Toby went on as if Cal hadn't said a word. "You find yourself a good woman and see if she isn't worth more than all that gold you keep winning and losing. With the right one, a man can build a life worth living."

It was an old argument, one in which neither of them ever gave an inch. "If you're so all fired up for me to find a wife, why aren't you looking harder for one for yourself?"

"Because we don't run into many of my kind. Once I get you settled down in one spot, I'll go looking for a wife myself."

Before Cal could think of a suitable response, Toby threw the shovel aside and stalked out.

"Well, I'll be damned." That was the first time Toby had ever made mention of wanting something more out of life than following Cal from town to town. There was one major flaw in his plans, though; Cal had no intention of tying himself down to one place or one woman.

There was no denying that women had their uses, but he sure as hell didn't have to marry one for that. He'd only cared about one woman in his life, and she'd left him to fend for himself in the gold camps of California. Hell of a thing for a mother to do, but he didn't really blame her.

From all he'd ever been able to learn about Eunice Preston, she'd been little more than a girl herself. He'd done all right without her and the nameless bastard who'd gotten her pregnant and then walked away. As far as he could remember, Eunice had never spoken a single word about her lover. Cal had never asked.

Along with the other camp brats, he'd scrambled through the daily sweepings from gambling halls for bits of gold dust and the occasional lost coin to keep himself in food and clothes.

He'd learned early how to play cards, knowing that there was far more gold to be found on top of the tables than beneath them. That had been a definite step up in lifestyles. He prided himself on knowing that he could survive on nothing at all, which gave him an edge over other, more cautious gamblers. They feared going broke more than they loved winning.

No, caution wasn't what won the big pots. A man had to be willing to lay it all on the line if necessary. Lady Luck wouldn't have it any other way.

For now, though, he needed to make peace with Toby.

The sun was edging its way down behind the mountains to the west. Lily kept an anxious eye on the horizon for some sign of Wade. There was always the chance that he would spend the night out with the herd. He'd done it before. Lately, they'd been losing too many head for it to be accidental. She hated to be alone at night, but lying awake and worrying about the herd wasn't much better.

The long summer day was just about gone when she caught sight of Wade coming in from the east. The last she'd seen of their unwanted guests, they were still hanging around the barn. Although they were nowhere in sight, there wasn't much chance that they'd given up and left.

Somehow, she had to warn Wade. Rather than risk going out the front door, she decided the best idea was to slip out through the side window. Once it was open, she pulled her skirt up past her knees and put one leg over the sill. Feeling awkward and ungainly, she shifted her weight to slide toward the ground on the outside. It was farther down than she'd figured, causing her to tumble down in a heap.

Before she could get up of her own accord, a pair of men's hands were around her waist, lifting her to her feet. She squawked in surprise.

"Who?" she sputtered. She looked up into the face of one of the handsomest men she'd ever seen. Humiliation at having been caught in such an embarrassing position made her flush hot and then cold.

"Beg pardon, ma'am," her rescuer said, touching the brim of his hat. "We haven't been properly introduced. Cal Preston, at your service."

Despite his pretty words, she was convinced that he was having fun at her expense. Something about the set of his mouth, not that he was smiling. But close.

"And you would be . . . ?" he prodded when she didn't immediately respond to his introduction.

She ignored his question as she tried to see around him, wanting to know if Wade had seen them. Although the stranger wasn't particularly tall, he had situated himself directly between her and her brother-in-law's approach.

Preston acted as if she had answered. "Pleased to meet you, Mrs. McCord. It is Mrs. McCord, isn't it?"

"Yes, of course." She wondered at the strange look he gave her, but she had other things on her mind. She couldn't very well go diving back into the house, and by now it was too late to warn Wade away from the ranch.

The stranger took the decision out of her hands completely. He offered her his arm. "Since we are both anxious to meet up with your husband, why don't we walk out to meet him together?"

Obviously, he'd made some wrong assumptions, but she wasn't about to correct them. Not until she found out what was going on.

Ignoring Preston and his arm, she brushed past him and hurried toward Wade. She knew the instant that he caught sight of her unwanted companion. He paled, looking terribly guilty and not a little afraid. Her heart sank. Whatever the men wanted, it didn't bode well for Wade.

He slowed his horse to a walk, as if delaying the inevitable as long as possible. After what seemed an eternity, he dismounted and waited for Lily to come to him. Even in the gathering shadows, she could see how frightened he was. And how very, very young he really was.

"I'm sorry, Lily."

"Wade, what have you done? Who are these men?" She tried to sound calm but feared that she failed miserably.

He looked beyond her to where Cal Preston was still waiting. "Men? How many of them are there besides him? Did they hurt you in any way?" His hand slid toward the revolver in his holster.

She hastened to reassure him. Although the stranger had yet to make a hostile move, she had no doubt that Wade was sorely overmatched. "The two of them showed up around noon but never came near the house all day after I told them you weren't here. They haven't bothered me at all."

That was a lie. The black man hadn't worried her, but Cal Preston was a different matter. She was still strangely aware of where his hands had touched her. And the way he'd offered his arm, as if daring her. No, that one was definitely trouble, but not in the way Wade meant.

When the second man stepped out of the shadows, Preston broke the silence. "Toby, why don't you escort Mrs. McCord back to the house while I have a talk with her husband?"

"She's not my . . ."

For reasons she didn't quite understand, Lily didn't want Preston to know the truth of her relationship with Wade. "I'll stay right here with him."

From the look Preston was giving her, she suspected that he'd picked up on what Wade had been about to say. But if he had any questions, he didn't voice them.

For the first time, Toby spoke up. "Ma'am, this is a matter best dealt with between the two of them. Why don't I help you finish up that laundry you started earlier?"

Lily turned to Wade, trying to gauge the seriousness of the situation, but he wouldn't look at her. His eyes were riveted on the man dressed all in black. It was obvious that neither of them would say another word until she left them alone.

She did her best to smile at the black man. "I'm sorry I didn't catch your name earlier."

"It's Toby, ma'am. Toby Thacker." Unknowingly copying his friend's gesture, he touched the brim of his hat in salute. Somehow, she knew he did it with far more sincerity.

"Well, Mr. Thacker, I would appreciate the help. Then afterwards perhaps you'd like to join me for dinner. These two are welcome to stand out here and glare at each other all night long, if that's what they want."

Toby's deep, rich laughter rang out, clear and full. It lightened Lily's heart as nothing had in a long time. He took the reins of Wade's weary-looking horse and followed Lily back around to the front of the house.

Together they made short work of the laundry, spreading it to finish drying on the bushes around the house. The night would be hot enough to do most of the work, and the morning sun would finish the job.

While Toby saw to the horse's needs, Lily served up the stew she'd made to go with the bread. Despite her earlier words, she set places for Wade and Preston. Even so, she was surprised when the two of them came inside seconds after she and Toby sat down. If anything, Preston looked grimmer than Wade. Whatever they'd talked about, things hadn't gone the way he'd wanted. Wade, though pale and silent, didn't look much the worse for wear.

From the way the three men tucked into their food, nothing was bothering any of them enough to affect their appetites. She, on the other hand, had trouble choking down even a minimal amount of the stew. Fresh bread was a particular favorite of hers, but tonight it had all the flavor of dust.

As the meal drew to a close, the tension began mounting again. First Toby and then Preston excused themselves, but they weren't going far. Wade didn't seem the least surprised by their decision to stay over and sleep in the barn. He seemed strangely resigned to their continued presence on the ranch.

She would allow him the dignity of waiting until he

helped the two men get settled, but then she'd demand answers. She half expected Wade to use some excuse to ride back out to the herd, but he didn't. She'd barely got the dishes done when she heard his step on the porch.

Bracing herself for the confrontation, she waited for him to come inside. When he did, all the anger drained away. It was clear at first glance that the only thing holding him together was stubborn pride.

It hurt to see him in that much pain. He looked away, as if unable to face her with the truth. She ached to put her arms around him, to comfort him like the boy he still was, but she knew the gesture wouldn't be welcome.

"Wade, I can't help you if I don't know what's wrong."

"No one can help. I'm sorry, Lily."

"You said that earlier, Wade." She kept her hands busy wiping down the table. "But you still haven't said what you have done to be sorry for." But it was bad, she knew that much—maybe really bad.

Wade put as much distance between them as he could by standing by the window and staring out into the darkness. "I lost it, Lily. All of it."

She made herself ask, even though suddenly she didn't want to know the answer at all. "Lost what?"

His shoulders hunched as if to ward off an expected blow. "Everything. The money, the ranch, everything."

All the strength went out of Lily's legs, forcing her to sink down onto the closest chair. She grabbed the edge of the table, clenching it hard enough that her knuckles ached.

"How?" The word came out a harsh whisper.

His voice caught, but he forged ahead as his words tore her world apart. "I couldn't stand it any longer, watching you work yourself to the bone around here. Every day, rain or shine, you're up before the sun and still working when it's dark. Hell, I don't know what

Thad was thinking, bringing a lady like you to a place like this."

"But Wade, the ranch wasn't just Thad's dream. We both wanted to build a life here for the three of us." That was true as far as it went. They just hadn't counted on Thad's dying. "I love our home."

Wade went on as if he hadn't heard a word she said. "Upton Boone's doing his best to get this place. We both know it. If he isn't trying to get you to marry him, he's trying to buy us out. Now, at the rate we're losing cattle, we won't make enough when we sell the herd to make the mortgage payment. You know he'll be the first one in line if the bank forecloses."

He wasn't telling her anything she didn't already know. It was when she'd refused both Boone's proposal and his offer to buy them out that the cattle started disappearing. There was no proof that he was behind the raids, but she and Wade had suspected him from the beginning.

"How much of the money is gone?"

"Half. I left your half in the bank."

It might as well all be gone. The bank manager had made it clear that he would not accept any partial payments. No doubt Upton was behind that as well. The sooner the bank could foreclose, the sooner he'd have title to the place.

She looked around the room, tears blurring the details, not that it mattered. There was little enough; she knew each piece by heart. Would they lay claim to it all or would she be able to keep the few things she brought with her when she married Thad? Her grandmother's teapot sat in a place of honor, and then there was the quilt her mother had stitched for her.

The thought of losing those two things pushed her over the edge. The tears flowed as she grieved for Thad and herself, and for Wade as well. She felt no anger toward him, only sorrow that he'd felt driven to such a desperate act.

After a few seconds, she felt his hand on her shoulder, offering what comfort he could. "I'm sorry, Lily. I know I keep saying that, but I only wanted to make things better for you."

Choking back her sobs, she tried to understand what had happened. "Why didn't you talk to me, Wade?"

"I was afraid." He moved away again.

"Of me?" This time she followed him to the window. "Please, Wade, won't you tell me what you were thinking?"

When he didn't respond, a surge of anger fought its way through her tears. "You can't just leave it at that. Explain yourself. I deserve that much."

Finally, he spoke, sounding farther away than just the few inches that separated them. "I was afraid you'd give up and leave. Boone told me that the only reason you'd stayed this long was because of me. That if it weren't for me, you'd have sold the ranch so you could live a better life."

Lily grabbed his arm and forced him to turn toward her. "Damn it, Wade!"

Her cursing shocked them both as she glared up at him. "I want you to listen to this: We're family, you and me. That means wherever I go, you go. What you do, I do. Even if we lose the ranch, I wouldn't leave without you. I trust you feel the same way."

He nodded. When she put her arms around him, he hugged her back. Their problems were far from over, but at least they had that settled. As they separated, it occurred to her that he still hadn't explained their guests.

"What do Cal Preston and Mr. Thacker have to do with any of this?"

"I already told you that I lost the money and the

ranch in a poker game. Cal Preston is the gambler who won it all."

"He's a professional gambler?" Now she had a proper target for her fury. She was still too upset to face him down, but tomorrow morning there would be a reckoning. She'd lay into him as soon as Wade rode out to the herd.

For now, the day's events had left her more exhausted than normal. She would do her best to get a good night's rest.

"We'll do some thinking tomorrow about what we can do next. You go on to bed while I take care of things."

He gave her an odd look, as if wondering why she was suddenly so calm. She hastened to reassure him that he was still in trouble. "I figure you probably haven't been sleeping well, wondering and worrying about when Mr. Preston would show up. Well, he's here now, and there's no changing that. Go on and get some sleep while you can. Morning comes early in these parts."

Wade managed to smile at that. Thadeus had always used it as an excuse for going to bed early with Lily. Of course, he wasn't really wanting to sleep. The memory of how they spent those nights in each other's arms threatened to make her blush.

Luckily, Wade had already disappeared into his room, leaving her to turn out the lamps.

Cal watched the lights in the house go out, one by one. He was used to much later hours, but he suspected that wasn't the case for the McCords. He watched the last light flickering in a room at the back of the house. He could see Lily moving around, her silhouette just a shadow through the curtains.

Although he couldn't see any details, the important thing was that there was no sign of Wade through that window. He refused to think too hard about why he found that bit information so satisfying. He had no interest in Lily McCord, outside of how to wring enough money out of her ranch to stake Toby and himself to a new start.

He'd heard the gambling halls in Kansas City were particularly nice. Maybe they'd head there next. That is, if he could pry Toby away from the place. Not only had his friend finished giving the barn a thorough cleaning, he'd helped Lily with the laundry. Who would have thought he had such a domestic side to him?

The thought occurred to Cal that when he rode out, he might very well be riding alone. Suddenly, the night air had a definite chill to it.

Morning was never his favorite time of day, but waking up with a chicken staring him in the eye had to be a new low. When the hen made a sudden lunge at his face, Cal jerked upright, banging his head on the stall door.

He let loose with a string of curses that would have done a bullwhacker proud. The chicken remained remarkably unpreturbed by the whole business. She continued pecking around in the hay, calmly ignoring both him and his threats. He figured a well-aimed kick might change that.

"Do you have something against chickens in general?"

He also hated being caught doing something stupid. "Only when they want to blind me."

"Well, if you insist on sleeping where you're not welcome, you have to expect some problems."

Lily McCord stepped out of the shadows across the barn, looking well-groomed and ready for the day. In fact, he suspected that she'd already accomplished more since sunup than he would all day. He felt decidedly at a disadvantage, but that didn't mean he was going to put up with the sharp side of her tongue.

"I would apologize for displacing the chicken, but since you didn't invite me to spend the night anywhere more comfortable, I had little choice."

Her gasp of outrage was particularly satisfying. He dusted some of the hay off his shirt. "What's for breakfast?"

"The rest of us had flapjacks about two hours ago. Dinner will be about seven tonight when Mr. Thacker and Wade come back in from the range." Her smile had a nasty edge to it. "The kitchen is closed until then."

Before he could think of a suitable reply, she stalked out of the barn, leaving him alone with the chicken. He didn't mind so much not having breakfast. Coffee, however, was an entirely different matter. Toby would have made some even if Mrs. McCord hadn't seen fit to.

Cal picked up his shaving gear and stepped out into the sunshine. Before going anywhere in particular, he looked around for some sign of where Lily had gone. She was on her knees, working in the vegetable garden out behind the house. It looked as if she was going to be there awhile, making it a perfect time for him to slip inside the house for some coffee and the chance to heat up some shaving water.

He angled his approach so that she wouldn't immediately see him invading her territory. Once inside, he poured himself a cup of coffee and then sliced himself off a couple of pieces of bread. It would be enough to hold him until later. He added more wood to the stove and set the kettle on to boil.

That done, he sat down at the table and put his feet up in the seat of another chair. He was quite sure that Lily McCord would be less than pleased to find him enjoying her hospitality without being invited.

He hoped she walked in soon.

The kettle whistled, forcing him into action. After slipping his shirt off, Cal lathered up his face. He ran his finger along the edge of his razor, deciding it would do for one more shave. More by feel than anything, he began stripping the two-day growth of beard off his face.

That done, he pulled out a sliver of sweet-smelling soap from his kit and used it to wash up with. It had been some time since he'd had the luxury of taking a hot bath, but he'd make do with what he had. He didn't mind making free with Lily McCord's hot water and mirror, but he drew the line at using her washtub without permission.

Besides, if she caught him buck naked in her kitchen, there was no telling what she'd do. Although, he had to admit, he sure wouldn't mind if she were willing to get naked with him. There wasn't much chance of that, though. She was still plenty angry about his taking advantage of Wade, or at least that was how she saw it.

He prodded that idea as he would a sore tooth. No way he was going to feel guilty about winning at poker. He'd been making his living with the cards since he was far younger than Wade McCord. It was hardly his fault that the boy had played with money he could ill afford to lose.

He wasn't the one in the wrong, no matter what the rest of them thought. It bothered him some that Toby had made it clear that he was siding with the McCords. Trouble was, even if they were right—which they weren't—it didn't matter. The money was gone, leaving only the ranch itself, and by the looks of things, that wasn't saying much.

The sound of horses approaching startled him out of his reverie. There were too many for it to be Toby and Wade returning early. Curious as to who would come calling this time of day, he stood by the front window and watched their approach. Lily came scurrying around the front of the house and stepped up on the porch, her back to him. When he opened the door, she stepped inside but left it open.

He wondered where she'd kept the rifle stashed. She hadn't had it with her in the barn, but it wouldn't have surprised him if she had. A woman alone had to be cautious. For all appearances, she handled it as if it were second nature to her.

The riders hadn't yet reached the house when she fired a shot into the dirt right in front of the lead rider, causing his horse to buck and shy. Once he'd fought his mount back under control, he didn't try to come any closer to the house. Interesting. Although Lily hadn't exactly been warm and friendly when he and Toby had ridden up, neither had she taken any shots at them.

Without thinking about why, Cal checked his revolver, making sure it was loaded and riding smoothly in its holster. Normally, he made a habit of staying out of other people's problems, but not this time. He didn't hold with a bunch of men terrifying a woman, no matter who she was. If Lily needed his help, he'd give it his best. While she kept them occupied, he looked around for another rifle.

He didn't find one, but there was a shotgun hanging on the back bedroom wall. A box of shells was on the shelf above it. What kind of mess were Lily and Wade in that they felt the need to keep loaded weapons so handy? He hurried back to the front door.

The front rider had dismounted as if to approach the house. Lily brought the muzzle of her rifle up, aiming dead center at the man's chest. It would give anyone pause, but this one laughed and shook his head, his long blond hair gleaming in the sun. Most women would find him handsome, Cal was sure, but Lily sure didn't seem to be overly impressed.

"Now, Lily, is that any way to treat guests?"

"It's *Mrs. McCord* to you, Boone. And you aren't guests. Now get on your horse and get off my property. All of you."

"Come on, now. We're old friends." He took another step forward, but stopped when she cocked the rifle again.

The four men with him started fanning out, making it impossible for a lone woman with a rifle to keep them all in her sights. Cursing himself for a fool, Cal knew he had to back Lily's action.

He took up a position beside her, being careful to stay just out of sight. No use in letting the others know that the two of them were alone. He answered for Lily: "Stop right there, mister. Mrs. McCord here doesn't seem to consider you a friend."

The slick smile was gone instantly. "Who the hell are you?"

"None of your damn business. Now, like the lady said, get back on your horse and ride on out of here."

"I came out here to talk over some business with Mrs. McCord. I'm not leaving until I do."

Lily shook her head. "Boone, I've told you before. We have no business to discuss."

Cal wondered if the other man could hear the hint of fear in Lily's voice from that distance. He hoped not. He also doubted the others had noticed that they were no longer alone. Toby was disappearing into the barn, working himself into a position to have a clear shot at the nearest two. Cal wouldn't be able to hit the others from this distance with the shotgun, but he could do considerable damage with his revolver if necessary.

First, he'd have to get Lily out of the line of fire. He tried to tug her back, intending to put himself between her and the others. She stood her ground, not even acknowledging Cal's presence.

"Boone, go back to town and leave me alone."

The blond's temper was starting to slip. "For the last time, I'm trying to do you a favor. I've already offered you more than this place is worth. You'd be a fool not to take it. Sooner or later, you're going to have to be sensible about things."

Lily remained calm, at least on the surface. "Leave, Boone. And take your friends with you."

Cal held his breath, hoping that the stranger did as she asked. Until he knew more about what was going on, he didn't want things to get out of control.

"You haven't heard the last of this, Lily," Boone drawled as he mounted up. "As for you, mister, I don't know who you are, but around here, folks don't go messing around in things that don't concern them."

One of the others used Boone's action to cover his own move toward the house. A shot rang out from the direction of the barn, surprising all of them. Toby had placed his bullet carefully, knocking the man's hat off but doing no real harm.

Evidently, the numbers were too evenly matched for Boone's comfort. He seemed more at ease frightening a single woman than facing an unknown number of armed men. He wheeled his horse around and cantered off without even a backward glance. The others followed him.

Cal watched until they were little more that a cloud of dust on the horizon. Toby stuck his head out of the barn loft. From that vantage point, he would be able to make sure that Boone and his friends kept going and didn't circle back.

Meanwhile, Lily disappeared out the door, probably to finish up whatever work she'd started in the garden. Cal followed her, determined to find out what was going on.

She was already on her knees, yanking at some straggling weeds as if her life depended on it. Although she gave no sign of it, he knew she was aware of his scrutiny.

"Does that happen often?"

Another weed died a violent death. She stubbornly refused to acknowledge his presence, but he could be just as determined. "Is that Boone fellow an old beau?"

That did it. Her head shot up, her fist clinching a dirt clod as if ready to throw it at him. Her dark eyes were flashing fire.

"No, he's not. Now leave me alone." She tossed the dirt aside and went back to her weeding.

Cal leaned against a nearby tree, making it clear that he wasn't going anywhere soon. "Why is he so interested in the ranch?"

"That's none of your business." Lily stopped mid-row and abruptly stood up. She pulled off her apron and used it to dust off the hem of her skirt. Without giving Cal a second glance, she marched toward the house.

He was hot on her trail, catching up with her before she reached the front porch. He took her by the arm and spun her around to face him.

"It is my business, Mrs. McCord."

She glared up at him and stood her ground. "No, it isn't. This ranch belongs to Wade and me, and it's going to stay that way."

"I have a piece of paper that says differently, unless you have the money Wade owes me."

There was nothing she could say to that. They both knew she didn't have it.

"That's what I thought." He let go of her and stepped back. "Tell me about this Boone. Who is he?"

"The nearest town to the north of us is his."

"You mean he lives there?"

"No, I mean the town of King's Creek is his. He

owns the saloon, the general store, the bank, and rumor has it, the sheriff."

"How likely is he to come gunning after me for standing with you?"

She shrugged. "Far as I know, he doesn't do his own dirty work because he doesn't need to. He has plenty of friends more than willing to kill for him."

Before Cal could ask any more questions, Toby joined them. "They kept going, Mrs. McCord. You're safe for now."

Cal watched as she smiled at Toby. "Thank you, Mr. Thacker. I appreciate your help. You timed that perfectly."

"Glad to be of service, Mrs. McCord." Toby took his hat off and wiped the sweat off his face with his sleeve. It was obvious he'd been riding hard all day. "I came back for some provisions for Mr. Wade and myself. It looks like someone else moved your herd. They had the cattle penned up in that small canyon out yonder. There was no sign of your two wranglers. We're going to keep watch to see if anyone comes back."

"I'll get some food together for you right away." Lily swept past Cal without a second glance.

"Do you need me?" Cal wasn't fond of all-night vigils, but he would help out if necessary. He didn't know whether to be relieved or insulted when Toby grinned and shook his head.

"Mr. Wade and I can handle it by ourselves." He nodded toward the house. "Besides, Mrs. McCord shouldn't be left alone. You'd be of more use here at the ranch in case that bunch comes back uninvited."

"I'm not sure that she trusts me any more than she does this Boone fellow. She thinks we're both after her ranch."

Toby quirked an eyebrow. "Aren't you?"

There wasn't anything he could say to that. If he didn't

get some money from the McCords, he'd be back to scraping by with whatever menial jobs he could find until he got enough money together for a stake. He didn't give a damn about the ranch. Lily and her brother-in-law were welcome to it, as long as he got his money.

"Lily says Boone owns a saloon in the fine town of King's Creek. Maybe one of us should spend some time in it."

Toby frowned. "Did he get a look at you?"

"I don't know. I tried to stay in the shadows."

"If he did, it might not be safe for you, especially if you go in alone. Why don't you let me check the place out first? If I wait a couple of days, he wouldn't have any reason to suspect that I'm involved with the McCords."

Cal had to admit that Toby was making sense, but he didn't like it. He never did like spending much time in one place, but at least in town there were certain diversions. He seriously doubted the delectable Lily McCord would consider making herself available for his entertainment.

As if he had conjured her up out of his imagination, Lily came bustling back out of the house with a burlap bag in her hand. She held it out to Toby.

"This should be enough for tonight and for break-fast in the morning. I'll cook you both a proper meal as soon as you get back."

Toby accepted her offering. "I'll keep an eye on young Wade for you, ma'am."

"I appreciate that, Mr. Thacker. I worry about him out there by himself. He means well, but he's too young to carry so much responsibility on his shoulders."

She shot Cal a knowing look, which closely echoed the one Toby had on his face. He'd heard enough on the subject of young Wade for one day. On the other hand, he wasn't about to let them know that their comments had scored a direct hit.

"Well, Toby, enjoy yourself." He tipped his hat toward Lily, knowing the gesture was more likely to make her mad than impress her with his good manners. "You can just give a holler when dinner is ready."

He could hear her sputtering with indignation as he walked toward the barn. For the first time all day, he felt like smiling.

Three

If that man thought she was going to cook him dinner, he could just forget it. On a ranch, people did more than shuffle a deck of cards to earn their keep. She didn't know what he'd been doing all day out there in the barn, but she knew he wasn't doing anything useful.

He wasn't the type. Not like his friend Toby.

Her conscience reminded her that Cal Preston had backed her up against Boone and his men, but pulling a gun probably came easy to him. Certainly, it didn't require any hard labor on his part. In fact, when he'd grabbed her arm earlier, she'd taken notice of his hands.

They definitely weren't the hands of a rancher or anyone else who earned their living with the sweat of their brow. No, he'd taken the easy way to make a living—stealing money from innocent young men with a deck of cards. He probably cheated.

No, that wasn't true. Even if she could picture him dealing off the bottom of the deck, Toby wouldn't have stayed with a man of such low character. Was there more to the man than she'd seen so far?

She closed her eyes and pictured Cal in her mind. Although he wasn't overly tall, there was a surprising amount of strength in the way he moved. His hair and eyes were the same shade of dark brown, making her wonder if he had some Indian blood. That would account for those striking cheekbones.

She had to give him some credit for taking care with his appearance, but none of that mattered. Fancy clothes and fancy manners didn't count for much in her estimation. She was, however, somewhat embarrassed by the fact that she was able to see him in such fine detail with so little effort.

A footstep on the porch warned her that she was about to have company. She waited to see whether he would knock or just stroll on in as if he owned the place. He probably thought he did.

She was right. Although Cal did her the courtesy of knocking first, he didn't wait for her to invite him inside the house before opening the door. She'd have to remember to throw the lock as long as Cal Preston was underfoot.

"I thought dinner might be about ready." When he spied the empty stove, he frowned. "Shouldn't you be cooking?"

Lily gave him a nasty smile. "I only cook for people I welcome at my table."

"And that wouldn't be me, I take it."

She didn't like the look in his eyes or his tone of voice.

"You'd take it right."

"I assume you wouldn't mind if I cooked for myself." Before she could answer, he was already picking up wood to stoke up the fire.

She took a position in front of the stove, her hands on her hips. "Get out of my kitchen and my house."

"No—to both counts." He put his hands on her waist and picked her up as if she weighed nothing at all. Then he set her out of his way and calmly went back to fussing with the stove.

That was the second time he'd done that to her. She

really hated men who used their strength against a woman. Her temper flared up, bright and hot. "I told you to get out of my kitchen and my house. I meant it."

"And I said no. I own part of the house and that includes the kitchen. Now, if you're willing to put some supper on the table for the two of us, fine. Otherwise, stay out of my way."

She'd lost the fight, and she knew it. "Get out of my kitchen. I'll feed you, but only if you stay away from me."

He handed her the chunk of wood that he was holding and stepped back. Not that he left the house or even the room. Instead, he walked around to the far side of the table and sat down, obviously ready to wait her out.

She got to work, throwing together a quick meal of bacon and fried potatoes. Along with some fresh milk, it would do. She could feel the weight of his gaze following each move that she made. Did he think she was going to do something to his dinner? The thought had crossed her mind, but her thrifty nature wouldn't let her waste food unnecessarily. Even so, he was making her nervous.

In her hurry, she got careless with the cast iron skillet and almost dropped it. She managed to keep it on the stove, but the grease splashed over the side and onto her hand, burning it in several spots. None of them were serious injuries, but they were painful.

Before she could think of what to do, Cal was beside her. He picked up a towel and soaked it with cool, fresh water from the pump. Without a word, he wrapped it around her hand with a surprisingly gentle touch. The water went a long way toward easing the pain, even if his nearness made her uncomfortable in ways she didn't care to think about.

"Sit down." He pulled out a chair from the table and pushed her toward it. "I'll finish up."

She wanted to argue, but her hand was hurting enough for her to know that she'd have a difficult time lifting anything right then. Besides, she was rather taken aback by the ease with which Cal was handling the cooking.

"You've done that before."

He shrugged as he chopped an onion and threw the pieces into the skillet with some of the bacon fat. Next he turned his attention to the potatoes. Peelings flew as he wielded the paring knife with some authority.

"If Toby and I waited around for a woman to cook for us, we'd have starved to death years ago."

"Sounds like you've known each other a long time."

"Long enough."

The potatoes went into the skillet next, followed by a sprinkling of salt and pepper. Her stomach rumbled in anticipation. If Cal heard, he was enough of a gentleman not to say so.

"How is your hand?" he asked without looking at her.

"Better. I don't think it will blister."

His response was more a grunt than a comment. She took it to mean that he was pleased that she wasn't hurt worse. He was probably worried that he'd also have to stoop to doing dishes or some other useful occupation if her hand was badly hurt.

The potatoes were sizzling nicely, and the fragrance of the onions and bacon smelled heavenly. She couldn't remember the last time that someone cooked for her. It felt strange to be a guest in her own kitchen. More out of habit than anything, she got to her feet to set the table.

"Sit down. I'll take care of it."

His voice was gruff, as if he wasn't used to common courtesy, and perhaps he wasn't. Gamblers weren't known for frequenting civilized society. Even a ranch in a newly settled area must seem pretty tame by his standards.

She noticed that he'd rolled up his sleeves, revealing sleekly muscled forearms. Even the towel he'd tied around his waist like an apron didn't take away from his masculinity. She'd been a long time without a man, but that didn't mean she'd forgotten what attraction felt like.

She drew a shuddering breath, forcing her mind away from those wayward thoughts. Even if she were ready to accept another man into her life, it wouldn't be a man who made his living in such a questionable manner.

With sure strokes, he sliced off a few pieces of bread and held them to the flames to toast. At last, dinner was ready. Cal set a plate heaping with potatoes and bacon in front of her, along with a cup of milk. She was prepared for the food to be half-cooked or overseasoned. Instead, everything was as good or even better than she could have prepared it herself.

Despite her reluctance to accept Cal's presence, good manners dictated that she make some effort to thank him for taking over for her.

"Everything is delicious. Thank you."

"You're welcome."

That was the sum total of their conversation at the table. Only a short time later, Cal pushed his plate away and leaned back in his chair. Her eyes followed the long line of his legs with some interest.

Unfortunately, he caught her staring. In order to hide her embarrassment, she immediately got up to clear the table. Although he didn't say a word, she was almost painfully aware of his continued presence. It wasn't hard to figure out what kept him hanging around when it was obvious that he wasn't interested in conversation with her.

His only alternative was retreating to his stall in the barn. Although he wasn't particularly thrilled to be with her, evidently her company was preferable to the milk cow and the chickens. She fought hard to resist the urge to giggle. The look on his face that morning when he woke up eye to eye with her best laying hen had been pretty funny.

She didn't know him very well, but she was willing to bet that he wouldn't appreciate being laughed at.

"So have you and the chickens worked out sleeping arrangements for tonight?"

That got his attention. His head snapped, his eyes narrowed in suspicion. Without a word, he got up and walked out, slamming the door behind him.

Lily immediately regretted her wayward tongue. Although Cal hadn't been exactly what she'd call a charming dinner companion, he had treated her burn gently and had done a credible job finishing the meal for her. She'd meant to tease him a little, but her goal hadn't really been to drive him off.

She wavered on whether to follow him but decided not to, for fear he would think she was inviting him back for the wrong reasons. Once again, his image flashed through her mind, stirring feelings in her that had lain dormant since Thad's death.

Out of habit, she threw the lock on the door and set about finishing up her nightly chores. She was used to being alone. But for the first time in a long while, she was also lonely.

Toby slowed as he reached the edge of town. If Lily was to be believed, anything could happen in King's Creek, and probably had. A black man had to be careful whenever he approached unfamiliar territory. When a man was unsure of his welcome, it paid to be cautious.

He'd waited until early evening to make the trip into town. Once the saloons got busy, chances were that he'd just be another customer in the crowd. He tied his horse up in front of the nearest hitching rail. Until he got the layout of the place straight in his head, he wanted his mount close at hand.

It felt good to be out of the saddle. He and Cal had been on the trail more than usual lately. He didn't know what was pushing his friend to keep on the move, and he doubted that Cal did himself. It wasn't as if either of them had ever had a place to call his own; perhaps that was why Cal was driven to keep moving.

Or maybe the man was looking for something and wasn't smart enough to recognize it when he found it.

A reluctant smile tugged at his mouth when he thought of Lily McCord and Cal Preston. The sparks certainly flew whenever they got within twenty feet of each other. Personally, he was surprised that she hadn't filled Cal's backside with a load of buckshot for the way he acted around her.

For certain, there was something going on. Cal's insistence on hanging on at the McCord ranch until he got his money just didn't hold up. They'd been flat broke before and would no doubt be so again. Why was it so important for Cal to get the money out of Wade McCord and his pretty sister-in-law?

He'd have to ponder that situation later because he'd come up even with the nearest saloon. He looked over the swinging doors and rejected the place immediately for being too quiet. There was no way he could slip in without being noticed. Maybe he'd try again later, but for now he'd move on down the street. He could count at least three more similar establishments within easy walking distance.

He struck pay dirt on his second try. The Silver Slipper was almost bursting at the seams. Before he stepped inside, he took the time to get the lay of the place. The bar was of highly polished wood, with a large mirror on the wall behind it. This place had been built with a lot of money and an eye for comfort.

The man standing behind the bar polishing glasses looked friendly enough, but there was more to him than just a smile. His eyes were never still, flickering from table to table and then back to the door. Toby knew when he'd been spotted.

The man gave him a quick nod, a clear signal that Toby was welcome to venture inside. He accepted the invitation with little reluctance. As he came in, the bartender tipped his head toward the back corner.

Toby followed his line of sight. There was an empty table right where the bartender was looking. It was clear that although he was welcome, he'd be better off in an inconspicuous corner.

That was fine with him. He was here to observe, not to get into the middle of the action. For that matter, he'd always been glad to leave the gambling to Cal. More than one black man had lost his life for winning too much at cards.

He stopped at the bar long enough to buy a bottle. He picked the seat that afforded him the best view of the room while keeping his own back to the wall. After pouring himself a glass of the amber liquid, he settled back to nurse his drink as he tried to learn more about King's Creek in general and Upton Boone in particular.

Along about sundown, he was well into his second drink. So far, he hadn't seen anything out of the ordinary. Some men were winning at the tables; most were losing. Some things never changed. He was watching a nearby table where a couple of cowboys were losing heavily. It paid to keep an eye out for such things because it was just the sort of situation that could turn violent.

It took awhile for him to realize that the level of excitement in the whole saloon had been increasing over the past few minutes. He pulled his eyes away from the card game and looked around for the source of the heightened interest.

Women. There were women in the room. No wonder the men were craning their necks to get a better look at the brightly dressed fancy ladies, who were lined up along the staircase. Although civilization was slowly moving west, there was still a shortage of the fairer sex.

After spending one's days eating dust following behind cattle, the sight of a woman all dressed up in lace and feathers was sheer pleasure. Even Toby, a loner by nature, was all too glad to drink in the sight. The first two women were brunettes, neither of them extraordinarily pretty, but the smiles they were flashing were bright and welcoming.

His gaze continued up the stairs, studying each woman in turn. It was the last one in line who made his heart skip a beat. Her skin was the color of sweet chocolate. Lord of mercy, she was the prettiest thing he'd seen in ten years!

As if she felt the weight of his gaze, she glanced in his direction. If she noticed him at all, she didn't give any sign of it that he could see. Just then, loud piano music started up and the women, having made their dramatic entrance, started down the steps and out into the crowd.

It took all the willpower he could muster to keep from leaping to his feet and tracking her down. He wasn't here to waste his time or his money on a woman. Even so, every move she made as she worked her way from one table to the next caught his eye. After a bit, he gave up all pretense of doing anything but watching her.

Finally, she was on his side of the room. He sat up straighter in his chair, wishing he'd taken the time to clean up some before riding into town. He'd wanted to blend in with all the other trail hands and drifters passing through King's Creek. If he'd shown up clean-shaven and sporting his best clothes, he could have drawn unwanted attention to himself.

Her eyes flickered in his direction once and then again, causing his pulse to race. It was as if she was being drawn toward him, but only reluctantly. Finally, she gave up and walked straight toward him.

"Want to buy a girl a drink, mister?"

Her voice had a huskiness to it that crawled over his skin and into his soul. He would bet from her accent that she had started life somewhere in the South. Her words sounded like home.

"Sure, but unless you want to share my glass, you'll need to bring one to the table."

She stopped to talk to a couple of cowboys at a nearby table, but then did as he suggested and asked the bartender for a glass. He handed her one, but then stopped her long enough to say something.

She shook her head and snatched the glass away from his hand. Turning her back on him, she marched straight toward Toby. The expression on the bartender's face was anything but happy. No doubt there would be trouble following close behind her, but for a few minutes alone with her, he was willing to risk it.

She pulled out the chair closest to him and sat down. Pasting a bright smile on her face, she announced, "You're new around here."

"How do you know that?"

She leaned forward, running her hand up his thigh. "I would remember someone who looked like you."

He stopped her wandering hand and placed it back up on the tabletop while he still had the strength of character to do so. "And how is that?"

"You know, like my kind."

"You mean colored."

She batted her lashes at him and gave him a smile that reminded him of a cat with a bowl of cream. "Partly. But mostly I mean someone as handsome as you are."

Toby's honesty extended to his own looks. "Do they pay you to tell that to all the men that come in here?"

For a second her smile slipped. It was almost as if he saw another woman peeking out from behind a mask, one who looked angry and hurt. But just as quickly, the smile was firmly back in place.

She started to stand up. "Well, if you aren't interested in what I have to offer, I'll find someone else who is."

Before she'd gone one step, Toby grabbed her by the arm and tugged her back toward him. This time, she surprised him by tumbling onto his lap. The sweet feel of her backside pressing against him sent a flash of hot hunger storming through him. Another few seconds of the sweet torture of having her so near, and he'd give in to the urge to haul her up those tempting stairs. Whatever it cost, both in money and his soul.

Oh, he was interested all right, but he was more intrigued by the woman behind the paint and gaudy dress. He gave her a gentle shove, one meant to give them both some room, not to reject her completely.

But she took it that way. She took a couple of short steps away from him, but it might as well have been a mile. "Like I said, mister, if you're not interested in going upstairs with me for a little fun, then I'm moving on."

She was lost in the crowd again before he realized that he hadn't even found out her name. Disgusted with himself and the whole situation, he tossed back the last of his drink and then carried the empty bottle back up to the bar.

"Want another one?" It was the same bartender.

"No, I've had my limit for the night." If he had a lick of sense he'd walk away, but he had to ask. "What's her name?"

The bartender didn't bother to pretend he didn't know who Toby meant. "Her name is Thea. Want some advice?"

Toby met the man's gaze head on. "Not particularly. Why should I want to listen to someone when I don't even know his name."

"It's James."

Toby allowed himself a small smile. "Nice to meet you, James. I'm Toby."

"Now that we've got the introductions out of the way"—he leaned over the bar and dropped his voice—"I wouldn't act too interested, if I were you."

Frustration shortened Toby's control over his temper. Her womanly scent and the feel of her skin was too fresh in his memory. "Why? Aren't I good enough for her?"

He almost hoped James would agree, so he'd have an excuse to punch him. But instead of offering insult, he gave Toby a strangely sympathetic look.

"I'm not saying anything, mister, but your attention might cause her problems. She doesn't need any more trouble than she already has."

He made a pretense of wiping the counter, while at the same time gesturing toward the other side of the saloon. "That blond man is the boss around here. He takes a personal interest in Thea, if you get my meaning."

Toby knew without looking that he was talking about Upton Boone. It had to be. He slowly glanced in the direction the bartender had indicated. Sure enough, it was the same man who had been at the McCord place the day before. He'd been too far from the barn for Toby

to have gotten a good look at his face, but there was no
mistaking that hair or that arrogance.

And now the bastard had his arm around Thea, fon-
dling her in a way that made Toby sick inside. It wasn't
as if he'd been fooling himself about how she made
her living. But knowing the truth and having it shoved
in his face were two different things. He pushed away
from the bar, intent on getting away from there, but
thought better of it.

After all, he was here to get more information on
Boone. What better source of information than a sympathetic bartender?

"So, he owns a saloon. In most parts, that wouldn't
make him a man to be reckoned with."

"It does when he owns four saloons, the bank, and
anything else in the town of value."

That confirmed what Lily had told them. It wasn't
the first time that he and Cal had run into a one-man
town. They made a habit of spending as little time as
possible in such places. When one man wielded all the
power, he could pretty much commit any number of
crimes and get away with it.

Like robbing a man who'd had a run of good luck
at the poker table. Cal still had the fading bruises from
his late night encounter with the law in one such town.

"What's Boone like to work for?"

The bartender shrugged. "He pays top dollar."

"And what does he expect in return?"

"Loyalty."

Interesting. "Is that why you're warning me away
from Thea? Because he wants her?"

For the first time, the man showed more than
friendly disinterest. "Don't fool yourself. He already
has her. He doesn't like to share."

"Seems strange since he has her working in here."

"Yeah, well, few men have the nerve to do more

than look." His voice dropped to a whisper. "And even if you're feeling nervy, remember that she's the one who'll pay for any trouble you cause. And you won't be around to protect her."

"What makes you say that? I might just decide to settle around these parts."

"Not for long. He'd have you killed for even thinking what you're thinking." Evidently, he'd had his say because the man walked away, taking a new position farther down the bar, leaving Toby on his own.

It was time to leave, anyway. But before he did, he took one last look at Boone, memorizing every detail about the man. A wise man learned everything about his enemy that he could.

Despite his best efforts, his eyes strayed into forbidden territory. Thea stood with her back toward him, but that didn't matter. He already knew the exact shade of brown of her eyes, the way her lashes curled, and the texture of her skin.

He drank in the sight of her, knowing the images would haunt his dreams for nights to come. Feeling years older than he had only hours ago, he headed out into the night.

It would be a long, cold ride back to the ranch.

Something was bothering Toby, but so far Cal hadn't been able to pry it out of him. He'd been fine when he left for King's Creek, but he'd been grouchier than a bear with a thorn in its paw ever since. The only person Toby was civil to was Lily McCord, and even she seemed to sense that something was wrong. More than once he'd caught her staring after Toby with a puzzled look on her face.

When Cal had approached his friend that morning, hoping to find out what was wrong, Toby had grunted and walked away. When Cal started to follow him,

Toby had turned on him, threatening to knock him three ways from Sunday.

Normally, Cal knew they were an even match. But whatever was driving Toby might change that. Since he was just getting over the last fight he'd been in, Cal was in no hurry to repeat the experience. Maybe there was some other way to get Toby to talk.

Cal left the barn in search of Lily. As usual, she was working in her garden. She picked up a bucket and headed toward the water pump. He caught up with her there.

"You hold the bucket. I'll pump."

Lily looked surprised at his offer of help, but did as he asked. When the bucket was filled, he held out his hand for it.

"I'll carry it back for you."

Reluctantly, she relinquished control of the pail to him. He fell into step next to her, trying to bring up the subject of Toby without betraying their friendship. He set the water down and stepped back.

"Did Toby say anything to you about his trip into town?" He tried to sound casual, but he didn't fool her for a minute.

"You were right there with me when he got back, so you know everything that I do."

"That's right. I forgot."

She shaded her eyes with her hand as she looked up at him. "No, you didn't. What's this all about?"

Cal looked past her to where Toby was checking his horse's feet. "He seems to have something on his mind. I wondered if he'd said anything else to you."

She followed his gaze. "No, he hasn't, but I've noticed it, too. Would you like me to talk to him?"

He considered her offer. "No, better not. He wouldn't appreciate us talking about him. He'll come around eventually."

Lily gently poured the water over the first row of plants. Cal waited for her to finish and then held out his hand again.

"I can pump my own water."

"That doesn't mean you have to." He pulled the bucket handle out of her grasp and headed for the pump. It was worth the cost of some manual labor to see Lily McCord at a loss for words. Whistling an off-key melody, he headed back to the pump.

Wade McCord was waiting for him.

"Give me that bucket. If Lily needs water, I'll get it for her." The youth stood with his feet planted firmly apart, as if ready to defend the pump with his fists if necessary.

Cal was in no mood to argue. He wasn't all that set on toting water, but damned if he'd take orders from Wade. "Why don't you go see if Toby needs help with the horses?"

He moved to step around Wade to get to the pump. Wade responded by shoving Cal with both hands. Cal dropped the bucket and grabbed his attacker by the shirtfront, jerking Wade off balance. When Cal let go, Wade went sprawling down in the dust. The younger man came up swinging his fists.

There wasn't much difference in their size, but Cal had years of experience in fighting behind him. Wade had only his anger. Even so, it was enough to help him land a few telling blows before Cal managed to subdue him up against the side of the house.

Lily and Toby reached them at the same time. Toby manhandled Cal off of Wade while Lily put herself between the two angry men. Naturally, she sided with her brother-in-law.

"Wade, did he hurt you?"

The boy shot Cal a triumphant look. "No, I'm fine."

Toby, on the other hand, lit into Cal. "What the hell

were you thinking of, picking a fight with the boy like that?"

"I didn't start it. He did." Cal wiped his mouth with the back of his hand. It came away bloody. He glared at Wade over Lily's head.

Evidently satisfied that Wade wasn't badly hurt, she turned on Cal. "Isn't it bad enough that you cheated him out of his money? Now you have to beat him up, too?"

That did it. Cal shoved Toby out of his way to get at Lily. "Nobody calls me a cheat and gets away with it. The only reason why you're not facing my gun right this minute is that you are a woman. Apologize."

Seconds ticked by as the two of them stood glaring at each other, neither one ready to give an inch.

Much to Cal's disgust, it was Wade who defended him. "He didn't cheat at cards, Lily. I've already told you that."

Lily threw her hands up in the air. "He should have known you were too young to be playing in the game. What do you call that?"

"For the last time, Lily, quit saying that. I'm not a kid."

"Fine. But if it wasn't the money, what were you fighting over?"

There was no way Cal was going to tell her that they came to blows over who got to carry her bucket. It was obvious to everyone but Lily that Wade was harboring strong feelings for her. If she hadn't noticed on her own, he wasn't going to be the one to point it out.

Besides, he wasn't too clear on his own motives.

Toby came to Wade's rescue. "You come with me, Mr. Wade. I need your help with my horse. He picked up a stone somewhere." He grabbed the boy by the sleeve and dragged Wade along behind him. Wade gave Cal one more ugly look before disappearing into the barn with Toby.

No doubt he was relieved not to have to explain himself further to Lily, but he clearly wasn't happy to see Cal standing so close to her.

It was a victory of sorts, but one that was short-lived. When he turned around, it was to find that once again he was alone. He heard the front door of the house slam, a clear indication that his company was no longer welcome. With Toby and Wade in the barn, he didn't particularly want to go there.

Finally, wondering if he'd lost his mind, he picked up the bucket and headed for the pump. At least the garden plants might be grateful for his attention.

Four

"What are you going to do about that woman and her problems?"

Cal pretended not to hear, but he knew that Toby would get his answer one way or another. Trouble was, he didn't know the answer himself. Maybe honesty would stun his friend into silence.

"I don't know." He met Toby's eyes over the glow of the lantern. The two of them were still spending most of their time in the barn. Right now, Toby was mending some tack while Cal played solitaire on a makeshift table made from an old board and a bucket.

"Why are we still here?"

He should have known Toby well enough to know he would go right to the heart of the matter. Hell, he'd been asking himself the same question for the past week.

"Maybe I like the hospitality." He made a show of looking around the barn, as if it had suddenly transformed itself into a luxury hotel.

Toby chuckled in response, laughing for the first time in days. As far as Cal could tell, Toby had yet to tell anyone what had happened in King's Creek that had affected him so strongly. At first, he'd wondered if he'd had problems with someone because of the color of his skin. It wouldn't be the first time, or likely the last.

But considering the strength of Toby's reaction, that

idea didn't ring true. He'd been insulted, even attacked before, but he got over it in less time than it took for the bruises to fade. Toby figured some folks were fools and went out of their way to prove it.

No, whatever this was, it ran deeper.

Cal dealt himself another game. He tossed a red six on a black seven and then started running through the pile. Trying to sound casual, he suggested, "Why don't the two of us make a trip into King's Creek tonight?"

"No." Toby's tone of voice left little room for discussion.

Cal didn't look up from the cards. "Why not? I'm sure Lily would be relieved to be rid of us for an evening. Besides, I've had about as much of this barn as I can stand."

Toby held the bridle up to his teeth and bit through the thread he'd been using to mend it. "I've had all of you I can stand, so go by yourself."

"Now what the hell have I done?"

"Not a damn thing."

Truly puzzled, Cal asked, "Then why are you so damn mad?"

"Because this place is falling down around Mrs. McCord's head, and you sit there without doing anything to stop it." Toby rose to his feet and glared down at Cal.

"You're so all-fired proud of yourself for winning that boy's money, not to mention holding it over their heads that he owes you even more. Never thought I'd see the day that I'd be ashamed to claim you as a friend."

Cal jumped up, his own temper flaring up hot and bright. "Don't go all holy on me, Toby. You knew I was a gambler when you hooked up with me. I've never claimed to be anything else." He took a step closer to his friend. "There have been a lot of times that my luck with the cards was all that stood between you and an empty belly."

Toby didn't back up, not one inch. "That might be true, but I'm none too proud of it. And at least you were winning money from others just like you."

"And what is that supposed to mean?"

"It means . . . it means . . . Aw, hell, Cal, I don't know what it means." He held his hands out and waved them in the air. "This place is somebody's home. It doesn't set well with me to be a party to taking it away from her and the boy."

"Damn it, Toby, I keep telling you that Wade isn't a boy. Hell, I'd been on my own for ten years when I was his age." He ran his fingers through his hair in frustration. "And contrary to what you're thinking, I haven't made a single move toward taking anything from your precious Mrs. McCord."

"Maybe not, but you also haven't done anything to convince that woman otherwise. She has a enough on her mind just worrying about what that son of a bitch Upton Boone is up to. She works herself to exhaustion while he stands there in his fancy saloon acting like he owns the whole damn world."

Now that last comment was interesting. That was the first time Toby had made mention of seeing Boone while he was in King's Creek.

"To hear Lily tell it, he does own a sizable piece of the world around here." Cal stooped to pick up his cards and started shuffling them, a habit that often soothed his frustrations. "So, did you talk to him?"

"Hell no."

"So what were you doing when you saw him?"

Toby made a pretense of straightening out the motley collection of bridles and bits of harness hanging on the wall. "I was washing the trail dust out of my throat and minding my own business."

"Were you close enough to hear anything he might have been saying?"

"I didn't get within spitting distance of him or any-one foolish enough to be involved with him."

Knowing Toby's way of expressing his disgust with that particular habit, it was probably best for everyone that he hadn't got close to Boone. But even more inter-esting was his comment about someone being involved with Boone. Toby usually figured most men deserved whatever happened because of their own actions.

Women and children were a different matter. Since it was unlikely that Boone let children run loose in his saloon, it had to be a woman. Thinking back to Toby's recent comments about looking for a woman to settle down with, Cal felt sure he had the right of it.

Ordinarily, he would take some pleasure in seeing Toby infatuated with some woman. But the fact that this one was involved somehow with Upton Boone had far reaching implications. By all reports, Boone was a man who liked to own things, including the people around him. He'd already threatened Toby and Cal for standing by Lily. If they tried to interfere with yet an-other woman he considered his, Cal had no doubt that those hired guns of his would come riding this way.

He'd about made up his mind not to make the trip into King's Creek by himself. But in light of this new development, he thought he'd better go.

"Make my apologies to Lily for not joining her at dinner tonight. I'm sure she'll get over her disappoint-ment quickly."

Toby was standing in the barn doorway and staring up at the evening sky. "Where the hell do you think you're going?"

"I told you. I need some time away. I'm going to take one of my last two dollars and buy myself a bot-tle." He picked up his gear and headed out back to the corral to saddle up his horse.

Toby was right on his heels with his own tack. When

Cal gave him a questioning look, he blustered, "You'll get yourself killed going in there alone."

"Fine. Saddle up."

It never hurt to have someone along for backup. Besides, he'd have a better chance of figuring out which woman had caught Toby's eye.

In only a few minutes, the horses were ready. The two men led them toward the house. Evidently, Lily had seen them coming because she was standing on the porch wiping her hands on her apron.

"Going somewhere?"

Cal let Toby answer.

"Yes, ma'am. We thought it was time to make another trip into town. See if we could pick up any more information on what Boone is up to."

Lily frowned. "It's been quiet this past week. Wade says that no one has bothered the herd. Maybe it really was some rustlers who have moved on for some reason."

Cal shook his head. "Maybe, maybe not. Either way, that wouldn't explain Boone's interest in buying you out." Or in marrying her, he added silently.

Without waiting for her to say anything more, he mounted up and Toby did the same. Lily stepped down off the porch and put her hand on the neck of Toby's horse and murmured something. Cal heard every word despite her efforts to keep it from him. He jerked on the reins and rode away without looking back.

Just as he had predicted, Lily wasn't at all upset about his leaving the ranch. It rankled that she had taken the time to warn Toby to be careful. Evidently, she didn't give a damn if something happened to him.

He urged his horse into a trot. The sooner he put some distance between himself and the McCords, the happier he would be. He was damn sick and tired of Lily's attitude. Although it was Wade who'd risked both her money and the ranch, somehow Cal had ended up being the bad guy. How was any of it his fault?

And why wasn't he leaving for good instead of for the evening? That was a question he hadn't an answer for and didn't want to think about very hard.

He glanced back at his companion. Toby was doing some brooding of his own. For a man about to see a woman who had caught his eye, Toby looked more as if he was on his way to a funeral. What about her had him so riled up?

Damn women, anyway. He'd never known one yet who wasn't trouble, starting with his own mother, although Toby had always insisted that his mother was different. In a time when colored folks weren't supposed to be educated, she'd managed to learn to read by herself and had passed the skill along to her son. A devout Christian woman, she'd instilled a sense of right and wrong in him as well. One strong enough that Toby felt driven to try to impose her teachings on Cal, whether he wanted the advice or not.

Cal had always suspected that she wouldn't have approved of Toby's choice of companions. Considering the two of them were on their way to spend yet another evening drinking and perhaps gambling, he was almost certain of it.

The sun was sinking out of sight as they cleared the final rise before King's Creek. He hadn't been sure what to expect, but the place was considerably bigger than he'd figured. Toby had mentioned that the town had at least four saloons, but that hadn't meant much. Drinking establishments were often the first sign of civilization in an area. It wasn't at all unusual for a town to grow up around them.

While many saloons were crudely built, these surely weren't. If Upton Boone was behind the design of King's Creek, he'd done it as a long-term investment if the quality of the materials used counted for anything. The man must have spent a fortune, which made Cal wonder where he'd gotten the money to do so.

Toby passed the first saloon and headed straight for the one down the road on the other side. If Boone did own all the saloons, it probably didn't matter which one they started in. They were bound to run into him somewhere along the line.

However, Toby must have a reason for what he was doing, but he didn't offer any explanation. After they had their horses tied up, Toby walked right in the door, but Cal stopped outside long enough to look around.

The bank was across the street; a hotel was beyond that. All in all, there was little about King's Creek to distinguish it from a hundred other towns he'd seen. Nothing, except that the others didn't have Lily McCord. With that unsettling idea, he followed Toby inside.

He found his friend at a table in the back corner. He'd already poured himself a drink. Cal pulled out a chair and sat down. Even if Toby hadn't waited for him before starting in, at least he'd gotten Cal a glass as well.

Cal filled it and then sipped. Not bad. The whiskey burned down his throat, smooth and smoky-tasting. For the moment, he was content to sit in companionable silence and study their surroundings. The saloon fit Toby's description well enough.

Finally, Cal broke the silence. "Nice place."

"I guess." Although he wasn't moving, Toby's eyes were anything but still. They kept flickering in the direction of the staircase that led to the second floor of the building.

Cal was about to ask if Toby was expecting someone to come down the steps anytime soon when he got his answer. First one and then another woman appeared at the top. They were dressed in gaudy dresses that were cut too low and worn too short to be acceptable in polite company. Cal heartily approved of their attire.

He started to say so to Toby when he realized that Toby's gaze was no longer wandering around the room. No, he'd definitely focused on one person. Cal followed his line of vision.

Damn, she was a looker, all right. Even though her bright smile was brittle around the edges, there was no arguing that she was one of the prettiest women he'd ever seen. No wonder Toby looked stunned. Interesting.

Cal couldn't blame the man for hankering after her, even if she meant nothing but trouble for him. Did she, as he suspected, belong to Upton Boone in some way?

The women came down the stairs as a group, but quickly dispersed into the crowd of avid admirers. Only the dusky-skinned beauty paused on the steps long enough to really look around the room. When she glanced in their direction, her eyes slid by them, but immediately returned for a closer look, as if unsure what she'd really seen.

Toby sat up straighter in his chair as she started in their direction. Although there were several tables between them and where she stood, he had no doubt which table was her destination. Oh, she paused here and there, talking to someone she knew. Smiling when a couple of cowhands asked her to join them. She was an expert in making each man feel special, as if she'd singled him out.

But not once did she more than pause as she worked her way through the crowded saloon. He could feel Toby's tension building, the closer she got. It would have been almost funny, if his friend hadn't looked quite so grim. It was as if the mere sight of the woman was painful to him in some way.

"Did you find out her name last time you were here?"

Toby nodded. "Thea. Her name is Thea."

At last she gave up all pretense and walked straight for their table. Without bothering to ask permission, she sat down on the opposite side from Toby.

"So who's your handsome friend?" She offered a practiced smile to Cal.

When Toby didn't answer, Cal spoke up for himself. "Cal Preston at your service, ma'am. Forgive my friend's poor manners for not introducing us."

She allowed him to take her hand. "I'm Thea. Thea Jones."

"Pleased to meet you, Miss Jones. Your beauty brightens an otherwise dreary day." Cal didn't have to look at Toby to know how disgusted he was. Too bad.

Thea, on the other hand, seemed all too ready to accept Cal's attentions. Both of them acted as if they were alone, ignoring the glowering presence across the table.

"I would gather from your accent that you hail from somewhere south of here."

"Yes, I do." Then she changed the subject, as if unwilling to discuss her past. "You look like a gambler. Why aren't you trying your luck at one of the tables?"

He had his own secrets. Being damn near busted was one of them. "I would rather spend time with a beautiful woman anytime."

She rolled her eyes, clearly having heard it before. Cal didn't miss the fact that, although she was careful not to look in Toby's direction, everything about her made it clear that she was all too aware of him.

It would be funny if it weren't so painful to watch. Cal wanted to kick his friend for not speaking up. Before he could think of a way to prod Toby into action, the bartender appeared at the table.

"Thea, you might want to start moving around some. The boss will be coming around soon." He made a pretense of wiping the table down before walking away.

She paid no attention to the warning, instead turning her attention to Toby.

"I'm surprised to see you back here. I thought you were passing through. You didn't even bother to tell me your name."

For a second or two, Cal thought Toby was going to ignore her. But finally, he spoke up.

"It's Toby Thacker, and I found reasons to stick around."

Her smile was warmer this time. "That's nice. I like this part of the country myself. In fact, some days I like to go riding when I can get away."

She didn't say who she needed to get away from, but Cal figured they all knew.

"What direction do you like to ride?" If Toby wasn't going to ask for himself, Cal would.

"There's a river that runs south of town. I like to follow it out to where it pools up. There's a nice stand of trees there, giving a person some privacy. You know, for thinking and things."

Toby looked up from his drink. "Would you be riding out that way anytime soon?"

"Tomorrow, maybe the next day. I like to leave around midmorning, so I can get back just after lunch."

"I like to ride about then myself."

Thea gave Toby an approving nod. She looked as if she wanted to say more, but a loud argument broke out at the top of the stairs, capturing everyone's attention. Cal had only heard Boone's voice once but recognized it immediately.

"I told you to get down there and earn your keep. And don't try telling me you're sick again." His fists were clenched as he glared at a young blonde.

She meekly nodded and tried to slip past him to the stairs. Boone let her think that she'd gotten by and then grabbed her by the arm, causing her to wince in pain.

Cal and Toby both started to get up, sickened by a whole roomful of men watching her plight without lifting a finger to help her.

Thea stood in front of them, preventing them from leaving the table. "Don't. It will only make it worse for her. I'll see to her in a bit." Her voice was calm and quiet, but the fury in her dark eyes was unmistakable. The two of them sank back down on their chairs, unhappy with the situation.

By now, Boone had let go of his victim. She scuttled down the stairs and immediately disappeared into the crowd. Satisfied that he'd made his point, her tormentor made his own descent, taking his time. Cal noticed the bartender was giving Thea a worried look.

It was Toby who spoke up. "Miss Thea, looks like your friend behind the bar thinks you'd better be moving on."

Thea shot Boone an ugly look but did get up. "It has been a pleasure, gentlemen. I hope you enjoy your stay here in King's Creek."

"I hope you get the chance to go for that ride you mention, Miss Thea."

"Me, too, Mr. Thacker. Me, too."

She was gone in a swirl of color and perfume. Toby watched her walk away and then drained his glass. He immediately filled it up and drank that as well. When he reached for the bottle again, Cal grabbed it and held it out of reach.

"That's more than you usually drink in a whole evening."

"So?" Toby glared at both him and the bottle.

"Getting drunk won't help her, and it'll only make you sick. Besides, we've got a long way to ride tonight." Aware that their actions were drawing some attention from nearby tables, Cal set the bottle back down.

Toby left it alone, turning his anger in the direction

of a better target. "Why hasn't somebody shot that son of a bitch?" At least he'd kept his voice low enough to reach Cal's ears only.

"Don't know. Either he normally keeps his nasty side hidden, or else he has enough guns backing him up to keep anyone from trying."

He didn't miss the fact that Toby's hand was currently resting right on the grip of his revolver. Maybe it would be better if they got out of there before things got out of hand.

"Why don't we go somewhere else for a while?"

Another voice joined in. "Leaving so soon?"

Cal looked up to see Upton Boone himself smiling down at him. Without waiting to be invited, their host pulled out the chair recently vacated by Thea and sat down. He stretched out his legs and leaned back in his chair.

"Don't you like my establishment? I serve the best liquor, and I have the prettiest girls in town."

"Nothing is wrong, Mr. Boone. I just hear you own several saloons in town. Thought we might check out a couple more before the night's over."

"The others aren't near as nice, although I'll let you decide that for yourselves. But you have me at a disadvantage since you already know my name."

"I'm Cal Preston, and my friend here is Toby Thacker."

Boone nodded toward Toby. "You've been in before." It wasn't a question, nor was it meant to be welcoming. "What brings the two of you to these parts?"

"The usual. Heard the gambling is good."

"But you're not playing."

Cal wondered if Boone pressed all newcomers so hard about their business. "Not tonight. I like to get the feel of a place before I lay my money down."

"Makes sense. Where are you staying?"

"Nowhere in particular. We set up camp outside town." True enough, thinking about the makeshift arrangements they had in Lily's barn.

"Why not get a room at the hotel across the street?"

"Well, unless they're free, I can't afford one. Besides, we weren't sure Toby here would be welcome."

Boone shrugged. "One man's money is as good as another's."

"Not everyone sees things that way."

"Since I own the hotel," Boone said with a particularly self-satisfied smile, "my opinion is the only one that counts around here. You'd be welcome there, Mr. Thacker, I'm sure. After all, I keep a close eye on things I own."

It was impossible to tell if his slight emphasis on the word *there* meant anything. Was he trying to warn Toby away from the saloon? Cal worried about Toby's reaction to what could be a veiled warning about Thea, but he needn't have. Toby offered Boone a friendly smile.

"I appreciate you saying that, Mr. Boone. It always helps to know where a man stands."

"Indeed it does." Their host rose to his feet. "Well, I have other guests to see to. It has been a pleasure meeting you both. I don't often get a man of your caliber through here, Preston. I would enjoy a friendly game of cards with you sometime."

"I'll keep that in mind."

Cal tossed back the last of his drink while he watched Boone walk away. He'd known men like Boone before; men who wielded their money as a weapon. Despite his easy charm, he was not a man to be underestimated. If he felt threatened, he would lash out with all the strength his money could buy.

Although at this point he didn't have a problem with Cal himself, there was little doubt that he'd noticed that

Thea had sat down with Toby not once but twice. If she was his private stock, he wouldn't take kindly to that.

"Let's get out of here."

Toby led the way out the door. Cal wondered how much effort it took his friend to resist one last look at Thea. For both their sakes, he hoped that Boone would assume that Toby had picked up on his warning and would heed it.

Once outside, they decided to try at least one more saloon before leaving town. Although they had met Boone, they still were no closer to solving the mystery of his interest in the McCord place.

They struck pay dirt in the third saloon they tried. Off the main street, this place didn't have the look of the others they'd been in. The floors were rough hewn, the tables mismatched, and the liquor vile. All that added up to men who couldn't afford better and were likely to be less than happy about their lot in life.

Discontented drinkers tended to be right friendly if someone else was paying for the liquor. Cal went in by himself. Toby followed a few minutes later, having pointed out that they would appear less threatening alone. Each of them picked a likely candidate, paid for a bottle, and sat down.

Cal had tasted worse whiskey, but he couldn't remember when. If it wouldn't have appeared odd for him to buy liquor and then not drink it, he wouldn't have touched the stuff after the first sip. Damn the McCords, anyway. What had they done for him to make it worth risking being poisoned?

On the other hand, the poor bastard he'd sat down with was downing the stuff as fast as Cal poured it.

"You seem troubled, friend. Feeling down on your luck?"

The man turned his bleary eyes toward Cal. "What

do you care?" That didn't keep him from holding his glass out for more.

"This town seems prosperous enough for a man interested in making some money."

The man snorted. "It is, if you're that son of bitch Boone and already own everything." He waved an unsteady hand around his head. " 'Ceptin' this place. Be glad it's not good enough for the likes of him because he'd steal it, too."

"Steal? Why would he have to steal anything? I would think Boone had enough money to buy whatever he wants."

"Call it what you want. But offering a man half what his ranch is worth is stealing to me."

"Offering is one thing; accepting it is another. Why would a man take so little for his place?" Cal already knew the answer, but he wanted to hear it anyway.

A single tear rolled down the man's cheek. "You try saying no to Upton Boone backed up by half a dozen rifles pointed right at your chest." With that, he lurched to his feet and wound his way through the tables and out the back door of the saloon.

Cal had no desire to spend another depressing minute in the man's company, but he figured the least he could do was leave the bottle for him. He picked up his hat, the signal he and Toby had arranged, and then headed out into the night air. He drew a couple of deep breaths, glad to rid himself of the scent of despair that had clung to his drinking companion.

Toby joined him a minute later, looking no happier than Cal felt about what he'd found out. "Did you learn anything?"

After taking a careful look up and down the street, Toby nodded. "We'd better wait to talk about it until we're out of town."

Cal couldn't agree more. If Boone did have that

many guns at his disposal, they were probably all somewhere close at hand. Men like that got bored easily. It wouldn't take much to prod one of them into action, especially if Boone had one or more of them watching Cal and Toby.

With that in mind, the two of them wasted no time in mounting up and riding out of town. They'd been careful to approach King's Creek from the opposite direction of the McCord ranch, although if someone were to trail them, they wouldn't be fooled for long.

Even so, it seemed a reasonable precaution to take, even if it did lengthen the time it took them to get back. He wondered if Lily would be waiting up to make sure they got back safely. He hurried his horse along, just in case.

Wade watched and waited until Toby and that bastard Preston were out of sight before riding in. Although he really liked Toby, he wished the gambler would go straight to perdition. It wasn't enough that he'd won all of Wade's money and the rights to half the ranch. No, he had to make Wade look bad in front of Lily.

Wade unsaddled his horse and turned it loose in its stall, making sure it had fresh hay and water. No doubt it was Toby who had seen to that. The other one wouldn't lift a finger to do anything useful around the ranch.

Except to tote water for Lily. Even after she'd gone inside to get away from Cal, he'd seen to her garden for her. Just the thought of it had Wade wanting to punch something—or someone, although he had some doubt that he could win against the gambler. In the brief tussle they'd had, he'd been surprised at the other man's strength.

Who would have thought that a man who made his living shuffling cards and smoking cigars would have such power in his punches? His jaw still ached from one particularly lucky blow. Wade had landed a few of his own, though, and that brought him some satisfaction. He'd even drawn blood.

The fight hadn't solved a damn thing. Lily hadn't seen them as equals. No, she'd lit into Preston for picking on Wade, like he was a child or something. How many times did he have to tell her that he was a man, all grown up?

He stopped near the house to watch her through the window. She was working in the kitchen, unaware that she was being observed. Ignoring a twinge of conscience, he took the opportunity to study her.

As usual, she was singing to herself while she stirred something on the stove. She'd stop as soon as anyone walked in the room, saying she sounded worse than a bunch of crows hassling an owl. He thought she had a sweet voice, but there was no convincing her otherwise.

He worried because she was so thin. Ranch work was too hard for a woman as delicate as Lily. She would deny that, he knew, but he had eyes. He could see how tired she was at the end of the day. Though he was sorry about losing the money, he didn't regret taking the chance. If the cards had fallen differently, he would've had enough money to take care of her the way she deserved.

Instead, he had only added to her worries and brought that damn gambler into their lives. Preston was sure enough a puzzle. The man was up to something, but damned if Wade could figure out what it was. He was so obviously not cut out for ranching. But then, in some ways neither had Wade's brother. Thad had all the big ideas, but no real sense of how to accomplish them.

The three of them would have been better off on a small farm somewhere, but that would never have satisfied Thad. No, he wanted wide-open spaces, a herd of cattle, and some high-strung horses to breed. He figured they'd learn the business as they went along. It had taken time, but things had been looking up for them.

Then one of those precious horses of his had ended all their dreams, leaving Lily a widow. Wade wondered if she ever realized how jealous he'd been of his own brother, although Thad had known. In fact, he'd made a special effort to make sure that Wade knew exactly what the two of them were doing during those long nights behind closed doors. He'd had a mean streak sometimes. Making his young brother green-eyed jealous had been just part of it.

There had been times Wade had come damn close to hating his only blood relative. And now, with Thad out of the way and Wade finally old enough to make Lily see him as something more than a kid, the gambler had to show up, making eyes at her. Yeah, he'd have to figure out what to do about Cal, and soon.

If anyone was going to take Thad's place in Lily's life, it sure as hell wasn't going to be a tumbleweed drifter like Cal Preston. No sir, not if he could help it.

Suddenly, Wade realized that Lily was looking out the window right at him. She motioned for him to come in to supper. Damn, what a fool he was, getting caught staring at her like that. He pantomimed washing up; she nodded and turned back to her cooking.

Wade walked around to the pump, wishing cold water could wash away all his improper thoughts about Lily along with the day's dirt. He didn't hold out much hope, though.

Five

Lily had promised herself she wouldn't wait up to make sure her two guests made it back to the ranch safely. And if she did worry some, it was only about Toby. He was such a nice man, polite and a hard worker. Cal Preston was a different matter. He could stay in town gambling, and goodness knows what else, all night long and that would be fine with her.

Not tired enough to feel like retiring for the night, she set aside the shirt she was mending for Wade and stood up. Stretching from side to side, she tried to work some of the stiffness out of her back.

The air in the house felt stifling, so she made a quick decision. "I'm going outside for a walk."

She didn't wait for Wade to respond. He hadn't said more than ten words all evening and had shut himself up in his room as soon as dinner was over. For all she knew, he was asleep. With that in mind, she slipped out the door and gently pulled it closed behind her.

Stepping off the porch, she looked up into the night sky. Seeing how high the moon was, she realized that it was later than she'd thought. She smiled up at the white-gold ball, loving the way its light made everything all silvery and black. The air had cooled considerably since the sun had gone down, making it feel good on her skin.

She stopped long enough to pull out her hairpins and shook her head. The night breeze playfully teased at her hair, making her feel wickedly free with it hanging to her waist. With renewed energy, she made the rounds, checking on the chickens and the corral. That brought her up short.

There were two more horses in the corral than there had been at dinnertime, which meant Toby and Cal were home. Not home, she quickly assured herself. They were back from town; that's what she really meant. Everything must have gone all right if they'd come back so quietly that she hadn't heard them ride in.

A sense of relief washed over her, warning her that she'd been more worried about the two of them than she'd let on, even to herself. No doubt they'd turned in for the night, too. It was clearly time for her to seek her own bed.

She was about to head back to the house when something in the night air warned her that she was no longer alone. The heady scent of tobacco, leather, and something that was pure man surrounded her. It had to be Cal. Toby didn't smoke, at least not that she'd seen.

Nor would he intrude on a woman's privacy without warning her.

"Kind of late for a lady to be out walking by herself." His voice seemed to come out of nowhere until he stepped out of the shadows next to the barn.

Lily fought the urge to scurry back to the house. She stood her ground and demanded, "What do you mean by that?"

"Only what I said. It's late to be out walking alone."

"Well, I'm not alone now, am I?"

He stepped closer, not at all what she intended for

him to do. "No, you're not. Did this little foray of yours have some purpose?"

"I was restless." Truth was, the restlessness didn't start until she saw Cal step out of the shadows. She felt edgy, as if her skin hurt.

Cal taunted her as he moved even nearer. "Why? Worried about Toby?"

"If you must know, yes. I wanted to know if he got back safe and sound."

"He did, and so did I, but I guess you don't care about that."

He was standing close enough now for her to hear the rhythm of his breathing. He sounded as if he'd been running hard. The warmth of his body raised the temperature around her and deep down inside her where her womanly feelings were stirring to life. She stepped back, stumbling over nothing.

Cal caught her by the shoulders to keep her from falling, but that didn't explain why he had to pull her up to his chest. His heart stuttered and then raced to catch up with her own pulse.

Confused by what she was feeling, she made the mistake of looking up into Cal's eyes. They glittered with the reflected light of the moon. If she didn't know better, she would have thought he was about to kiss her. But that couldn't be true. They didn't even like each other.

But that didn't stop her from waiting through the seconds that it took him to dip his mouth down to meet hers.

"Cal, what the hell are you doing out here?" Toby had almost walked right into them. Now he was backing away, shaking his head as if to deny the truth of what was right in front of him. "Well, I'll be damned."

Lily didn't know who was more embarrassed at that moment. Toby was clearly at a loss what to say. She was grateful for the darkness that hid both her shame and her blush. Not that they'd really done anything wrong—or even anything at all. Cal eased back into the deep shadows.

His voice was like the crack of a whip. "Toby, get the hell away from here now."

"Good idea," was his friend's response as he disappeared around the corner toward the door of the barn. He muttered disapprovingly each step of the way.

They both waited until Toby was gone, doing their best not to acknowledge each other's presence. All Lily wanted to do was run for the house and hope that she woke up in the morning to find this had all been a dream.

Or a nightmare. But Cal was all too real.

"Are you all right?"

She managed to nod, but that was all.

"I'll walk you back to the house." He reached out to take her by the arm.

"That's not necessary."

"Maybe not, but I'm doing it anyway." He tugged her along beside him.

It felt less like being escorted and more like being dragged, but she appreciated the gesture. The whole experience had shaken her more than she cared to admit. Had she misread Cal's intentions? She didn't even understand her own. Would she have allowed him to kiss her?

She risked a glance at her companion, but it was too dark now to see the expression on his face. Perhaps that was best for both of them.

Once they reached the porch, he let go of her arm, allowing her the dignity of walking the rest of the way on her own. Before opening the door, she turned back to thank him for seeing her back to the house, but he was already halfway back to the barn. She didn't envy him having to face Toby; she was only too glad not to have to talk to anyone at that moment.

With what resolve she could muster, she tried to put Cal Preston out of her mind. It worked for the time it took for her to make her final preparations for going to bed. But once she climbed into bed and saw the empty pillow next to her, the sensations all came rushing back.

It had been a long time since she'd shared the intimacy of her bed with a man. Thad had never been much for talking, but still the time they'd spent together behind the closed bedroom door had been special to her. All of it, not only the rare time when he'd been willing to talk about his dreams for their future.

And she missed being touched. The simplicity of a kiss or a hug had meant far more to her than she'd realized until it was too late. But Cal Preston was anything but simple. A kiss from him would complicate her life far beyond the momentary pleasure of the embrace.

She kicked off the blankets. Even the thin cotton of her nightgown felt hot, but it had little to do with the temperature in the room. The moonlight filtered through the curtains, casting shadows in the room, but they didn't contain the two-legged menace that the ones by the barn had.

But more than she cared to admit, she wished they did. Turning her back on the window and everything outside, she finally fell asleep.

Cal was up at first light. He thought about slipping inside the house to make some coffee but didn't want to risk running into Lily. He'd be lucky to be away before Toby woke up. His friend had lectured him long and loud about the stupidity of Cal's actions last night.

He'd denied everything Toby had accused him of,

but they'd both known the intent had been there, shimmering in the air between Cal and Lily. For that moment in time, Cal had ached with the need to kiss her. What would have happened beyond the kiss was anyone's guess.

He suspected that Toby hadn't run out of things to say to him, only the energy to say them. Chances were he'd start in as soon as he opened his eyes. Cal had no intention of being there to hear them.

Besides, Toby wasn't saying anything that Cal wasn't already telling himself. Only a fool got involved with a good woman. He was sure that despite her sharp tongue, Lily McCord would make some man an excellent wife. But Cal didn't want a wife, excellent or otherwise. Rare was the gambler who made a good husband. They were a nomadic lot, moving from town to town, seeking out Lady Luck, the only woman who really mattered in their lives.

But damned if he didn't wish he'd gotten to taste Lily's kiss. Her mouth was temptation itself. And underneath those drab everyday dresses of her, she had womanly curves enough to make a man lose all common sense. He'd only felt her against him for a few seconds, but his body remembered the sensation all too clearly.

This line of thought wasn't getting him anywhere. He picked up his saddle and slipped out to the corral. His horse didn't seem too happy to see him, sidling away when Cal tossed the chilly blanket and saddle up on his back.

"Come back here, you miserable animal," Cal crooned. At least his horse didn't care what he said to him as long as Cal fed him regularly. The big sorrel edged closer, begging for an ear scratch. Cal gave him what he wanted and then finished saddling him.

He regretted taking the time when he heard footsteps coming right in his direction. If it wouldn't appear cowardly, he would have mounted up and taken off at a gallop. He braced himself for Toby's tirade, but to his surprise it was Wade.

The boy looked startled when he realized that he wasn't alone.

"What are you doing up this early?" he demanded.

Cal was in no mood to argue with anyone. "I thought I'd ride out and check on the herd."

"Why? You haven't shown any interest in the cattle up to this point."

He couldn't very well tell Wade why he was avoiding both Toby and Lily, so he lied. "I want to check on my investment."

Wade flushed, but nodded. "Fine, but only if I go with you."

Cal led his horse out of the corral. "What's the matter? Don't you trust me?"

"Hell no." Wade started saddling up his own horse.

His frank answer made Cal chuckle. "Well, at least you're honest about how you feel." Once outside the gate, he mounted up. "I'm going to start without you, but I'm not going anywhere fast. Catch up with me when you're ready."

With that, Cal urged his horse into a slow trot. Almost immediately, he eased back to a walk. He'd had little sleep during the night and was up far earlier than was normal for him. As a result, he had a headache lurking around the edges of his mind. It wouldn't take much encouragement for it to come into full blossom.

He'd only gone about half a mile when he heard the sound of horses approaching. Just as he feared, Toby was with Wade. That was all right, though. With the youngster along, Toby wouldn't be able to tear into Cal, not without explaining why. For some reason, Toby had taken a sort of fatherly attitude toward the boy. He wouldn't want to distress him over an incident that didn't amount to much.

He might as well wait for them. Once they caught up with him, Wade led the way to the valley where he and Toby had moved the cattle. Even though Cal had never worked on a ranch, a man couldn't play cards against ranchers and cowhands for years without picking up some knowledge along the way.

He could see why they'd chosen this particular valley for the herd. The only way in was fairly narrow, keeping the herd from spreading out too far. The creek running along the western edge was ample for the small herd, and the grass was still lush and green. One or two men would have little difficulty in keeping the cattle penned in.

Cal offered his compliments to Toby on his choice of locations for the herd.

"It wasn't my idea. Wade here had already figured it out for himself. When it comes to cattle, the boy sure enough knows what he is doing."

The younger man flushed with pleasure at Toby's praise. "Thad and I always meant to build up the size of the herd and hire more help. About the time we could afford a couple of hands, Thad died. Since then all the men and about a fourth of the cattle have run off."

Toby shook his head. "No use feeling bad about that. No man could have done more by himself than you have."

Wade seemed to sit up straighter in his saddle as they surveyed the valley from where they sat. Cal felt an unexpected surge of sympathy for the younger man. There'd been no mention of any other family, so losing his brother had left Wade alone in the world except for Lily. No wonder the boy was attached to her. Trying to run a ranch, even one of modest size, was difficult enough with help. Alone, a job that size could use a man up pretty damn fast.

Toby interrupted his thoughts. "I'm sorry to leave you alone today, Mr. Wade, but I've got business elsewhere." He urged his horse forward, leading the way into the valley and closer to the herd. The cattle paid the three horsemen little heed.

Meanwhile, Wade followed Toby, clearly puzzled by Toby's plans for the day. Cal didn't blame him. As far as the McCords knew, neither Cal nor Toby had any other ties to the area other than their tenuous interest in their ranch. Wade could stay confused as far as Cal was concerned. He wasn't about to tell the McCords that Toby was fool enough to get himself tied up in knots over a woman, especially one connected to Upton Boone.

Toby shifted in his saddle and then stood in the stirrups to get a better look. "Don't seem to be any more missing."

Wade agreed. "I've been watching for signs that the rustlers have been back. Either they've moved on, or they've been busy elsewhere."

"I still hate leaving you alone out here."

"He won't be alone." Cal wasn't sure which of them was the more surprised by his announcement, them or himself.

Wade narrowed his eyes in suspicion. "You don't know anything about riding herd."

"More than you think, but that isn't important. I do know a lot about guns." Cal patted the grip of his revolver. "If unwanted company shows up, you tell me which skill would be more helpful."

Wade answered by spurring his horse forward. Cal and Toby let him go.

"I'll be back this afternoon sometime. I don't much like him being out here by himself, but Mrs. McCord shouldn't be alone either. We surprised Boone last time. I'm thinking he won't be run off so easily next time he comes calling."

"At least he doesn't know who was helping her. As long as we can keep that bit of information from him, we can still check up on him in town." He didn't say what he was thinking, but Toby guessed.

"Thea doesn't know where we're staying." He sounded defensive.

"Not yet, but she's a smart woman. Eventually, you'll either let something slip or else just up and tell her." Cal had firsthand experience how easy it was for a man to make a fool of himself around the right woman. It was even easier when it was the wrong woman.

Toby's eyes narrowed in anger. "Since when don't you trust me to keep my mouth shut?"

"Since you started thinking with something other than your brain." Cal smiled to lessen the sting of his words. "You know your own self how much trouble I've gotten into doing the same damn thing. After that poker game, if I'd gone to the stable instead of upstairs with Mary, we wouldn't be sitting here now."

"You got that right." He watched Wade working his way down the south side of the valley, looking for strays. "I need to see her."

"Then go."

"You sure you'll be all right out here?"

"I figure I'm smarter than a damn cow. A little, anyway." Just as he intended, Toby laughed.

"Then I'll be going." Toby wheeled his horse around and headed back to the entrance to the valley.

When he rode out of sight, Cal positioned himself on the opposite side of the valley from Wade and began imitating his actions. The work was hot and dusty, but it beat sitting at the ranch and thinking impure thoughts about Lily McCord.

His gut ached and his hands trembled. What if she came? And what if she didn't? Could he get his nerve up to ride out here again?

Cursing himself for a fool, Toby swung down out of the saddle to give both himself and his horse a rest. He led the animal down to the river's edge and let him drink a little. Once he cooled down, he could have his fill from the ice-cold stream.

There was plenty of grass, so he hobbled the animal and let him wander at will. He wouldn't go far. That done, Toby sat down on a nearby log and settled in to wait. He closed his eyes and let the image of Thea Jones fill his mind. Damn, she was beautiful. Those eyes of hers were enough for a man to drown in. And those lips were made for sin and would taste like heaven. Her beauty, while considerable, wasn't all there was to her.

She probably thought he would hold her profession against her, but he didn't. She wouldn't be the first woman who had turned to prostitution just to keep food in her belly and a roof over her head. The fact that she still held her head up high and had some pride about herself was a testament to her strength.

A woman like that would make a man a good partner. He opened his eyes and shook his head at the foolish thought. Cal would tell him that women only complicated a man's life, but then Cal hadn't had a mamma like Toby's. She'd ruled their family with an iron hand, but no one ever doubted her goodness.

God rest her soul, he still missed her.

His horse stopped eating and held his nose up to test the wind. At first, Toby didn't hear anything, but he kept his eyes pinned on the cluster of trees that his horse was watching with such interest. Sure enough, he could just make out something moving through the trees heading in his direction.

He stood and dusted off the seat of his pants. Once he'd straightened his clothes as best he could, he slipped back into the undergrowth. There was no telling who might be riding through the area. He might be a fool for coming all this distance on the small chance he would see Thea, but that didn't mean he was foolish enough to make a target of himself.

When the rider finally came into sight, a sense of disappointment washed over Toby. Though he couldn't yet make out any details, the stranger was definitely wearing trousers and a man's jacket. He pulled out his pocket watch. If she didn't show up within the next half an hour, he might as well ride on back to the ranch.

That was when he noticed that the rider had stopped to water his horse. No, wait. Make that *her* horse. The clothes might have belonged on a man, but that was all that did. That slender build was definitely feminine. When she took her hat off to fan her face, he knew for sure.

She'd come.

He worked his way closer to where Thea stood with her back to him. Now that she was right there in front of him, he hesitated to approach her.

She made the decision for him. "You might as well come on out here, Toby Thacker. I don't have much time and I would rather not waste it playing hide-and-seek with the likes of you."

When she turned to face him, a playful smile was tugging at the corner of her mouth. Damn, she looked good. Even without the makeup and fancy clothes, she was a beautiful woman. Her eyes were enough to capture a man's soul forever. And what those men's trou-

sers did to show off her lush curves should be against
the law.

His mouth felt too dry for words. "Morning, Miss
Thea," was all he managed to get out.

"I brought us some lunch, if you've a mind to do
something besides stand there gawking at me."

No doubt she got enough of that from the men who
frequented Boone's Silver Slipper. She deserved better.

"That was right thoughtful of you, Miss Thea." He
hurried forward to lift down the saddlebags from her
horse. He set them on the ground near the log he'd sat
on earlier. "I'll hobble your horse near mine, if that is
all right with you."

When he got back, she had a tablecloth spread out
and was putting fried chicken on a plate. His mouth
watered, but it had little do with the food.

"That looks delicious."

She smiled. "Don't thank me. I got the cook at the
hotel to put this together for me." She held out a plate
to him.

He accepted it, but then wasn't sure where to sit.
Thea, with that same half smile, patted the ground next
to her. "Sit here by me."

Toby crossed his legs and sank down on the blanket
next to her. For the moment, eating chicken seemed to
be the safest thing to do, because he wasn't sure he
could carry on a conversation yet.

All too quickly, the two of them finished the last of
the chicken and the apples she'd brought along. She
didn't seem to be anxious to talk much, either.

"Let's walk by the river." After he stood up, he offered her a hand up, but she got to her feet without
his help. Side by side they walked in silence along the
river. Occasionally, he'd stop and toss a few rocks in
the river, trying to skip them across to the other side.
She surprised him by tossing a few herself.

Finally, she was the one to break the silence between them. "I wasn't sure you'd come."

Her quiet statement came as a shock to him, but the uncertainty in her eyes testified to the truth of it.

"A man would have to be a fool not to want to spend time with you."

She met his gaze head on. "Lots of men have spent time with me over the years."

No doubt Thea meant the words to be a challenge. That was fine with him. He'd rather have things out in the open. For a few seconds, he let her words hang there between them before he spoke. Then, reaching out to take her dainty hand in his rough, work-hardened one, he gave her a solemn look. "They've spent time with the show you put on along with those fancy dresses of yours. I'm talking about the real you."

She tried to jerk free of his grasp, but he wouldn't let her. "I'm not two women, Toby. Don't fool yourself about that."

"I won't, but don't you go foolin' yourself, either. There's a lot more to you than what Upton Boone shows off in the saloon. That part you hold back from him and the others, that's the part I want all to myself. I know I have to share the rest, for now."

"That's something else you have to know, Toby. I belong to him in ways you don't know and wouldn't understand."

"Explain it to me, Thea. I can't help you if I don't know what the problem is."

This time he let go when she wanted to be free of his touch. She wrapped her arms around herself, as if to ward off cold. She looked up at the sun and shivered in its warmth. "I owe him. That's all you need to know."

She drew a deep breath. "Now, maybe we can spend a little time together like this. I can't give you more than that. If it isn't enough, then ride on out of here and let me have some peace."

It hurt that she didn't trust him with the truth. He wanted to walk away; damned if he didn't. But he wouldn't, not after he looked down into her pretty face and saw that it was exactly what she expected him to do. He wondered who else had walked away and left her hurting in the past, leading her to expect the same from him.

"I'm not going anywhere soon." He risked touching the side of her face. When she didn't flinch away, he cupped her chin to tilt it up a bit. Gently, very slowly, he leaned down to kiss that mouth with all the need he'd been feeling since he'd first laid eyes on her.

She didn't stir, just stood there and let him make the first move. But once their lips met, she sighed and leaned into him. Her hands found his shoulders and held on for dear life. He pulled her into his arms and groaned with the pleasure of it all. She tasted of sweetness he'd never known before.

Probably most men she had known had come to her in a hurry with only their own satisfaction on their minds. He promised himself he'd make their time together good for them both. So for the moment, he would take his time and make the most of their kiss and not go rushing along the path that the heat between them would lead them down.

Oh, he wanted her all right; he sure enough did. But as he'd told her, he wanted the whole woman, the real woman she was. He let her be the one to make the next move. When her tongue traced the shape of his mouth, he almost lost his sanity with the effort it took to maintain control.

She moved back and smiled at him. Pleased with both her and himself, Toby planted a quick kiss on her nose and then moved just far enough away from her to give himself room to breathe.

"Want to walk some more?"

When she nodded, he put his arm around her shoulders and led the way along the dappled shadows by the river. When their way was blocked by a tumble of boulders, they turned back.

When they reached the horses, she frowned. "I need to be getting back to town."

To Boone was what she really meant, but now wasn't the time for that argument. He wasn't about to spoil the last minutes of their day together.

"How often can you get away?"

She frowned. "Most weeks, I go riding one day, maybe two. So far, no one has objected. If I were to start disappearing more often, I don't know what would happen."

He fought down the frustration he felt. He didn't want to beg for her time or settle for the scraps that Boone didn't want. He also knew he had no right to demand more than she could safely give him.

"Why don't we plan on meeting up here again in three days' time?" He'd settle for four days, but five was too long to wait.

Evidently, she needed time to think about it, because she abruptly changed the subject. "I thought you and that friend of yours were passing through."

So they both had their own secrets. "Not exactly. We're staying with friends."

"Anyone I know?" She was asking for more than information.

He hesitated before answering. But realizing that if he wanted her trust, he had to be willing to offer up his. "Lily and Wade McCord."

Thea frowned and narrowed her eyes. "Don't they own a ranch not far from town?"

He nodded. "That's them. Do you know them?"

"Not likely. Decent women the likes of her wouldn't have nothing to do with my kind."

"Don't do that!" He clenched his fists at his side to keep from shaking her.

She jumped at the harshness in his voice. "Don't do what?"

"Put yourself down like that. Miss Lily is a good woman, a strong one, too, like you. I can see the two of you getting along right fine."

"Well, since there isn't much chance of us ever meeting up, I won't argue the point. It doesn't matter anyway. Since women like her don't come into where I work, I wouldn't have any way of meeting her. I think I've seen the boy around town, though."

"Handsome with reddish-brown hair and hazel eyes."

"That sounds like the one I'm thinking of." She stopped, as if trying to think of something that just wouldn't come clear. "I know I've heard their name somewhere recently."

"Boone stopped by their ranch awhile back. He wants to buy it from Miss Lily."

"That doesn't mean anything," Thea said, shaking her head. "He's always wanting to buy somebody out. Maybe I'm thinking of something else."

"If you think of something you've heard about the McCords, make sure you tell me. They are nice people." That settled, he tried again to get an answer to his earlier question. "Three days?"

"I can't promise, Toby, but I'll try. If not three, then four for sure. That's the best I can do."

"A man can't ask for more." He tugged her back into his arms. She went willingly, turning her face up to his, ready for his kiss.

This time he didn't coax; he took her mouth with

the same intensity that he wanted to take her to bed. Maybe he'd scare her with his need; it sure enough scared him. But it was the only way he had of telling her how much he wanted her.

When she didn't object or back away, he risked letting his hands do a little exploring on their own. He traced a pattern, circling closer and closer to learning the feel of her breasts. Someone moaned in pleasure when he gave a gentle squeeze, but he couldn't have said which one of them it was. Maybe it was both.

Thea let him taste and let him touch. He struggled to memorize each sensation because it would be three long days before he could enjoy them again. It took all his strength and nearly his sanity to stop and let her go.

Back to town and back to Boone, while Toby went back to being alone. And when Thea rode out of sight, she took the day's beauty with her.

Six

Lily spent the morning hours alone. Although Cal seemed content to do little of value with his time, she'd gotten used to having him underfoot while she did her own chores. But when she had gotten up that morning, everyone else was already gone, leaving no word as to where they were or when they'd be back.

Of course, it was only Wade that she was worried about. The other two may have decided that it was time for them to give up and move on. That was fine with her. She and Wade had enough on their plates without being hounded for money they didn't have.

To be fair, neither Toby nor Cal had seriously pressed them to pay off Wade's debt. She wasn't sure what that meant. Toby seemed to be a decent man, but Cal was a gambler. In her limited experience, men who made their living with a deck of cards only worshiped one thing—cold, hard cash.

To satisfy her curiosity, she detoured from her normal routine and walked straight to the barn. A glance at the corral verified that three horses were missing. Once inside the barn, she knew immediately that her unwanted guests weren't gone for good. Although they didn't have much in the way of personal possessions, some of their things were still scattered around their temporary living quarters.

As she checked her hens' favorite nesting spots for eggs, she tried not to think about why she suddenly felt like smiling. She didn't know where the three men were, but at least she knew they would all be coming back.

Even Cal Preston.

For the hundredth time, she replayed last night's events in her mind. Even though the whole thing had taken on dreamlike qualities, the emotions stirred up inside her were painfully real. Perhaps if they had kissed, she would have been able to put it all behind her as a bad experience.

But somehow, she knew it wouldn't have been. Although she didn't approve of either him or his profession, she didn't doubt that he took his cards seriously. She could only conclude that whatever he chose to pursue, he did so with single-minded purpose.

Which made her wonder if he brought that same intensity to lovemaking, not that it was any concern of hers. It was obvious that he'd never found anyone or anything that made him want to settle down. She could not afford to risk her reputation by getting involved with a man like Preston. It wasn't as if she were really interested in him anyway. Her reaction to him was due to the fact he was close, not that he was worthy of her affections.

Although she'd been content with Thad, the sharp pain of grief had faded over time. Maybe her reaction to Cal was her mind's way of saying that it was time to get on with her life. That thought made her feel better about the whole situation. It wasn't Cal she wanted at all. No, she missed having a husband. There was no way the gambler could fill that void.

Turning her back on his meager pile of belongings felt right, as if she was walking away from the man himself. Once outside, she settled into the routine of her morning chores. The chickens fluttered around her feet as she scattered their feed in the dust. She milked the dairy cow and was carrying the milk to the house when a series of shots rang out, all aimed into the dirt right behind her.

Without concern for the waste, she dropped the pail and took off running for the house. The shots continued until she reached the porch and dove through the front door. Her hands were shaking so badly at first that she couldn't shove the bolt. The second time she tried, it slid into place, making her feel a little safer. Picking up her rifle, she prepared to return fire, if necessary. It would be a waste of ammunition, though, until she could figure out where the shots were coming from.

After what seemed an eternity, she realized that the only noise was the sound of her heart pounding. Edging closer to the front window, she risked a quick glance outside. Nothing was stirring. That didn't mean that it was over, because whoever was out there could afford to wait her out.

It wouldn't be the first time she had spent the day locked in her house. The last time was only a few days before when Toby and Cal had come riding into her life. This time she wasn't going to bake bread or any of the other chores that needed doing. No, she'd stand guard and pray that Wade came home early.

Cal figured it was safe to go back to the house. With Toby off with Thea and Wade riding herd on the cattle, he'd have the barn to himself. Actually, though he wouldn't admit it under pain of death, he'd actually enjoyed the morning's work. If Wade had brought enough lunch for them both, he would have stayed even longer. No doubt he'd probably get bored with chasing cows pretty damn quick, but it had been an interesting experience.

He'd even managed to round up a couple of steers that had wandered off from the others. It had felt like a game, trying to outguess their next move and countering it. One had been particularly wily, but Cal had bested the beast in the end. The memory made him smile.

He reached the corral before he realized that something was wrong. It was quiet, almost unnaturally so. Looking around, he saw the milk pail lying on its side, its contents soaking into the ground. That was scary enough. Then he saw blood on the ground, and his own froze in his veins.

"Lily!" he shouted as he took off for the house, drawing his revolver as he ran. "Lily, where the hell are you?"

Once on the porch, he tried the door and found it wouldn't open. He pounded on it with his fist before it dawned on him that he was making a pretty big target of himself, especially if someone was in the house with Lily.

He was working his way toward the window when he heard the bolt slide. Slowly the door opened and a rifle barrel appeared in the crack. He flattened himself against the wall and with his free hand grabbed the gun by the barrel and gave it a yank.

Lily came stumbling out the door, fighting to keep control of her rifle. Only a quick move on his part kept her from falling to her knees. She lit into him, flailing fists and feet.

He tossed her rifle off the porch and tried to holster his own gun before attempting to calm her down. Finally, he wrapped his arms around her, trapping the struggling woman against his chest.

"Damn it, Lily, it's Cal. Quit fighting me." When

she landed a nasty kick to his shin, he almost dropped her. He let out a string of curses and tried again.

"Lily, stop it. I can't help you if you don't calm down." Evidently, something was getting through to her, because as quickly as she had attacked, she stopped. She sagged in his arms. He did his best to soothe her, awkwardly stroking her back with one hand while he supported her with the other.

"Are you hurt?"

She shook her head, her eyes wide with remembered fear. "No, I think they were shooting in the dirt to chase me into the house. You know, trying to scare me, and they did."

No wonder. He'd have been running like hell for cover himself, but she didn't need to know that. "Can you stand? I need to go see where the blood in the dirt out there came from."

Obviously unwilling to be left behind, Lily stumbled along in his tracks. It wasn't hard to figure out what had happened. One of the chickens was lying dead in the dirt by the barn. He half expected Lily to break down, but she surprised him.

Picking the dead bird up by its feet, she announced, "It looks like chicken for dinner. Do you like it fried or stewed with dumplings?"

Relieved that he didn't have a hysterical female on his hands, he smiled. "I'm right fond of chicken and dumplings. Besides, it's one of Toby's favorites."

Then he got serious. "How long ago did this happen?"

Lily looked up at the sun. "It seemed like I was hiding in the house forever, but it couldn't have been all that long. Maybe half an hour or so."

"I want you to go back in the house and lock the door while I have a look around." He took her by the arm and walked with her, matching his long strides to her shorter ones.

"What do you hope to find?"

"How many of them were there, maybe which direction they came from. I don't hold out much hope that I'll find anything really helpful, but you never know. Maybe someone got careless."

He walked her back to the house. On the way, he'd handed her back her rifle. After making sure she'd bolted the door again, he drew his own gun and went back out to study the ground where the shots had hit.

He followed the line of fire as best he could out beyond the corral. Atop a small rise, the grass was still mashed down where someone had lain down to take aim. If he had to hazard a guess, it looked as if one man had held the horses while the other did the shooting.

If he ever found out who put that fear in Lily's eyes, he'd shoot the bastard himself. That is, if Toby didn't get to him first. What kind of coward took pleasure in scaring a lone woman?

The answer was simple, to Cal's way of thinking. It had to be another ploy of Boone's to get the McCords to sell. They'd never prove it, though. Even if they knew who'd pulled the trigger, Boone probably had a half-dozen paid witnesses ready to swear the two men had been in town all day long.

For now, there wasn't much he could do but go back to the house so Lily wouldn't be alone. Once Toby returned, they would set up a plan so that one of them was always with her.

As if he'd conjured his friend up out of thin air, Toby rode into sight just as Cal finished unsaddling his horse. This time, he put the animal in a stall in the barn rather than turning it loose in the corral. If someone was going to shoot animals, it only made sense to keep them out of sight as much as possible.

He waited for Toby to reach him.

"Let's get out of sight," he said by way of greeting.

Toby waited until they were inside the barn before asking questions. Cal filled him in on the morning's events in short order.

"Is Miss Lily all right?" Toby asked as he checked his guns over.

"She was when I sent her into the house. By now, I figure she's trying to decide if it could have been me shooting at her. My arrival could be viewed as being pretty damned convenient."

Toby didn't laugh.

Hell, he was only half kidding anyway. After all she had little reason to trust him. Toby made quick work of seeing to his horse. The two of them picked up their rifles and ammunition and cautiously approached the house in case Lily was feeling jittery enough to shoot first.

Toby called out before they approached the door, wanting to give fair warning of their presence outside the house. "Miss Lily, can you let us in? Cal and I want to make sure that you are all right in there."

Lily peeked out the window before unlocking the door. Cal couldn't fault her caution. She opened it far enough for them to slip inside and then just as quickly locked it behind them. It was clear that the incident had shaken her badly.

"I'm right sorry this happened, Miss Lily." Toby shook his head. "I can't imagine what kind of fool would go tormenting women and animals like that."

Lily sank down onto a nearby chair. "I can't either. It's meanness, plain and simple." Her eyes flickered in Cal's direction, but then slid away.

Damn, he was right. She was wondering if it had

been him all along. It was doubtful that she'd believe a word he said, but he tried.

"I don't scare women and children."

She almost managed to hide the guilty look in her eyes, but it was there, all right. His temper, already shaky from the fear he'd felt when he'd seen the splashes of blood outside, started to slip.

Toby started to say something, but Cal held up his hand to stop him. This was between him and Lily.

"I don't know what I ever did to give you such a low opinion of me, Mrs. McCord, but I'm telling you, I did not shoot at you or your damn chicken."

She nodded, but hesitantly.

He strode over to where she still sat perched on the edge of the chair and jerked her up to face him. "I'll only repeat this one more time. It wasn't me."

Lily stared up into Cal's eyes. Something in his gaze must have convinced her of his innocence. Slowly, she nodded again, this time with more assurance.

"I'm sorry, Mr. Preston. I know you wouldn't do something like this. This has all the earmarks of Upton Boone's tactics. I should have known better than to doubt you."

"Damn straight, you should have." He eased his hold on her and then allowed her to sit back down. She seemed relieved when he took several steps away from her. A part of him resented it, but he couldn't really blame her. With everything that had happened lately, she must feel as if her life was out of her control.

"Toby, why don't you make Mrs. McCord a cup of tea while we make some plans."

She tried to protest, but Toby stopped her. "It's no trouble, Miss Lily, and I could use a cup myself. This has been a trying day for us all."

Cal shot his friend a questioning look, but Toby wouldn't look at him. Unless Cal missed his guess,

Thea had shown up for their rendezvous. Although now wasn't the time, he resolved to pry the details out of his friend before the day was over.

His interest was only partly due to curiosity, because Thea also had ties to Upton Boone. Toby was obviously taken with the woman, but neither of them knew enough about her relationship with Boone to trust her. Had she met up with Toby as a means of luring him away from the McCord ranch, or solely for her own reasons?

On second thought, that seemed a little far fetched. For one thing, as far as they knew, she didn't know of their connection with Lily and Wade. Toby might have told her today, but there was no reason to think she had anything to do with today's incident.

He wandered from window to window, trying to see if there was any activity around the ranch. Everything appeared to be back to normal. For now.

Lily spoke. "I'll be back in a few moments."

He was about to ask her where she was going when he noticed the blush staining her cheeks. She obviously had some personal needs to see to. "Don't be gone long. We'll leave the door unlocked until you get back."

She slipped out the door. He wouldn't have been surprised if she'd taken off running, but if she did, it was after she left the front porch. He took advantage of her absence to talk to Toby.

"One of us should ride out and make sure Wade is all right. There's no reason to think he isn't, but it pays to be safe."

"I had the same idea, but I didn't want to worry Miss Lily. I'll go and check up on the boy. If everything is quiet out there, I'll bring him back in time to have dinner."

Cal frowned. "Do you think they'd attack more than once today?"

Toby was busy setting the teapot and three cups on the table. He added a heaping spoonful of sugar to each cup and then poured the hot liquid. It wasn't Cal's drink of choice, but even he had to admit that it tasted good after the day's events.

Finally, Toby answered his question. "We have no way of knowing. Hell, we don't even know for sure if Boone is behind all this."

Neither of them had heard Lily come back in. "Even if it is him, it doesn't make sense. If he just waits us out, he stands a good chance of buying the ranch from the bank. Why send someone to scare us?"

Toby pulled a chair out for her at the table and waited for her to sit down before he answered her question. "I've been giving that some thought. There has to be a deadline of some kind for him. Like you said, scare tactics don't make sense otherwise. You've turned down every offer so far. Pushing you like this won't make you any more willing to listen to him."

"But what kind of deadline could there be? He knows that we're barely scraping by. If the herd doesn't bring enough money at market, we'll lose the ranch for sure."

Cal was relieved to see that there was some spark back in her eyes and color in her cheeks. Her outrage at Boone's behavior had done much to restore her normal energy.

"Maybe there is some reason for his rush, but remember that things have changed." Cal nodded toward Toby. "Last time Boone tried a direct approach, he found that you have someone helping you."

He stopped to consider his next words. "Personally, I've been wondering if those two hands that took off were his men to begin with. He no doubt figured that when they ran out on you, you and Wade wouldn't keep things going alone."

"Maybe he panicked." Lily sounded almost hopeful.

Cal hated to disillusion her, but that idea didn't work for him. "He has no reason to. So far, he's been able to buy or steal everything he wants. He wouldn't strike out like this unless it suited his long-term purpose, whatever it is."

He glanced at Toby, who wouldn't meet his eyes. "We need better information. Someone on the inside."

Lily didn't pick up on the sudden tension in Toby's face. "How would we do that? None of his men are going to help us."

"You're right about that. None of his men would."

Toby's scowl made it very clear that he was not happy with the way this conversation was going.

"Damn it, Cal, I can't ask it of her and I won't. She's taking a big chance as it is."

"Ask me what?" Lily finally noticed the anger in Toby's face. She looked to Cal for an explanation.

"Not you," Cal told her. "Boone has a woman working for him in the saloon."

"Why would she help us?"

Toby pushed away from the table and stalked out, putting an immediate end to the discussion. "I'm going to see if Mr. Wade needs help." He shot a venomous look in Cal's direction. "Get that idea out of your head before we get back for dinner."

On his way out, he slammed the door hard enough to rattle the windows. The two still at the table sat in stunned silence. Considering the days events, Cal had half expected Toby's display of temper to upset Lily, but instead she laughed.

"She must be some woman."

"Toby thinks so."

Lily left the table to watch Toby ride out. "You said

she works in the saloon. Does that mean . . ." She let her words trail off, as if unwilling to give voice to so indelicate a question.

"I suspect it does, but Toby doesn't seem to care. A lot of good women have done that sort of work. Most had no choice in the matter."

"That sounds like personal experience. Who was she?"

Her voice was gentle, but it didn't make it any easier for him to answer her. He surprised himself when he did.

"My mother." He held up his hand to forestall any more questions. "And before you ask, I never knew my father. She was pretty sure who it was, but he was long gone before I was born. I was better off without either of them."

He had to get out of the house before she did something stupid, like offering him sympathy. Or worse yet, pity. He'd done just fine without any sort of family.

Picking up his rifle, he walked out without a word. He knew he was being a bastard, but then he came by it rightly.

Lily watched him go, hurting for him even though she suspected he wouldn't have appreciated it one bit. She doubted that he realized how much of his childhood pain he still carried around with him. It was easy enough to say he didn't care, but it was there, hidden underneath his pride and tough hide.

She couldn't imagine growing up without the warmth she'd known in her own family, even when they were constantly on the move. But he was right; he'd done better than many who'd had the advantages he lacked. There was far more to Cal Preston than he wanted anyone except maybe Toby to know.

At first, she had thought that he'd cheated Wade out

of their money and the ranch. Now, she was inclined to believe her brother-in-law when he said that the game had been fairly played. His idea of right and wrong might not be exactly like hers, but Cal clearly followed his own rules. Now that she knew that Cal had been on his own since he was a boy, it was little wonder that he'd thought Wade was old enough to know what he was risking at the poker table.

Well, there was nothing to be gained sitting there mooning over a man who had no interest sticking around for the long haul. She'd promised him chicken and dumplings, and the meal wouldn't cook itself. With that in mind, she began plucking the dead chicken, readying it for the stew pot.

Four days later, Toby couldn't stand it any longer. He'd ridden out to the river the day before and again that morning. Although Thea had told him that she couldn't promise to meet him, he'd been sure that she would. Both times, he'd waited well into the afternoon, but with no luck.

Cal hadn't said another word about trying to enlist Thea's help in finding out what was behind Boone's interest in the McCord ranch. That didn't mean that he'd forgotten about the idea. He didn't understand what a risk she was taking in just seeing Toby. He wasn't about to ask her to endanger herself any more than was necessary.

Something was wrong. He had no proof, but deep down inside he knew that Thea would've come if she'd been able. He wouldn't be able to rest until he knew what was wrong. Maybe she simply hadn't been able to slip away from Boone. If that was the case, he would understand, or at least try to.

Once he saw with his own eyes that she was all

right, then he would risk a word or two with her to set another time to meet. But he needed to know for sure.

The day had dragged on seemingly forever. He managed to choke down the lunch Miss Lily had set before them, but he couldn't have said what it was. Finally, the sun started on its way down behind the mountains to the west. He headed for the barn to saddle up his horse.

Cal followed him. "Do you want company?"

"No, but you should probably come anyway. It would look better if we showed up to play poker."

"Not if we don't have any money. I doubt Boone was so taken with my charm that he'd loan me a stake."

Toby gave his friend a disgusted look. "I'm not fool enough to risk every dime I have on a deck of cards. You're the one who does that." He dug into the bottom of his saddlebags and pulled a small roll of bills and tossed it to Cal.

"That should get you started. Lose it and we really will be flat broke."

Cal muttered something under his breath as he finished saddling up his horse. No doubt he was furious that Toby had been holding out on him, but one of them had to be sensible about money. Cal had grown up in the California gambling dens where men won and lost fortunes every day. He'd never learned what a man could do with money if he held onto it long enough.

To Cal, money was good for buying his way into another game. If he had enough of it, they slept in clean beds and ate decent food. If times were bad, the two of them made do with stables and beans.

But that was behind them now, even if Cal didn't know it yet. Only a blind man wouldn't see that something special was brewing between him and Lily McCord, even though neither of them was willing to admit it. The night he'd caught them leaning in toward each other outside the barn, there'd been enough heat lightning flashing between them to start a fire. The memory made him smile.

He gave the cinch on his saddle one more tug and then led his horse out into the fading daylight. Cal would catch up with him soon enough. Something was driving Toby to reach King's Creek as soon as possible. Nudging his horse with his heels, he took off at a steady canter, hoping that the sick feeling in his gut was only nerves.

Lily waylaid Cal before he could charge off after Toby. She stood squarely in the middle of the barn door, hands on her hips.

"So which one of you was supposed to tell me that you wouldn't be home for dinner?"

He was already mad about the money Toby had thrown at him. Coupled with Toby taking off on him, he was in no mood to put up with her tearing a strip off his hide.

"Get out of my way. Please." He added the last in an attempt to be civil. When he tried to lead his horse past her, Lily grabbed the reins and stopped him.

"Not until you tell me where you are going."

"Why didn't you ask Toby? He's the one you worry about." He glared down at her, his frustration growing by the minute. He needed to catch up with Toby before he reached town. He figured Toby was jumping to conclusions about Thea because he wasn't thinking his best. Even so, he'd need backup if there was a problem brewing in King's Creek.

"I don't appreciate cooking a meal when there's no one to eat it."

"Feed it to Wade."

"He's leaving for the night. Someone around here

has to look after the cattle, you know." She looked him up and down, sneering as she did so. "And now because of you, my dinner is going to waste."

She'd conveniently forgotten that he'd been out helping Wade for the past three days, not that her beloved brother-in-law appreciated his efforts. The only reason he put up with Cal riding along was that Wade didn't want Cal anywhere near Lily. Not for the first time, he wondered how she'd managed to remain oblivious to her brother-in-law's feelings for her.

"Well?" she demanded in the perfect tone of voice to send a man right over the edge.

His temper shattered. "I didn't realize that you were so anxious for me to stick around." He closed the two steps between them, until only a few inches separated them. Her eyes widened as the awareness between them flared once again. "You've got two seconds to get out of my way."

"And if I don't?" The woman had more guts than common sense.

"Then this," he growled as he caught her by the shoulders and pulled her into his arms. His lips crushed down on hers. When she opened her mouth to protest this newest outrage, he immediately deepened the kiss.

She tasted sweet and spicy, a flavor like nothing he'd ever sampled before. To his surprise, she quit struggling to get loose as her arms found their way around his neck. Her fingers tangled in his hair as she moaned. Or maybe it was him. Hell, right now he didn't know where he stopped and she began.

He was vaguely aware of dropping the reins, and his horse wandering outside to nibble at some grass. The animal could look after himself for all Cal cared at that moment. He had other, more important things on his mind. Like dragging Lily inside the barn and tumbling her down into the pile of hay that had been serving as his bed.

She went willingly. Damn, it felt good to pin her down long enough to learn the feel of her beneath him. She fit perfectly, or would when he'd stripped them both naked. As much as he wanted to do just that, he did his best to slow things down because he knew it had been a long time for her. The least he could do was make it good for her.

His hand molded her breast and gently squeezed. Her response was all a man could ask for. He rained a series of nibbling kisses on her mouth, following the curve of her jaw to the sweet length of her neck as his fingers loosened the top few buttons of her dress.

"Cal, please!" Her head tossed restlessly back and forth.

"Yes, ma'am." Only too glad to oblige, he tasted each sweet inch of her flesh as it was revealed. The top curve of her breasts sent a new surge of heavy heat through him. He wanted more. Needed more. None too gently, he pulled the dress down far enough to un-cover her breasts completely.

She arched up in invitation. He wasn't about to deny either of them the pleasure. He swirled his tongue around one sweet peak before taking it completely in his mouth and suckling. In response, Lily bucked so hard, she almost threw him off.

Her hands were busy as well. She already had his shirt pulled free from his pants. Her hand slid under-neath and her sharp nails dug into his skin. No doubt she'd leave her mark on him, but he didn't give a damn. All that mattered right that moment was finishing what they'd started.

He reached down for the hem of her skirt and pulled it up to her waist. The sight of her bare thigh above her garters almost stopped his heart. The smooth expanse of skin felt like silk to his hand. When he touched the damp core at the juncture of her thighs, he knew for certain that she wanted him as badly as he wanted her. Nothing in his life had scared him more.

For both their sakes, he needed to be honest. "Lily, this won't change things."

She stilled. Looking up at him in the dim light of the barn, she studied his face as if looking for something. It must not have been there because after one second, maybe two, she pulled back slightly.

"I'm not like those women who work for Boone."

"I know that." He twined a lock of her hair around his finger, then tucked it back behind her ear. "Even a bastard like me knows a lady when he sees one."

Lily reached up to put her finger over his lips. "Don't call yourself that."

He kissed her finger. "But that's what I am; make no mistake about that. I have no family and no roots. I like it that way."

This time, she was the one who started the kiss. As her tongue danced with his, her hand strayed down the center of his chest to his belt and below. He gasped at the almost painful need that followed her touch. He'd given her the chance to stop, and she hadn't wanted it. Consequences be damned, he was going to take her.

He reached for the buttons on his pants. The first one had slipped free when he heard someone calling Lily's name. Not for the first time, he cursed Wade's very existence.

Lily had heard him at the same time and was struggling to get free from Cal's embrace. He grabbed her hands to still their frantic attempts to push him away.

"I'll distract him. You straighten yourself up and slip out the back."

Her dark eyes were huge against her pale skin.

"He'll know that we've . . . you and I were about to . . ."

Cal managed to get to his feet, tugging Lily up along with him. He quickly brushed the hay from his clothes. He had only seconds at best before Wade would come charging through the door. Sometime soon he and the boy would no doubt come to blows again over Lily, but now was not the time.

Her mouth was swollen with the aftereffects of his kiss. Not finishing what they'd started would be another of his life's regrets. He pulled another piece of hay from her hair. She'd managed to rebutton the front of her dress and was looking over her shoulder, trying to see if she'd managed to straighten her dress.

"Turn around."

Silently she did as he asked. With a few quick strokes, he brushed away the last evidence that they'd been rolling in the hay together. It was a damned shame.

"Lily, where are you?" Wade was almost to the barn.

Lily drew a sharp breath. "Go on out. I'll be all right."

"I'd rather stay here with you tonight, but I have to catch up to Toby. He might need my help."

"Go, then."

She sounded businesslike and all too ready for him to disappear for the night. He knew he shouldn't do it, but he wanted to make sure she didn't forget the feel of him quite so quickly. Knowing they were only a heartbeat from discovery, he put both hands on her face and tilted it to the right angle for one last kiss.

Using his lips and his tongue, he promised her without words that some time soon they'd finish what they'd started. Just as abruptly, he broke off the embrace, leaving both of them wanting more. He'd gone less than two steps out the door when he ran into Wade.

Wade glared at him. "Why is your horse just wandering around?" The younger man looked past him into the barn. "What were you doing in there?"

"In answer to your first question, my horse was restless. The answer to your second question is none of your damn business. Now get out of my way, boy. I have places to go."

Wade rose to the bait, just as Cal had planned. "I'm not a damn boy, and you can go to hell as far as I'm concerned."

"I probably will. If you're looking for Lily, I haven't seen her."

Not enough of her, though he'd come damn close. The memory of what he had seen and touched was enough to make him ache with need all over again. For such a small woman, Lily McCord had the power to bring him to his knees. He had to get away before he forgot that Toby might need him.

In short order, he caught up with his horse and took off in the direction of King's Creek at a full gallop.

Seven

Cal considered following Toby's roundabout approach to King's Creek but rejected the idea. He'd rather risk someone's noticing where he came from than get there too late to keep his friend from acting rashly. Luck was with him, because he found Toby tying his horse outside the Silver Slipper just as he rode in from the opposite direction.

He urged his horse into a quick trot in order to catch up with him. Toby had evidently seen him coming, because he waited before going inside.

"Thought maybe you weren't coming."

"I said I'd be here." He swung down out of the saddle and stepped up onto the boardwalk, hoping Toby wouldn't ask any more questions. As usual, he wasn't that lucky.

"What took you so long? I'd stopped to wait for you after a while but gave up on you." With a look of disgust, he reached over and plucked a piece of hay from the back of Cal's collar. "Kind of a funny time of day to take a nap."

"If you know what's good for you, you won't say another word." He hadn't come to terms with the explosion of passion himself, and there was no way in hell he wanted to give Toby a chance to tear into him about it.

Toby shook his head and sighed. "I hope you know what you're doing. I wouldn't want to see Miss Lily hurt."

"Shut up, Toby." He led the way to the door, knowing that it would distract his friend.

Once inside, they made their way to the back tables. Despite Toby's apparent casual disregard for the crowd surrounding them, Cal wasn't fooled for a minute. There was considerable tension in the set of Toby's shoulders and in the way his eyes kept flickering from side to side.

Once again, they'd arrived before the women joined the customers for the evening. For the moment, the two of them took up positions that would allow them to keep an eye on the entire room while they waited.

It didn't take long. Cal had just sat back down from buying them both a drink when the first of the girls appeared at the top of the steps. One by one, they filed down the staircase to be absorbed into the press of men around them.

Thea wasn't among them.

He grabbed Toby's arm to keep him from immediately surging to his feet. "She may be running late. She may be with Boone. Give her time."

Reluctantly Toby settled back. "If she doesn't show soon, I'm going to go find her."

"Don't be a fool. As far as you know, Boone's got some of his guns right here in this room. You won't be of much help to anyone dead." He looked around the room.

"Come on. Let's see if we can get into a game."

"I didn't come here to play cards."

"Well, I did. Besides, it'll give us an excuse to hang around in here without anyone wondering why we're nursing just one drink all night." A shared bottle might have worked as well as a game of poker, but they both needed to keep their wits about them.

About twenty minutes later, a couple of seats opened up at the nearest table. Cal approached the remaining players and asked if they'd like some new money in the game. The familiar pattern of shuffling and dealing helped him keep Toby occupied. It wasn't a high-stakes game, which was a good thing since neither of them could afford it.

For a short time, the cards were not going his way, but then the tide turned. After he'd won three hands in a row, he had enough to cover his own play. It felt good to have more than a few coins standing between him and being flat busted. Toby's mind clearly wasn't on the game, and he dropped out after the first few rounds of cards.

The others didn't seem to mind that he sat a little behind Cal, especially since he wasn't saying a word to anyone. Whenever the door opened, he craned his neck to see if it was Thea coming in.

His mood worsened with each disappointment. Cal had already suggested that he ask the bartender, but the one they'd met before was nowhere to be seen. His replacement hadn't said more than ten words to anyone all night as far as Cal could tell. He wished there was something he could do, because he wasn't sure how much longer he could control Toby.

Finally, he tossed down his cards and cashed in his chips. He tucked the resulting stack of bills out of sight in his wallet. This time, he wasn't going to make the mistake of flashing his winnings around a strange town.

He was about to suggest that they give up for the night when a ruckus started at the top of the stairs, drawing everyone's attention. The noise in the room made it difficult to make out what was happening, but then a woman's terrified scream rang out over the room.

"That's Thea!"

Toby was up and running before Cal could stop him. Luckily for them both, no one else made a move toward the staircase. Taking the steps two at a time, they reached the top of the steps in a matter of seconds.

They would have known where the screams were coming from even without the cluster of frightened-looking women standing outside the door. Something heavy either fell or was knocked over as man yelled out a string of obscenities.

"You bitch! I'll take my money's worth out of your hide if you don't hold still."

The sound of a fist hitting soft flesh was all too clear through the thin wood of the door. Toby shoved the other women out of the way and then tried the door handle. It was locked. He looked back at Cal.

Cal knew they were getting in way over their heads, but it didn't matter. He didn't give a damn who was behind that door. Any bastard who would hurt a woman deserved to be shot where he stood. Toby turned his shoulder toward the door, and Cal did the same. On a count of three, they lunged forward, hitting the door at the same time.

It took one more try before the thin wood gave way. They charged inside, only to find Toby's worst fears hadn't been anywhere near the truth. The room reeked of liquor and fear. A man stood swaying over Thea, his hands clenched in fists. Before they could stop him, he swung again. He was too intent on what he was doing to notice that he was no longer alone in the room with the woman.

Toby pulled his gun, ready to blow the son of a bitch to hell.

Cal stepped in front of him. "They'll hang you for

it, Toby. Let me." Instead of reaching for his own gun, Cal picked up the leg of a broken chair and swung. It made a satisfying crack as it broke over the cowhand's head. He dropped to the floor in a heap. He was still breathing, not that either of them cared.

Thea was huddled in the corner of the room, bleeding from her mouth and nose, her clothes in tatters. Both eyes were swollen shut, and she cradled her arm against her. Immediately, Toby shoved past Cal to reach Thea.

"Don't rush. No use in frightening her even more." There was no telling if she even recognized who was in the room with her.

Toby nodded that he understood what Cal was telling him. With the utmost care, he knelt in front of Thea and held out his hand. "Honey, it's me, Toby. I'm going to get you out of here."

At first she didn't respond, but finally her hand slowly moved out to touch Toby's. Gently he eased her out of the corner and then picked her up in his arms. She nestled her head against his shoulder, and he stepped over the still unconscious body of her attacker. The bastard deserved more than a cracked skull, but this wasn't the time for vengeance. Thea needed medical care, not more violence.

Most of the crowd outside the room was gone, but two of the other women hovered just down the hall. "We'll take care of her."

"Like hell you will." The barely contained fury in Toby's voice had them backing up quickly.

There was no way Cal wanted to face the crowd downstairs. He wasn't even sure they'd make it as far as the door with their burden. "Is there another way out of here?"

One of the girls spoke up. "I'll show you."

They slipped down the back staircase, which led out

to the alley behind the saloon. A man was coming in as they reached the door. Cal's gun was in his hand almost before he realized that he'd reached for it.

The bartender stepped inside. It only took him one look at Cal's gun and Thea in Toby's arms for him to raise his hands and start backing out of their way.

"Is she all right?" There was no mistaking his concern.

"She will be once I get her the hell out of this place." Toby pushed past him out into the fresh air.

The bartender grabbed Cal's sleeve. "Boone won't be happy about this. If whoever did this is dumb enough to stick around, he won't live long enough to get out of Boone's way. But don't think for a moment he'll appreciate your friend out there helping Thea. He'll see it as someone stealing his personal property." He shook his head. "He's out of town for a few days, but someone's bound to tell him as soon as he gets back. Personally, I didn't see anything, for all the good that will do you."

"Thanks for the warning."

They both froze at the sound of footsteps behind them on the staircase. It was one of the girls, carrying a sack. She shoved it at Cal.

"Thea's things. She'll be wanting them." Without waiting for a response, she turned and ran back up the stairs.

"Thank her for us."

"I will. Now you'd better get the hell out of here."

Toby was waiting for him a short distance from the door. Neither of them had thought much past getting out of the building. They needed a minute or two to assess the situation.

"Is she hurt bad enough to need a doctor?" Cal hoped she didn't, because it would only increase the chance of being caught. There was no doubt that they'd take the risk if it became necessary.

"I don't know. She can't go far riding double on horseback."

Thea whispered through her swollen lips, "No doctor. Boone owns him, too."

That settled it. "You stay in the shadows and wait for me. I'll bring the horses around. We'll ride until we're good and clear of this place. When it looks safe, I'll go on ahead and get the wagon and come back for you."

He didn't wait to see if Toby had any objections to his plan. One way or another, they needed to put some distance between themselves and King's Creek. He loped down the alley for the distance of about six buildings before cutting back over to the main road through town. Then, slowing his steps, he did his best to blend into the flow of folks walking along the boardwalk.

Once he reached the front of Boone's place, he mounted his horse and led Toby's by the reins. No one paid him any undue attention. A couple of blocks down the street, he cut through to where Toby was waiting. He dismounted in order to hand Thea up to Toby. When she was once again settled in Toby's lap, they left town, keeping to the less traveled streets as much as possible.

Once the lights of the town had faded out of sight, they cut back around to ride directly for the ranch.

After about twenty minutes, Toby called a halt. "Cal, I can't tell if she's unconscious or just asleep. I'm afraid to keep jolting her along like this."

"I'd be a damn sight happier if we were farther from town, but we can't risk hurting her any more, either." Cal tried to gauge how much farther they had to go.

"I'll cut across country. You keep to the road and

go as slow as you need to. If you have to, stop and I'll find you. The farther you go, the safer you'll both be."

"Hurry, Cal. I don't know how much more of this she can take. Maybe I should wait here."

Thea stirred and tried to lift her head. "I can take whatever I need to. Keep going."

"Hush, woman. You're in no shape to know what's best for you."

Cal decided there was nothing to be gained by sticking around long enough for them to settle their argument. If Thea still had enough sass in her to fuss at Toby, she'd hold up a while longer. He urged his horse into a fast trot. In only seconds, he'd left the road and his friend behind.

Lily awoke to the sound of a rider approaching at a dead run. Her first reaction was fear, both for herself and for Wade. Boone and his men had never bothered them at night before, but there was always a first time. She grabbed her wrapper and the loaded rifle and scurried to the front windows. As dark as it was, she couldn't see much past the window, but the hoofbeats were coming closer.

And unless she was mistaken, they were headed right for the house.

"Lily, wake up!"

Relief washed over her as she recognized Cal's voice, but it was short-lived. Something was wrong or he wouldn't have come charging up to the house like that. Knowing Cal had left with Toby and now he was alone, it was only logical that something had happened to his friend. She threw the bolt and pulled the door open.

"Is it Toby? Is he hurt?"

Cal was breathless. "Not him. Thea. We need the wagon."

"I'll get dressed and meet you in the barn."

She ran for her room. This was another of those occasions when Wade's old castoffs would serve her better than struggling into her dress. Once she was clothed, she sat down to pull on her boots. Meanwhile, she made a mental list of things to take with her.

She grabbed a couple of quilts and a pillow, as well as an old sheet for bandages. If this Thea was badly injured, she'd need to be kept warm until they could get her back to the house. With that in mind, she also dug out the bottle of whiskey that she kept around for medicinal purposes.

She piled everything on the porch and then ran back for an extra lantern and the matches. Cal pulled up by the porch just as she came out. He jumped down and helped her load everything into the back of the wagon.

He looked surprised when she climbed up in the seat beside him. "You don't have to come."

"She might need a woman's touch."

She halfway expected him to argue, but he responded by slapping the reins, guiding the horses out into the darkness.

"Where is she?"

"Toby has her. They were riding double along the road. I came ahead to get the wagon."

A hundred questions went through her mind. Who was Thea, exactly? How had she been hurt? Why were they bringing her to the ranch instead of to the doctor in town? Now didn't seem to be the time to pester Cal with everything she wanted to know. He had enough on his mind trying to keep the horses moving at a good pace without risking injuring them.

Besides, he wouldn't be doing things this way if it weren't absolutely necessary. The realization that she'd come to trust him on some level came as a surprise to her. She considered the matter, wondering when that had happened.

Maybe it was because he hadn't pressed them for the money, but more likely it was the way he kept warning her about his questionable background. She smiled into the darkness. He wouldn't like it if he knew that she found his attempts to frighten her off refreshing. Only a true scoundrel like Upton Boone tried to hide his true nature behind a slick smile and fancy manners.

Oh, she wasn't fool enough to think he had it in him to stick around. He had itchy feet, sure enough—a gambler through and through. But he had honor even if he didn't recognize it as such.

The wagon hit a rut, throwing her off balance. Cal's long arm snaked out and caught her, pulling her upright. His teeth gleamed brightly in the dim moonlight as he grinned down at her.

"You'd better hold on to something. I wouldn't want you to go bouncing down the road without me."

Lily surprised him by wrapping her arm through his and holding on. Not only did it make the ride smoother, but the warmth of his body next to hers did much to ward off the damp chill of the night.

Every so often, Cal slowed the horses so he could better listen for Toby. It was hard to judge the passage of time, but it seemed to have taken the better part of an hour before they caught the sound of a horse approaching at a slow walk.

Without warning, Cal gave a long whistle, startling both Lily and the horses. Almost immediately, there came an answering call from up ahead on the road. Cal slapped the reins against the horses, hurrying them along.

Lily clambered over the seat into the bed of the

wagon and fumbled for the lantern and matches. They might not need the extra light for long, but it would help in getting the injured woman safely tucked into the wagon. Cal pulled up just shy of where Toby was waiting. After setting the brake, he climbed down and hurried over to his friend.

"How is she?"

Toby sounded worried. "Either asleep or unconscious."

"I'll take her."

Toby seemed reluctant to relinquish his burden, but eased her down into Cal's waiting arms. Toby wasted no time in dismounting. He followed Cal to the wagon.

"Miss Lily, I didn't expect to see you."

And wasn't pleased to, she was willing to bet. "I thought your friend might appreciate a woman to help take care of her. You know, to help settle her in once we get back to the house."

When he looked at her this time, some of the tension in his face had eased. "I know she'll appreciate your help then, Miss Lily."

The three of them got Thea tucked in the wagon bed. Toby didn't want to leave her, so he tied his horse's reins to the back of the wagon. Cal drove while Toby and Lily helped keep Thea from being jarred around unnecessarily. The injured woman moaned and whimpered a few times, but each time Toby was able to soothe her with a few soft words.

It was a good thing that Lily had brought along extra quilts. She spread one more over Thea and then wrapped the last one around her own shoulders. Neither of the men seemed to notice the temperature change, but then she doubted that Toby was noticing anything other than Thea.

The initial rush of excitement had long worn off, leaving Lily aching with exhaustion. Although she tried to remain alert, she found herself nodding off despite the constant jolting of the wagon. Finally, she gave up fighting the need to sleep. After all, there was little that could be done until they got Thea into the house.

She sank back against the side of the wagon, bracing her head against the edge. It seemed as if no time at all had passed when Toby shook her awake. Cal had already jumped down from his seat. Lily struggled to her feet. When she started to climb down, Cal surprised her by holding up his hands to lift her down.

Too tired to argue, she leaned down and trusted him to see her safely to the ground. If it seemed as if his hands lingered at her waist longer than necessary, she put it down to his making sure that she had her balance. After all, one injured woman was enough for them to handle.

And if the night suddenly felt colder when he stepped away, well, perhaps she was only imagining things. Besides, there was too much to be done to waste time worrying about it. She picked up one of the lanterns and took it inside to ready Wade's bed for their guest.

The men were right behind her, carrying the woman between them. Despite their efforts to be gentle, Thea was in obvious pain. Lily had thrown an old sheet over the top quilt to protect the bedding until she could doctor Thea's wounds. Once that was done, Cal and Toby could help get her settled under clean covers.

As they maneuvered their burden through the bedroom door, Thea regained consciousness enough to realize where she was, or at least where she wasn't.

"This isn't my room." She struggled against their determined efforts to lay her on the bed.

"Settle down, Thea. You're safe."

Despite her injuries, she managed to put up quite a

fight. "I don't care if I'm safe or not. I don't belong here. Take me back."

"Damn it, woman, don't be a fool. That bastard almost killed you. Given the chance, he might just finish the job."

Equal measures of worry and fury warred in Toby's dark eyes. If Lily had any doubts about the strength of his feelings about this particular woman, they disappeared in the face of such passionate emotion.

Since the two men weren't getting anywhere in their efforts to do what was best for Thea, it was time for Lily to take control. "Dump her on the bed and then get out of here."

Cal looked only too glad to unburden himself. Toby didn't look so sure.

"Miss Lily, I don't know. . . ."

Lily held up her hand. "Well, I do. If I can't convince her to stay the night, then she can walk back to town. I figure she's smarter than that."

Lily wasn't sure, but she thought Cal's sudden coughing spell sounded more like suppressed laughter. Toby hesitated another second, maybe two, before doing Lily's bidding. Once they decided to use their combined strength against Thea, she was no match for them. Rather abruptly, they tossed her on the bed, still managing to cushion her fall to prevent further injury.

"I'm going to take care of the horses."

Cal beat a hasty retreat and disappeared down the hallway to do her bidding. Toby wasn't as quick to leave.

"You stay with her while I gather a few things. After that, you get out of here until I tell you different."

"Yes, ma'am."

When she returned, she overhead him saying, "You listen to Miss Lily. She's a nice lady."

Once he was gone, Lily closed the door behind him.

She drew a deep breath before turning to face her patient. Seeing the doubt in Lily's eyes, she knew she'd have to work hard to gain the woman's trust.

"I know you don't know me at all, but I think highly of Toby. Any friend of his is welcome in my home."

Then, before Thea could protest, Lily dipped a washcloth in the warm water and gently washed the blood and dirt from Thea's face. That done, she began removing Thea's torn clothing. She could have used Toby's help in lifting her to help with the dress and underclothing, but that would not have been proper.

It took longer for her to do it all herself, but it seemed to be the safest course. When she had the dress off and had loosened Thea's corset, she slipped one of her own gowns over Thea's head and tugged it gently down to provide decent cover for the woman. That done, Lily did her best to assess the nature of Thea's injuries.

She was no expert, but it appeared that most of them were bruises and superficial cuts. When she picked up Thea's left hand, her patient flinched in pain.

"I'll have to feel along your arm to see if it is broken or only sprained."

Thea bit down on her lip, trying not to cry out.

"I don't feel any breaks, so maybe we got lucky," Lily said as she tore off a long strip of fabric to make a bandage. Whether it was a sprain or a slight break, binding the arm would go a long way to easing the pain as well as protecting the arm from further injury.

Thea silently watched every move that Lily made. Try as she might, Lily couldn't quite decide what emotion was lurking in the depths of the dark eyes that stared up at her. When she'd cleaned the last cut, she gathered up the soap and dirty toweling.

"I hope that feels better." She didn't wait to see if Thea would answer. "I'm going to call Toby back in here to help me get you under the blankets. After that, I think we all should get some sleep."

Before she reached for the door, Thea spoke up. "Thank you, ma'am."

"Call me Lily." She patted Thea on her uninjured arm. "And you're welcome."

Just as she suspected, Toby was hovering right outside the door. "You can come in long enough to lift Thea up so I can get her under the covers."

Her heart ached to watch Toby's gentle strength as he tenderly lifted Thea and held her still as Lily pulled the covers down. Before she could pull them over Thea, Toby was already tugging them into place.

"I'll stay with her, if that's all right with you, Miss Lily." His eyes pleaded with her to agree. "She may need something during the night."

Lily looked to Thea before answering. Even though Thea's eyes were closed, she gave a small nod.

"That'll be fine, then. There isn't much left of the night, but I doubt any of us will be up at first light." She picked up the soiled clothes and water and started out of the room. "Don't hesitate to call me if you need anything."

She was surprised to find Cal sitting at the kitchen table, having expected him to turn in for the night after seeing to the horses. He held up a pot of coffee.

"I made fresh if you want some."

Despite her need for rest, she knew sleep would be awhile in coming. She took a cup down off the shelf and held it out for Cal to fill. Sitting down eased the ache in her back. She leaned back and allowed the warmth of the cup to soothe her tired hands.

"How is she?"

"I'm not sure. Some of the bruises and cuts were

pretty bad, especially along her ribs." She chose her next words carefully. "Do you or Toby know who did this to her?"

"We didn't exactly get his name."

"Well, we can wait until she's more alert and ask Thea if she knows who he is. Either way, we'll need to notify the sheriff."

Cal sat up straighter in his chair. "Why the hell would we do that?"

"Because whoever did this should be locked up."

"Don't be naive. No one is going to do a damn thing about it." He took a healthy swallow of his coffee before adding, "Especially not the sheriff."

How could he sit there, sounding so calm, especially when he'd seen how badly hurt Thea was? She might not mean anything to him, but she clearly did to Toby.

"Why not? A man who'd do that to a woman should be locked up."

"I'll tell you why, Mrs. McCord." This time he wasn't calm. Bitterness dripped from every word. "Because she's a whore, Mrs. McCord. The law protects decent folks like you, but it does damn little for anyone like Thea."

"Don't call her that!"

"Why not? That's what she is."

"I don't care. In my home she'll be treated with the respect any woman deserves."

"Fine, but remember this. The minute she walks out that door over there, she'll go back to working for Boone, most likely on her back."

He lurched to his feet and walked out the door, slamming it behind him. It wasn't the first time he'd done so, but this time Lily was hot on his heels. She caught up with him a few feet short of the barn and latched onto his arm, using his own movement to spin him around to face her.

"Cal Preston, this time you have gone too far!"

He shook her hand off his arm. "I said nothing but the truth."

She glared up at him, even though she knew the darkness hid her expression from him. "You said it for the sole purpose of shocking me."

"The world doesn't revolve around you, Lily McCord. But even if it did, you have no idea what we're dealing with here."

"I'm neither stupid nor naive. Thea was probably everything you accused her of and more, but that doesn't seem to matter to Toby. Did you see the expression on his face every time he looks at her?"

She gestured back toward the house, where Cal's best friend was standing vigil over Thea. "For his sake, we need to treat her as the lady she could be rather than what she's been before he brought her here."

Cal stood over her, his hands clenched in fists at his side. She wasn't sure whether he was considering her words or contemplating violence. A few seconds passed.

"Fine. She's a lady." Then he spun away from her and marched into the barn and out of sight.

Eight

Thea pried one eye open partway and then tried unsuccessfully to get the other one to cooperate. When she lifted her hand to her face, an agony of pain burned through her side, making her flinch.

She whimpered, hating herself for giving in to the need. It took all the courage she could muster to get past the pain in order to take inventory of her injuries. She was no stranger to beatings, given her past, but it had been a long time since she'd been hurt this badly.

Part of her confusion came from not knowing where she was. She remembered being cornered in her room, refusing to beg for mercy from some drunken drifter. Although that part was fairly clear in her mind, once his fist had landed the first blow to the side of her head, clarity was gone.

Someone, she wasn't sure who, had put a stop to the abuse. And now she was lying in a strange bed. As carefully as she could manage it, she turned her head, trying to take stock of her surroundings.

Sunlight streamed in through a small window, telling her that quite some time had passed since she'd lost consciousness. There was no telling if it had been a matter of hours or days, but she favored the shorter time. Although she hurt all over, none of the injuries seemed severe enough to have put her out for too long.

Other than that one clue, nothing else made sense. It was clear that this was someone's room, but she couldn't see well enough to know if the scattered belongings were masculine or feminine. Logically, she would assume it was a man. The only women she knew were the ones who worked in the Silver Slipper with her. While they might have been willing to see to her injuries, this room was far too nice to belong to one of them.

Approaching footsteps interrupting her inspection. Slowly she turned her head in the direction of the sound. Even the pain from that small movement was considerable, but this time she managed not to cry out.

She didn't know what—or rather who—to expect, but a woman carrying a tray full of food came as a surprise. Not knowing what to say, she remained silent.

"Miss Jones, are you awake?" the unknown woman whispered.

Thea almost didn't recognize her own name. As tempting as it was to feign sleep until she had a better idea what was going on, she responded to the gentle concern she heard in the stranger's voice.

"Yes, ma'am." The words sounded thick to her, no doubt owing to the fact her mouth felt swollen and bruised. She didn't ever get the drifter's name, but he had a real talent for using his fists.

The woman came closer. Her hand felt cool to Thea's forehead. She should protest being treated as an invalid, but in truth she was too weak to fight off even a newborn baby.

"No temperature. That's good."

The woman's face briefly swam into focus. She looked somewhat familiar, but surely wasn't anyone Thea knew by name.

She managed to get out her most pressing questions. "Who? Where?"

"I'm sorry, Miss Jones. I should have realized that

you might not remember me from last night." The woman busied herself dragging a chair closer to the bed even as she answered. "I'm Lily McCord. You're in my brother-in-law Wade's room in my house. He's out with our herd most of the time, so you're welcome to stay here as long as you need to."

The names rang a bell, but she still had no idea how she'd come be in a strange man's room.

"How?"

"I know you have lots of questions, and I'll try to answer them in a bit. Right now, though, I thought you might be able to sip some of this broth. I'm afraid to give you anything more solid until we see how this stays down."

The scent of rich chicken broth wafted toward Thea. It smelled heavenly.

"I'm going to prop you up on a couple of pillows to make it easier for you to swallow."

It hurt to move, even though Lily McCord's touch was gentle. Several seconds passed before Thea could muster the strength to open her eyes again. Her hostess was sitting patiently, giving her all the time she needed to marshal her strength.

"I'll try some of that broth now." It was a matter of some pride that her voice sounded stronger than it had only moments before.

Lily smiled approvingly as she held a spoonful of the clear broth to Thea's mouth. She savored its richness. Slowly she took in the nourishing liquid, knowing it would hurry along the healing process.

Once they'd worked out a rhythm, Lily did her best to answer Thea's questions.

"Well, near as I can figure, Cal Preston and Toby Thacker were both having a drink and playing cards at the Silver Slipper last night. Neither of them told me how they came to find out that you were in trouble, but they were the ones who got you out of there."

The mention of Toby's name startled Thea into jumping, spilling the spoonful of broth Lily had been about to feed her. Rather than getting angry over the mess, Lily surprised her by laughing.

"I guess you don't remember that part either." She dabbed at the quilt and sheet with a napkin. "Why don't I tell you the rest of what I know before you finish the broth? You'll stay dryer that way."

Thea could only nod. Her body might be slow to move, but her mind was whirling like a dust devil. What could Toby have been thinking of, coming back to the saloon like that?

"Where did I leave off? Oh, yes. Cal said Toby carried you out the back door. Toby rode double with you on his horse while Cal came ahead to fetch our wagon. I came along to help out. The three of us settled you in here."

Lily's voice dropped to a whisper, as if to make sure no one else heard her next words. "Toby sat up all night, making sure that you were all right."

The crazy woman sounded as if she thought Toby was doing something special, taking care of her like that. Stupid was more like it. Boone would kill him for sure, right after he shot the drifter who did this to her. Boone had many faults, but he took care of everything he owned, even her. Tears burned her eyes. She should have turned her back the first time Toby Thacker caught her eye. She'd known from a single glance that the man would cause her trouble.

She struggled to sit up. Maybe if she got back to the saloon today, Boone wouldn't know she'd ever been gone. He wasn't due back for another day, maybe two.

Lily did her best to hold her down. "I didn't mean

to upset you, Miss Jones. I thought you should know what happened."

Her futile attempts exhausted Thea's last bit of energy. She went limp, letting her body sink back into the comfort of the bed. Her mind found no such ease. Even so, she feigned the sleep she so badly needed to avoid answering any more of Lily McCord's questions.

"Stop that damn pacing!"

Cal ignored that order just as he had all Toby's other demands. He made two more trips the length of the barn before Toby roused himself enough to complain again.

"If you won't sit still, then can't you at least do something useful?" Toby turned over in the pile of hay he'd claimed as his bed and glared up at Cal.

"Like what?"

"I don't know—hell, there's got to be something you can do around here. Water the garden. Ride out and check on young Wade. He's been out with the herd for the past three days. He might appreciate some company."

"Not mine, he wouldn't. He'd as soon take up company with a rattlesnake." Even so, the idea had some appeal. If he didn't get away from the confines of the barn, he was likely to do something rash, such as trying to entice Lily McCord into finishing what they'd started the other day. That could very well be the dumbest thing he'd ever done.

He'd never lied to himself before and he wasn't going to start now. Lily affected him in ways he'd never before experienced with a woman, and it scared him. He spent most of his time trying to figure out which would bring him the most pleasure: wringing her neck or bedding her for a week.

At this point, either one would satisfy his need to get his hands on her again.

Toby had fallen back to sleep, leaving Cal no handy target for his bad temper. Maybe he should go check on Wade. He could pretty much count on getting a fight out of him. Maybe pounding on Lily's precious brother-in-law would help his mood. It would also encourage her to keep her distance.

He yanked his oldest clothes out of his saddlebags and changed into them before he had a chance to talk himself out of going. Toby did no more than grunt in his sleep when Cal led his horse right past him, saying he was going to meet up with Wade. On the whole, Cal was glad. Toby was better off right where he was instead of in the house mooning over Thea Jones.

Outside, he was tempted to leave without telling Lily where he was headed, but he couldn't be sure if Toby would remember anything of their one-sided conversation. No sense in worrying his friend any more than he had to.

He threw the reins over the porch rail and walked into the house without knocking. Just as he expected, Lily complained, although there was no real heat in her words.

She didn't bother to look up from her mending. "Next time knock."

"What's wrong?" He stood over her and waited until she answered.

"I'm worried about Thea." She clipped a thread and then glanced toward the bedroom door. "Something is wrong."

Cal walked closer to where Thea lay sleeping. From the little bit he'd seen the night before, he would have guessed that her injuries were mostly painful, but not serious.

"Was she sensible when you talked to her? Or are you thinking she might be busted up inside, like she needs a doctor?" He hated to draw attention to where the injured woman had been taken, but he'd fetch help if it was needed.

"No, I don't think so. She's bruised and cut, and I wouldn't be surprised if her ribs are cracked, but that's not what I'm worried about."

Lily pursed her lips as she gave the matter some thought. "She got really upset when she found out how she'd gotten here. Soon as I told her that it was Toby who brought her here, she tried to get out of the bed, you know, like she was terrified. She's in no shape to go anywhere, but I think if I hadn't held her down, she would have crawled to get away."

"Toby would never hurt her."

"If I had to guess, I'd say she wasn't afraid of him as much as she was afraid *for* him." Lily looked puzzled. "She never said a word about her own injuries, like they didn't matter."

Memories of his early childhood stirred in the back of his mind, bringing back images of his mother's sweet face distorted and swollen as she tried to convince him that she was all right. The sound of fists pounding on her had haunted his childhood nightmares. The memories made him sick to his stomach.

More gruffly than he meant to, he shocked Lily with the truth. "That's because this is not the first time that one of her customers has done this to her, and it won't be the last. Whores get used to it after awhile, if they live through the first few times. That, and they generally learn to avoid the mean drunks."

Instead of being offended, Lily placed a comforting hand on his shoulder. He shook it off and stepped back, glaring down into her wide eyes. Damn the woman, anyway. He'd survived better than most would have, and he sure as hell didn't need anyone's damn pity, especially hers.

Cursing himself for a fool and Lily for prying out

another of his shameful secrets, he stormed out of the house. He hadn't gone two steps before he realized he hadn't told her where he was going. He turned back to do so and ran right into her. Instinctively he caught her up close to him to keep from knocking her down.

His mouth found hers before he found the words to speak. She accepted his anger, his heat, and his need to taste her sweet mouth. The mere touch of her hands on him banished the bitter-cold memories haunting his mind. In their place, she left a trail of fire that had him aching with the need to take her, to lose himself in her arms.

He managed to rein in the urgency long enough to ask her, "Where?"

She didn't pretend not to understand. "Inside, my room."

He shoved the door open and pulled her inside the house, wishing he had it in him to be gentle. Maybe later, but for now, it was all he could do to wait until they were behind closed doors.

Lily knew she might very well regret what was about to happen between her and Cal, but that wasn't going to stop her. Once and for all, she had to know firsthand the feel of this man in her bed and in her arms.

He reached out and she went willingly. Those wonderful hands of his, so deft with a deck of cards, played over her with a master's touch. She'd almost forgotten how her breasts felt when molded to fit a man's hands. Whimpering with the pleasure learning the feel of Cal's fingers sliding over her skin, she did her best to match him touch for touch, caress for caress.

Clothing was loosened and then lost. His chest was smoothly muscled, with a smattering of dark hair that felt like heaven. He cupped her bottom and lifted her against the center of his need. Instinctively, she wrapped her legs around his waist, moaning with the sweet agony of having him so close.

He closed the short distance to her bed and sent them tumbling down onto the quilt. The soft cotton felt cool to her overheated skin, but then the sensation was lost among all the others that were threatening to overwhelm her.

His mouth found her breast at the same time his hand slipped between them to test her readiness to accept him. He petted her in counterpoint to his sweet kisses, teasing her into begging for more.

When she feared for her sanity, she cried out, "Please, Cal, now! Please!"

He rose above her, settling himself between her legs. With one thrust, he took her. His shoulders trembled as he fought for control, trying to give her time to adjust to his sudden invasion. It had been a long time for her, but her body remembered the sweet feel of being one with a man.

He rocked gently against her, learning the fit of their two bodies. But when she dug her nails into his back, he knew it was time. The ride he took her on was wild, but he was with her every step of the way. The tension built between them, until it burst, sending wave after wave of pleasure crashing over her. With a final thrust, Cal shuddered in her arms, leaving both of them spent in the tangle of her sheets.

Lily fought to keep her eyes closed, but the pounding wouldn't stop. Gradually, she began to make sense of the noise. Someone was knocking on her bedroom door. She prayed that whoever it was would give up and go away.

"Miss Lily, are you in there?"

Toby. She woke up enough to recognize who was calling her name. Rolling over onto her back, she stretched her arms over her head, trying to work some life back into her limbs. The movement caused her covers to slip down, revealing her naked breasts. She clutched the quilt around her and looked around in confusion.

Where was her nightgown, and why was she in bed with the sun still high in the sky?

Memories came flooding back. Her skin flushed with embarrassment and remembered passion. The pillow next to hers showed signs of being used, but Cal was nowhere to be seen. She'd like to think he'd left her alone out of consideration for propriety, but that didn't ring true somehow. However, finding his current whereabouts would have to wait until she was decently dressed.

"Give me a few minutes, Toby."

Scrambling out of the bed, she started searching for her underclothing. Lord of mercy, it was scattered all around the room, thrown about with casual disregard. One garter stared down at her from atop the shelf on the wall; its partner was floating in the bowl of water on the washstand.

Thad would never have acted in such a manner. He'd always treated her like the lady she was, allowing her the dignity of waiting until she was under the covers in her nightgown before joining her in the bed. He might have pushed her gown up to her waist or unbuttoned it from the top down, but never had she woken up hours later without a stitch of clothing left to cover herself decently.

Cal Preston had allowed her no such modesty. He'd invaded her bedroom and her body with a wildness she'd never before experienced. And the worst thing of all, she'd enjoyed every minute of it. A twinge of guilt pricked at her conscience. She'd been content in her marriage and had no business comparing her husband to another man—a gambler at that. She owed Thad's memory more respect than that.

Reaching for her dress, she slipped it over her head and then crossed to the small mirror on the wall to check her appearance. Her hair was a mess, bringing back the memory of Cal lying next to her, pulling the pins out one by one, and then running his fingers through the length of her hair as he kissed her deeply and long. That had been after the first time he'd made love to her. Or maybe it was the second.

She brushed the tangles out of her hair and quickly braided it. Checking in the mirror to see if her part was straight, she noticed a small bruise low on her neck. She gently touched it, knowing that Cal Preston had left his mark on her in more ways than one.

Tugging her collar up to hide the evidence of their ill-spent afternoon, she went out to see what Toby needed.

"She won't let me near her." Toby was clearly frustrated, glaring at the door to Wade's room. His attention was so clearly on the woman behind it that he didn't seem to wonder why Lily had been in bed. Or with whom.

"I'll check on her for you." Lily brushed past him and slipped inside the other room.

Thea was awake and glaring at the door with eyes still half swollen shut. She relaxed a bit when she saw it was Lily coming in and not Toby.

"How are you feeling?" Lily sat down on the chair near the head of the bed. Without warning, she reached out and touched Thea's forehead with her hand. Thea almost, but not quite, managed to not flinch.

"Still cool to the touch. I take that as a good sign." She tilted her head as she considered the look in Thea's eyes. "I'd guess you still aren't happy about being here. Since it's too late to change that, I would suggest we concentrate on getting you well."

"I'll be fine in a day, maybe two."

Stubborn pride had a lot to do with that particular lie, but Lily admired the woman's determination. She smiled down at her patient.

"For now, I would bet you have some needs to see to. Can you make it outside with some help?"

Thea nodded. "Yours, not Toby's."

"He won't like that idea, but that's all right. I think all men need an occasional reminder that we can do fine without them." She hoped Toby would forgive her for conspiring against him, but right now she felt it important to gain Thea's trust.

She'd already laid out one of Thea's own wrappers. With a great deal of effort, the two of them managed to get her to her feet, decently covered, and ready to make the long trip outside.

Neither of them was surprised to find Toby on the other side of the door when Lily pulled it open.

"Where the hell do you think you're going?"

Before Lily could think of a suitable reply, Thea snapped at him. "I'm sure if you'd use that head of yours for something other than your hat, you could figure it out. Now get out of my way."

Toby stood his ground, glaring at them both, but Thea paid him no heed. Since he wouldn't move, she worked her way around him. Lily did the same. Together they slowly walked outside, with Toby shadowing their every step. Thea might be stubborn, but she'd found her match in the man she was trying unsuccessfully to ignore.

Lily would have found the situation amusing if she hadn't been so worried that Thea was doing herself more harm than good by refusing his help. At long last, they made it to the small building out back. Thea disappeared inside, leaving Lily alone to face Toby's anger.

She tried distracting him by indirectly asking about Cal. "What would you and Cal like for dinner?"

He answered her without taking his eyes off the closed door. "It doesn't matter to me, and Cal's gone. He rode out to help Wade and didn't say when he'd be back."

Lily didn't know whether she was relieved or angry by Cal's desertion. Granted, Wade couldn't do all the work by himself. And then there was the little matter of where Cal would expect to sleep now that he'd been in her bed. If he stayed gone for the rest of the day, or even a couple of days, she'd have the time she needed to regain control of herself.

It dawned on her that Toby was muttering something under his breath. She strained to catch his words.

"She should be done by now. In two seconds, I'm going in after her." He punctuated his words by stepping right up to the door, ready to yank it open.

Lily pulled him back. She grabbed his collar and forced his face down to the level of hers. "If you have any hope of getting past her defenses, mister, you will not touch that door. The woman needs her pride; right now that's all she has." Although she whispered the words, it didn't lessen the strong feelings behind them.

Toby's eyes narrowed as he considered her statement. Finally, he nodded and backed away, doing so just in time. He'd barely gotten back to his original position when Thea stepped out the door. Lily rushed to her side, slipping her arm around Thea's waist. Toby, hung back, allowing them to hobble back to the house unaided.

His expression made it clear that he wasn't at all happy about it. Lily was proud of him for his forbearance, knowing that Thea appreciated it even if she didn't say so.

Once they were inside, Lily aimed Thea toward the kitchen table.

"You can keep me company while I start dinner."

Lily settled the other woman in a chair and then sent Toby to fetch a quilt to keep her warm. "If you get too tired, say so, but I always figure people heal faster out of bed."

Toby started to join them, but Lily stopped him. "Don't you have chores to see to?"

There was little he could say to that. He didn't slam the door as hard as Cal usually did, but he came close. Even so, Thea surprised Lily by laughing. The movement caused her to inhale sharply as she grabbed her side, but the smile revealed some of the beauty hidden by the bruises. It was easy to see why Toby was so taken with her.

Lily gave her a conspiratorial wink. "What is it about men that makes them think we can be intimidated by loud noises?"

Thea shook her head, but her eyes strayed to view outside the window where Toby was working off his frustrations by cutting firewood. Lily was willing to bet that Thea was unaware of the pure longing in her eyes when she thought no one was watching her. She allowed herself only a few seconds of weakness before turning away from watching him.

"Tomorrow I'm going back to town." Her voice was barely above a harsh whisper.

"I don't see how you can." Lily kept her tone reasonable as she calmly peeled vegetables for the stew she was putting together.

"I have to."

"You're in no shape for the long trip back to town, much less to go back to work."

Thea sat in miserable silence, staring at the tabletop. Lily was determined to get through to the woman.

"You don't know how nice it is for me to have another woman around. I'm tired of being so badly outnumbered."

"I don't belong here. I'm not your kind." Having said that, Thea pushed herself to her feet. She shook off Lily's attempt to help her, working her way back to Wade's bedroom alone. Once there, she firmly closed the door behind her, closing out Lily as much as she had Toby earlier.

Lily tried to convince herself that Thea hadn't meant to hurt her feelings, but she knew that she was fooling herself. Thea had no intentions of letting anyone close, especially someone she felt was too different from herself either because of her race or her profession or both.

Peeling potatoes was a poor substitute for good company. Toby was mad, Thea was sulking, and Cal was out with Wade. She tried to tell herself that the tears stinging her eyes were due to the onions she was cutting up. Not even the vegetables believed her.

Cal was in no hurry to reach the valley that sheltered what was left of the McCord herd. His nerves felt raw, bruised, and battered from the aftermath of the afternoon's activities.

Even a life-long gambler like him would never have bet on the chances of his ending up in Lily's bed. He'd had his fair share of women over the years, though not nearly as many as Toby had accused him of. Whatever their number, not one of them measured up to the experience he'd had rolling around in the sheets with Lily.

Not one. Not ever. And not again, he kept telling himself.

His horse had been plodding along, content to follow the trail at a slow walk since Cal was in no hurry to get anywhere. Wade wouldn't be thrilled to see him, and Cal wasn't ready to face Lily, and maybe never would be.

Suddenly, the animal's ears flicked forward and its head came up to scent the wind. Cal strained to see what had upset the horse, but whatever it was, was too far away for his human ears and eyes to detect.

Even so, he urged the horse into a fast canter, drawing his pistol as he did so. Though it might be a pack of wolves or a big cat making his mount nervous, it was wiser to assume that the trouble was two-legged. With that in mind, he left the trail and worked his way through the cover of a stand of trees rather than approaching the entrance to the valley directly.

He stopped at the edge of the woods and listened. His horse was still acting nervous, dancing sideways when Cal tried to leave the scant protection the trees offered. Once again, he listened, trying to figure out what had the horse so spooked.

This time he heard it. The sound of pounding hooves scared him as little in this life did. Where the hell was Wade? If the boy was caught in the stampede, there would be little Cal could do to save him. His horse resisted his first signal to ride into the valley, but it gave in when Cal dug in his heels.

The sorrel leapt forward into a full-out run. Once inside the valley proper, there would be room to maneuver. If the cattle reached them while they were in the bottleneck of the entrance, it could be disastrous.

He caught sight of the first few head just as he cleared the opening. If he didn't turn them to the side, the herd would scatter everywhere outside the valley. Without really thinking it through, he pointed his pistol in the air and fired three shots. The first few cows hesitated and then veered away from him.

Rather than waste all his ammunition, he yanked his hat off his head and began waving it and hollering pure nonsense at the top of his lungs. The next bunch of cattle were as confused by that as the first had been by the loud noises. He waited for a heartbeat for the rest of the herd to come thundering through the brush, but only a few stragglers came his way.

Whatever—or whoever—had set them off hadn't stampeded the entire herd. Even so, the cost to the McCords could have been devastating. But the cattle weren't his first priority. He had to find Wade McCord and make sure the youth was alive and well. Lily would never forgive him if something had happened to her brother-in-law, no matter who was responsible.

He was tempted to start yelling for Wade but decided caution was the wiser course. After all, he still didn't know why the cattle had panicked. The sky above was clear blue, ruling out lightning or thunder as the cause. The next most likely culprits were the rustlers who had been making off with the McCord cattle for some time.

He circled along the edge of the valley, following the route Wade had shown him the first time he'd helped the boy with the herd. The logical place to start was the sheltered clearing that Wade had been using for a camp.

Everything seemed quiet enough, but that didn't mean anything. As he neared the campsite, Cal dismounted and loosely tied his horse to a handy tree limb. It would hold the animal if things were quiet, but if the cattle came charging again, it would be able to pull free and get to safety. That done, he reloaded his pistol, filled his pockets with spare rounds, and pulled his rifle out of its scabbard.

Slipping from tree to tree, he worked his way to the back side of the camp. Every few feet he paused long enough to listen, hoping to get some idea of what laid ahead of him in the camp.

Finally the trees thinned out to the point where they offered very little cover. He stooped low, sticking to the shrubby undergrowth as much as he could. Finally, he got a clear view of Wade's makeshift home.

It wasn't good.

Wade was slumped next to a tree with his arms tied behind him. His head lolled forward, and a small trickle of dried blood crusted at the edge of his mouth. From where Cal stood, it appeared that the boy was breathing regularly. With luck, what injuries he had were fairly minor, since his attackers felt that he was still enough of a menace to require restraints.

For now, he appeared to be safe enough. Cal needed to do some scouting before he dared enter the camp. Since neither of them was expected back at the house any time soon, he couldn't risk being captured as well. Who knew when Toby would come looking for them?

There was an unfamiliar horse tied up near Wade's. It was still saddled and breathing heavily, a likely indication that someone was still in the immediate vicinity. Cal pondered what to do next. Before he could decide, the question was answered for him. A single man came back from the stream, carrying his canteen and a bucket of water. He looped the strap of the canteen over his saddle horn and led his horse over to where Wade was sprawled.

Taking the bucket in both hands, he poured it over the boy's head, a rude awakening that left Wade sputtering and choking. The bastard laughed at him.

"The boss said for you to tell that pretty widow that time has run out for you McCords. Up until now, we've been playing a friendly game. No more. She's next."

To give Wade credit, he cursed the bastard pretty damn solidly, questioning everything from the man's birth to his manhood. Cal was impressed, although all it accomplished was to get Wade kicked in the ribs again.

It was time Cal took over. He would have taken pleasure in beating the son of a bitch senseless for hurting

Wade and running the cattle off. For threatening Lily, though, he had to die. Painfully and long, if at all possible.

Cal managed to keep his approach unnoticed until he was only about twenty feet away. It was the horse that noticed him first, alerting Boone's man that they were no longer alone. He spun around, drawing his gun as he turned.

Both guns fired, but Cal was the better shot. The rustler hit the ground, dead.

Cursing his own aim, Cal hurried over to free Wade from his bonds. Since the man had assumed that the intruder was an enemy, Cal had to figure he'd been alone in his dirty work. However, they couldn't count on that remaining the case. He drew the small knife that he wore tucked the top of his right boot and cut through the rope wrapped around Wade's wrists.

"I thought you were going to let him go on kicking until he killed me." Wade glared up at Cal as he sat trying to rub some feeling back into his arms.

"You're alive; that's more than he can say." So much for gratitude. Any minute now, those numb hands and arms would burn like hell. Cal was feeling petty enough to hope it lasted some time.

"How long has he been hanging around?" What Cal really wanted to know was how long Wade had been tied up and unconscious. It wouldn't do to let Wade that know Cal was worried about him.

"The bastard jumped me a few hours ago. I'd come back to camp to get something to eat. He must have had his horse tied up farther away then, because I sure didn't hear any sign of either of them until after he'd jumped me." Wade touched the back of his head and winced. "He knocked me cold."

"Could have been worse. He could have shot you instead."

Wade struggled to his feet. "Wonder why he didn't. Without me around, Lily would never be able to hold onto the ranch."

Cal refrained from pointing out that she had him and Toby to help her now. He wasn't ready to think about that idea too closely himself. "Someone else is calling the shots; someone like Boone. Up until now, he wants you both scared more than he wants you dead."

Cal slipped his knife back in his boot. "Soon as you can ride, we'll go check on the cattle and see if you have any left. Your friend there," he said, nodding in the direction of the dead man, "stampeded a good part of the herd before he came back to check on you. I managed to turn one bunch before they made it out of the valley, but there's no telling what other mischief he'd been up to."

He had to admire Wade's grit. He had to be hurting, but that didn't stop him from immediately saddling his horse and mounting up. They spent the rest of the afternoon working the herd deeper into the valley. Just before dark, Cal talked Wade into riding back to the house to warn Lily and Toby about the dead man's threats. He hoped Toby would pry himself away from Thea long enough to join Cal in the valley.

Once Wade was gone, Cal dug the stranger a shallow grave, figuring to buy themselves some time that way. As long as Boone didn't know for certain what had happened, he might think the man was still on the job.

That done, Cal built himself a small fire and sat down to wait for Toby, wishing he'd thought to bring his deck of cards.

Nine

"Damn it, Lily, we've got to do something!"

"Watch your language, Wade. I don't need to hear a mouthful of cursing on top of everything else." Lily picked up her bread dough and slammed it down on the table. That felt so satisfying, she did it twice more before settling in to knead it properly.

Wade glared at her from across the table. He drew a deep breath and launched into his arguments all over again. "I tell you, the man as much as said they were going to come gunning after us. His boss said they were done playing around."

Deep down inside, Lily was stone cold with dread. It wasn't that she didn't believe Wade, but she wasn't ready to face any decision of that magnitude. The first priority had to be getting the cattle to market. Even if they didn't make enough to pay the mortgage, they'd need to raise some money, enough to start over somewhere else.

Once the herd was sold, they'd know how to plan for their future, no matter how bleak it might be.

The sound of a door opening was a welcome break to the darkness in her mood. She glanced over toward Thea, who stood in the doorway of Wade's room. From the look on Thea's face, she still wasn't sure of her welcome. Lily mustered up a smile.

"Come sit. We're just talking."

After another second or two of hesitation, Thea shuffled forward. A telling glance from Lily had Wade hurrying to pull out a chair for their guest. The gesture didn't please Thea, but Lily figured that if they kept acting as if she was welcome in their home, she'd eventually come to believe it.

Tossing another handful of flour onto the bread board, Lily kept up the soothing action of working the bread. "Would you like some coffee?"

Thea immediately started to rise. Ignoring Lily's protests, she poured a cup for herself. "I'm not helpless."

Pride was a touchy thing. Right now Lily didn't know which of her two companions was the harder one to deal with. "I know you're not."

Lily looked up from her dough and caught Wade looking at Thea with a puzzled look on his face. Since he hadn't set foot in the house since the night Thea had arrived, she realized that no one had explained her presence to him. Unexpected company was unusual in itself; a woman bearing evidence of recent injuries must seem curious indeed. At the very least, she could introduce the two of them.

"Wade, I'm sorry. Where are my manners? May I present a friend of Toby's, Miss Thea Jones? Thea, this is my brother-in-law, Wade McCord."

Wade nodded. Thea did the same, making Lily smile. Neither of them knew quite what to think of the other.

"Thea's going to be staying with us for a while." Before Thea could deny it or Wade could question it, Lily went right on talking. "Wade, there are things that need to be done. I'm sure Toby would appreciate not having much to do when he gets back from checking on the herd tonight."

Unless she was mistaken, quite a bit of the tension

went right out of Thea's posture upon hearing that Toby was away for the day. For a woman who denied any involvement with the man, Thea sure took a personal interest in his whereabouts.

Wade got to his feet, clearly frustrated with Lily's attitude. Without a word, he headed outside, presumably to do some chores. Maybe he'd work off some of his bad mood. She hoped so, because she was getting tired of having to tread carefully with everyone else.

She had problems of her own, ones that had nothing to do with Upton Boone, a shrinking herd of cattle, or the ranch. Cal had stayed out with the herd, choosing to send Wade back to the house instead of coming himself. Although she knew it was better that way, she didn't like knowing she was that easy to ride away from.

Not that there would be a repeat of yesterday afternoon. She had her reputation to consider, not to mention her heart. Despite her best efforts to convince herself otherwise, something about Cal Preston drew her in ways that not even Thadeus had been able to. After spending a childhood with a father who'd never understood that a family needed roots, she had no business even looking at a professional gambler.

"Men are sure enough a problem."

Lily looked up in surprise from the pile of flour and dough she was abusing. It was the first time Thea had spoken except out of necessity or to lash out at Toby. She was looking at Lily with a woman-to-woman smile playing around her lips. Lily smiled back as she wiped her hands clean of the sticky mess on a towel.

"That they are." She poured herself another cup of coffee and sat down across from her guest. "Most of the time, I like having them around, but sometimes . . ." she let the words trail off as she shook her head. "Wade tries so hard to be the man in charge. He forgets he's still mostly a boy."

"He wouldn't see it that way, not at all. He gets mad because he wants you to realize he's grown up. Which, by my reckoning, he is." Thea calmly sipped her own drink.

Her dark eyes sparkled with mischief. "But I wasn't talking about your brother-in-law. Even if you're worried about him, he wouldn't have you all knotted up inside. My guess is that Cal Preston is responsible for that."

Her knowing look made it all too clear that she knew exactly how Cal and Lily had spent yesterday afternoon. "I would deny knowing what you're talking about, but I'm not in the habit of lying."

"You're not the only woman who ever made a fool of herself over the wrong man. Besides, if you don't mind me saying so, he is good-looking enough to turn heads."

Lily couldn't remember the last time she'd had the pleasure of talking with another woman, especially one more worldly than she was. "He is that, isn't he?" Feeling daring, she added, "Of course, Toby isn't hard to look at either."

She immediately regretted her words when Thea's face went all stony cold again. Evidently, some subjects were off limits. "I'm sorry. I didn't mean to upset you."

Thea stared out the window for several seconds. Sighing, she spoke again, her words low and lonely. "He's not for me."

"Are you already married?" That was the only thing Lily could think of that would stand between Toby and Thea.

"Me married? Now that's a laugh, Miss Lily." Her words were as bitter as the look in her eyes. "When men ask for me, it isn't my hand in marriage that they're interested in."

"It can't have always been that way. Maybe with Toby's help, things can change for you."

"That's every whore's dream, you know. For a handsome man to come along and whisk her away, to start over pure and clean." She rose to her feet, pride alone keeping the tears from falling from her eyes full of pain. "Well, I haven't felt clean since the day my master dragged me to his bed and kept me there until another pretty face caught his attention. Then I got sold to a brothel to make room for her."

Lily wasn't going to let Thea walk away again, not if she could help it. She was up and after her before the other woman had gone more than two steps. She lacked the words that would ease that kind of pain, so she wrapped her arms around Thea's shoulders and pulled her close.

To her surprise, Thea didn't fight her off. Maybe they both needed the comfort of another woman's understanding. It didn't last long. When Thea tried to ease back, Lily let her go. She held out a handkerchief, which Thea accepted.

Dabbing at her eyes, Thea repeated her earlier words. "Men are sure enough a problem."

"That they are."

The exchange set both of them to laughing.

"Why don't you go check on Mr. Wade while I see if I can salvage that poor dough? The fresh air will do you good, and I need to feel useful."

Lily let herself be shooed out of the house, realizing that Thea needed some time alone. Despite the tears and laughter, she had a long way to go before she'd freely accept Lily's offer of friendship, much less anything Toby might want from her.

Outside, the day was hot and dusty. She'd been neglecting the garden. She tipped her hat forward to shade her face from the unrelenting sun and attacked

the few weeds that had invaded her vegetables. Once
that was done, there would be water to fetch, chickens
to feed, and dinner to cook.

And, oh yes, one man to get out of her mind.

Shots rang out only a few minutes after Lily stepped
into her bedroom for the night. She quickly extin-
guished her lamp to make less of a target of herself.
Instinctively, she dropped to the floor and crawled to
her bedroom door. In the dim light filtering in the windows, she could see that Wade already had the rifle in
his hand.

He risked a quick look outside and then dropped
back down.

"Where's Thea?" Lily asked, raising her voice to be
heard over the sporadic gunfire.

The other bedroom door opened just wide enough
for their guest to slip through. "Here I am."

Lily fought down panic, knowing clear minds were
needed, not mindless fear. She slipped into the other
room long enough to get the shotgun down off the
wall. It would do little good at any distance at all, but
up close was a different matter. She sent a prayer soaring to the night sky that this was just another game
Boone was playing.

Thea picked up Wade's revolver and checked it over
with a practiced hand.

"You've done that before." Wade took a couple of
quick shots out into the darkness with his rifle and
then traded it to Thea for the revolver.

The two of them worked as a team, leaving Lily free
to watch the back window of her room. No one had
yet actually attempted to come in the house, but there
was always a first time. It only stood to reason that if
the raiders were raising a ruckus out front, they could

have someone out back trying to sneak in while Lily and Wade were otherwise occupied.

Not for the first time, she wondered where Toby was and if he and Cal were all right. Despite his promise to return for dinner, there had been no sign of Toby or Cal all evening. If Thea was disappointed in Toby's failure to return, she'd given no sign of it.

They'd all worked hard to convince themselves that Toby had stayed away only because of Cal's inexperience handling cattle. Now, they had to wonder if something had gone horribly wrong.

The silence came as suddenly as the gunfire had. For several long minutes the three of them sat, weapons aimed out into the night at phantoms they could only hear and not see. When it seemed that the attack was over, another blast of gunfire hit the house.

The bullets splintered the wood, sending chips flying, but the shots were aimed high, another way to terrify without real damage. This time, the quiet didn't come as a relief. The silence built, the tension becoming almost unbearable.

Finally, a strange voice called out from somewhere out front. "This is your final warning. Either sell the ranch or walk away, we don't give a damn which. But be gone."

Once again, the sound of several riders laughing and shooting filled the night, leaving the three in the house huddled in corners, shaking in fear.

Or make that two, Lily realized. Wade was the calm one, still standing guard at the door, firing out into the night whenever a possible target presented itself. When one of the riders let out a yelp of pain, followed by a string of curses, Wade smiled grimly and took another couple of shots.

At least someone would regret attacking the McCord place. The last of the gunshots faded away along with the sound of several riders leaving. The three of them waited five minutes, and then ten, before moving from their chosen corners.

Thea was the first to speak. "Does that happen often?"

"Often enough." Wade was going from window to window, looking for any signs of movement. "That bastard Boone wants this ranch pretty damn bad."

"Upton? What would he want with a place like this?" Thea sounded truly puzzled. Realizing that she may have insulted her hosts, she apologized. "Sorry, I didn't mean it that way, but Upton takes pride in owning only the best. This place will be a fine ranch someday, but he's not one for getting his hands dirty. He pays others to do the hard work."

"What do you think he was doing tonight?" Wade offered Lily a hand up off the floor and then did the same for Thea. "His hands are dirty enough, even if he wasn't one of them out there tonight. Those men have his money in their pockets."

Lily kept waiting for her heart to slow down. Needing something to work off her nerves, she tried to assess the damage to the walls. Nothing looked too bad, not that it mattered if they couldn't figure out some way to put a stop to this harassment.

"Get down, both of you!" Wade was back at the window, his rifle aimed and ready to fire. "I hear horses coming this way."

These riders stopped some distance from the house. Wade shot in the direction where the sound had come from.

"Damn it, Wade, are you trying to kill us?"

Lily was up and running for the door, only to have Wade block the way.

"Stay where you are. I'm not about to let them in

now." Without taking his eye off the door, he pushed her back toward the kitchen.

"What's wrong with you?" Lily demanded, trying once again to get past him to open the door.

"It's pretty damn convenient, the two of them showing up right now, don't you think?"

"It's not their fault they weren't here when the shooting was going on."

"Who says they weren't?"

Realization was slow in coming, but Lily finally understood what Wade was thinking. "I know you don't think much of Cal, Wade, but how can you think such things about Toby?" She was truly disgusted with his attitude. "Now I would appreciate it if you'd get out of my way."

His temper outshone hers. "No, Lily, I won't. I'm tired of you thinking you can boss me around forever. I have as much say around here as you do, and it's damn well time you realized it."

For the first time, Lily looked at Wade and didn't see the boy she'd watched grow up. In his place was a man, one with angry eyes and his late brother's good looks. Shaken by the transformation, she backed away.

"You're right, Wade, but I consider those two men out there our friends."

"Like hell they are! You seemed to have forgotten that Cal was the one who took my money and the ranch."

Now who wasn't making sense? "Well, what did you expect? You're the one who risked it all in a poker game. You know that I don't approve of gambling, but that's what happens when you sit down across the table from a professional gambler." She glared up at him. "You told me yourself that it was a fair game."

"Tell me this—why are you defending Cal Preston? At first, you couldn't wait for him to leave. Now it's like he's part of the family."

Wade set the gun down and put his hands on Lily's arms. He didn't use enough force to leave bruises, but his touch hurt her all the same. With no warning, he dragged her closer and crushed his mouth down on hers. She had to fight to get free of his embrace. When he did release her, she stumbled back, wiping her mouth with the back of her hand.

"How dare you!"

"How dare I? That's a laugh. I've spent years watching you with my brother, knowing he didn't really appreciate what he had." Wade ran his hands through his hair, clearly frustrated. "Then when he died, I thought you needed some time, but that eventually you'd realize that I . . ." His words trailed off as he stared at someone over Lily's shoulder.

Only one person could put that look in Wade's eyes.

Without thinking first, Lily took a step back, closer to Cal. She regretted the action as soon as she saw Wade's reaction. He looked at the gambler and then at her.

"The bastard, what has he done to you? Isn't it bad enough he has my money and my ranch, did he have to take you from me as well?"

Guilt kept her from answering, but he saw the truth in her eyes. With that, he shoved past Lily, sending her reeling.

Cal kept her from falling, but Lily felt as if her world was spinning out of control. Bewildered, she looked from Cal to Thea and then back again, hoping one of them could explain how things had gotten so out of hand.

"I didn't know. . . . I swear, I didn't know."

Thea's expression was sympathetic. "Maybe you didn't want to."

"Wade!" she called, but he was already gone. "I've got to go after him." She tried to push past Cal.

He blocked her way. "Leave the boy some dignity. Right now, he has some more growing up to do."

Lily hesitated in the doorway, torn between the need to offer comfort and the need to adjust to her own shock. It was as if the cheerful boy she'd always loved had been replaced in an instant by a hard-eyed man, angry and bitter. He was all the family she had left. Somehow she'd find a way to make it right for him.

She had to.

A heavy footstep on the porch gave her hope that Wade had returned, but it was Toby. She looked past him, hoping that her brother-in-law was following behind. Instead, all she heard was the sound of a horse charging out of the barn.

"Where's that boy going all fired up like that? He'll break his fool neck riding like that at night."

Feeling numb, Lily did her best to answer. "I drove him away." With that, she barricaded herself in her room where she could cry in private.

Cal didn't know which McCord he wanted to throttle more: Wade for having the good sense to think of Lily as a woman rather than a sister, or Lily for not realizing sooner what the boy was feeling. Either way, he was right in the middle, the villain in both their eyes.

He was looking around for something to kick when he noticed the chips of wood on the floor. Looking up, he saw a row of holes that could only be caused by bullets.

"What the hell happened here tonight?"

Thea have him a superior look. "I wondered when you two idiots would notice."

Toby entered the fray. "So are you going to stand there feeling all smug or are you going to tell us?"

She wagged her finger in Toby's face. "Don't you

go trying to boss me around, Toby Thacker. I may owe you my life, but I will not be treated with disrespect."

Great, now the two of them were going after each other. Was he the only sane person left within fifty miles? "That's enough, you two."

He stepped between his friend and Thea, shoving them apart. "Toby, you keep quiet long enough for Thea to explain." Turning to her, he crossed his arms over his chest and did his best to look intimidating. It didn't work.

"I'll tell you the same thing I just said to your friend. Don't boss me around. If you want to know something, ask politely."

He prayed for patience. "Fine. Miss Jones, if it isn't asking too much, please tell me how this house came to be shot all to hell." He started off quietly enough, but the last was loud enough to rattle the windows.

A lesser woman might have cowered, but Thea gave him glare for glare. "Along about bedtime, another bunch of idiots, presumably Boone's men, came screaming around the house, shooting at everything in sight. They kept the bullets high, but the warning was clear. If Miss Lily and her brother-in-law don't sell or just plain leave, things will only get worse."

She drew a breath. "Not only that, it seemed pretty convenient to Mr. Wade that the two of you came riding back so soon after the shooting stopped. If I wasn't such a trusting sort, same as your Miss Lily, I would have to agree that it looked pretty suspicious."

"She's not my Miss Lily." He didn't like the knowing look that Thea gave him, although she didn't say any more. "Any chance that you recognized any of the voices?"

"No, I didn't."

She looked as if they would assume she was lying, but Cal figured she had nothing to gain by doing so.

"All right, so a bunch of unknown men decided to pay another call. What set off the fight between Lily and Wade?"

"You did."

His temper, fueled in part by guilt, flared up hot. "Like hell I did. I wasn't even here."

"Maybe not in person, but you were hovering right there between the two of them, sure enough." She tilted her head to one side, as if considering what else to say.

Toby prodded her. "You've got something stuck in your craw. Spit it out before you choke."

"You might have things to answer for, Cal Preston." She gave him a look that told him all too clearly that she knew what some of those might be. No doubt she'd gotten an earful when he and Lily had been in the room next to hers. His fears were confirmed when she smiled and nodded toward Lily's closed door.

"But what went on between those two tonight was bound to happen sooner or later. Wade McCord is a man—a young one, true enough, but still a man. Lily hasn't wanted to see what was right there in front of her eyes. Something was bound to bring the situation to a full boil sometime. You might have hurried it along a bit, but that's all."

"Earlier they were arguing over whether it was time to take the cattle to market or not. She tried to put her foot down, but all that did was put a lid on a boiling pot. He was building up steam since late this afternoon. It wasn't hard to see that a fight was brewing inside that boy."

He couldn't argue with her. He'd known for some time how Wade felt about Lily even if the woman herself hadn't had a clue. And no doubt Wade was tied up in knots over how he felt about her.

"Well, there's nothing to be done tonight. Wade will

have to come to his senses on his own. If he doesn't show up in the morning, we'll try tracking him."

"And Miss Lily?" Toby's eyes had that look about them that always foretold a long and lengthy lecture about the sins of the flesh and hell being Cal's ultimate destination.

He was in no mood for religion or lectures.

"She's safe enough in her room. For now, I'm hungry. Let's see what kind of meal we can scrape together."

Toby looked all set to argue when Thea stepped in. "I made fresh bread and there's some stew left from our dinner. You go wash up while I get it heated up."

Cal was only too glad to escape out into the cooling night air. He didn't need Toby to tell him that he'd screwed up badly this time. It wasn't the money that he'd lost or the ranch he could claim an interest in. Hell, he didn't give a damn about Wade's IOU.

Truth was that once they'd found out that there wasn't any cash to back it up, they should have saddled up and ridden out. There was always some way to earn another stake to a poker game. He'd been doing a fine job of that very thing for longer than he could remember. If he knew anything in this life, it was how to squeeze a living out of a deck of cards.

He'd been asking himself since the day after they'd reached the McCord ranch why they were still hanging around. It wasn't that he didn't know the answer; he just didn't want to own up to it. The answer was behind a closed door crying her heart out right that minute.

He hadn't left because Lily McCord, with all her problems and her firebrand personality, wouldn't let him go. She had her claws in him good and proper; damned if she didn't. And he still didn't know how she'd managed it. After all, for the first week or more, she hadn't had a civil word in her head for him.

The next thing he knew, they were at each other,

naked and needy. Even the memory of those hours in her bed were enough to make him aching-hard all over again. If for no other reason than that, he should saddle up, light out, and put as much distance as he could between himself and the siren Lily McCord. Instead, his wayward mind kept trying to figure his chances on sharing that big bed of hers again sometime soon.

Damn, he was an idiot.

And worse yet, Toby was on his way out to tell him that he thought so, too.

Ten

It took several nudges, but the persistent toe of Toby's boot finally was stirring some life into Wade. Mumbling a few curses, he pushed himself up from his bedroll and glared up at Toby. He blinked his eyes and then tried again to focus.

"You look like hell, son. Didn't you get any sleep last night?" Truth was, he looked as if he was suffering the aftereffects of too much alcohol, but there weren't any liquor bottles lying around, empty or otherwise.

Wade rubbed his unshaven jaw and then stretched his arms over his head. "Not very damn much."

Toby poured a cup of coffee and handed it to the younger man. He hid a smile at the way Wade grabbed on to the stuff as if it were his only lifeline. He hadn't been hard to find once Toby figured out his trail. Wade had ridden hard for a while out of sheer temper, but then turned back. After carefully bypassing the ranch house, he'd gone to ground at their camp in the valley.

"I don't suppose I need to tell you what a fool thing you did by riding out last night." Toby raised his hand to forestall the argument Wade was about to start. "I'm not saying you didn't have cause to be mad, but you risked both your neck and your horse riding like a crazy man after dark. It don't matter a damn bit how well you knew the terrain when you know you weren't thinking straight."

He mustered up a look like the ones his mother used to give him when she wanted him to know she didn't appreciate having an idiot for a son. "And if you'd managed to do yourself serious harm, how do you think Miss Lily would have felt?"

Just as he expected, Wade rose to the bait. "She doesn't care about me, not since you and that damn Cal Preston showed up."

"Now, boy, that's a lie and you know it."

Wade rolled to his feet, ready to fight if necessary. "I'm not a boy, damn it! I'm a man, full grown."

Toby allowed himself a brief smile. "You might well be, but you're not going to convince anyone of that fact until you start acting like one."

Glaring at Toby for all his worth, Wade sputtered, "I do a man's work. Who do you think has been taking care of things around here until you showed up?"

"You have. But doing a man's work doesn't always take a man to do it. You've been riding herd on cattle since you could sit a horse." Toby spit, taking careful aim to miss Wade's boots—barely. "Truth is, being a man don't have much at all to do with the kind of work a person does. It has a lot more to do with how well he cares for his animals, how he acts towards others, and"—he paused for effect—"how he treats the women in his life."

"But Lily and that damn gambler . . ."

"Shut up, boy!" Toby spit again. "What's between the two of them is exactly that—between them. The only thing you have a say in is how you treat Miss Lily." He let his sympathy show for the first time. "Now, I know your feelings for her run real deep, and I don't blame you for wanting her to feel the same. But if you're honest with yourself, you'll admit that she cares a whole passel about you, just not the way you want."

Toby gave Wade some time to ponder that. "Now if it were me, I'd do some serious thinking. Lily can't change how she thinks of you any more than you can change the fact that you love her. What you have to decide now is if she's important enough to you to accept what she *can* offer and be satisfied with it."

Figuring he'd lectured enough for one day, he finished off his own cup of coffee and tossed the dregs into the fire. "Now, let's see how the cattle are doing this fine morning. If we're going to get them to market any time soon, we need to get a head count so we know what we're dealing with."

Without waiting to see what Wade would do, he swung up in the saddle and slowly trotted off downstream. The boy would follow along soon enough. Meanwhile, he wondered if Wade had any idea what a joke it was for him to be handing out advice on women. Hell, Thea Jones had him tied up in knots, good and proper. Every time he looked at her, he wanted her that much more.

Her no-nonsense way of handling whatever was handed to her was worth admiring. There was no doubt in his mind that she'd had a hard time of things since early on in her life, but somehow she'd managed to hold on to her spirit and her pride.

But by damn, whenever she stood toe to toe with him, she got him so worked up that he didn't know whether to beat her or bed her. Not that he'd ever raise his hand to a woman, not even the flat of his hand to her backside, no matter how strong the temptation.

Those big eyes of hers spoke all too clearly of the ugliness she'd already lived through. He wanted—no, needed—to make it all better for her. He didn't give a damn what she'd done in the past. Neither of them had led blameless lives. What he wanted was to build a future with her and not look back.

It was going to take some convincing, but everyone who'd ever known Toby knew he was as stubborn as they came. For now, he'd let her taste what life was like outside Boone's Silver Slipper. With Miss Lily working so hard to make a friend of Thea, he figured he couldn't lose.

Please, God, let that be true.

He could hear Wade coming up behind him. There wasn't much he could do about Thea while he was out here punching cattle. All the more reason to get right to work, so he could head back to the house.

Besides, it was getting right entertaining to watch Cal and Lily tiptoeing around each other, pretending like nothing had happened between them. He didn't know for certain, but he'd bet his last dollar that it was more than just a few stolen kisses. Cal should know better than to mess with a decent woman like Miss Lily, and he'd told him so in no uncertain terms.

That didn't mean that he didn't understand what Cal was going through. Personally, he doubted even Miss Lily had figured out how she'd come to be involved with a gambler with the itch to wander. From what Wade had told him of her childhood, Cal's rootless nature must scare her.

Cal, on the other hand, had little experience with a decent woman, especially one whom most men would be right proud to call their wife. His mama hadn't given him any kind of upbringing at all and chasing Lady Luck from town to town hadn't helped, either. Toby could only hope that common sense and a little pushing on his part would get his partner to see the wisdom of grabbing hold of everything Lily McCord had to offer him and hanging on for dear life.

Of course, the fire was already heating up between

the two of them. All he had to do was fan the flames a bit.

Looking back, he saw that Wade was almost upon him. No doubt the boy wouldn't appreciate the direction that Toby's thoughts were headed. He was harboring some pretty strong feelings for Lily himself. It would take some time and distance for him to get any perspective on the subject.

Toby figured on Wade hurting a lot more before he started to get any better, but there was no helping that. It wasn't easy for anyone to guide a heart in a direction it didn't want to go on its own.

Damn, wasn't he the philosophical one today! His horse spooked up a couple of stray cattle. Getting them back to the herd was something he could do without any arguments. It was time to get some work done.

The way Cal figured it, he had two choices. First, he could pack up and ride off without looking back. By himself, of course, because Toby wasn't going anywhere soon. He kept reminding himself that he'd been alone when he'd hooked up with Toby and could handle being alone again, no matter how much he hated the idea. Although he and Toby might squabble, he'd gotten used to having a friend by his side—and sometimes at his back. There would be a hole in his life, that was for sure.

The second choice wasn't much better. He could stick around long enough to help Wade and Lily get their cattle to market. Then he could pack up and ride off without looking back.

Either way, he ended up alone. It was all a matter of how much dust he was willing to eat before he turned his back on his friend and the McCords. He kicked a rock, sending it flying. He looked around for another one, needing some way to vent his frustration with the entire situation.

Someone stepped out onto the front porch. Cursing the sudden surge in his pulse, he was relieved to see that it was Thea and not Lily. She brought her own set of problems along with her, but at least they didn't tear at his guts the way Lily McCord did.

He watched as she gingerly stepped down from the porch. She was moving better every time he saw her. Either she was a fast healer, or she had more willpower than most. It was probably a combination of the two.

Still, he couldn't stand by and watch her tottering along unaided. He might not like the threat she posed to his friend, but he could sure understand the appeal she had for Toby. In several long strides, he reached her and held out his arm.

"I can get around on my own," she snapped.

"I know, but you don't have to." He continued to hold out his elbow until she gave in and slipped her arm through his.

As they started forward, he matched his stride to hers. "Are we headed anywhere in particular, or are we just out for a stroll?"

"Nowhere special. I just needed some fresh air."

He smiled. "Lily fussing too much?"

Thea shook her head. "That woman needs a houseful of children to worry over. Then maybe she'd leave me alone." She shot Cal a curious look. "You going to stick around and give them to her?"

The shock of that idea caused him to stumble over his own feet. He didn't appreciate Thea's laughter any more than he did the image of Lily cuddling a baby, one with his hair and her smile. Something stirred deep inside him, warning him that if he didn't ride out soon, he might not be able to.

"That's what I thought. She's not like me, Cal Preston. You've got no right to go sniffing around her if you don't mean to stick by her."

Out of desperation, he tried turning the tables on his tormentor. "And what about you? What are you going to do about Toby? I don't want to see him hurt."

If he was expecting a fight, he didn't get it. "Neither do I. He's a good man."

"Yeah, he is." Probably the most decent man he'd ever met, but he suspected Thea knew that without his telling her.

They reached the small creek behind the barn. He led Thea over to a log and helped her to ease down on it. The shade of a nearby tree provided them some relief from the hot sun. Cal stretched out on the ground near her feet. The quiet murmur of the cool, clear water rippling over the rocks soothed away the worst of Cal's mood.

"God must have a sense of humor."

Cal chewed on a piece of grass and considered Thea's words. "How so?"

"He takes three good people like Toby and the McCords and makes them all wrong for each other." She laughed softly. "Then he throws a couple of misfits like us into the mix and sits back to see what happens."

He couldn't fault her logic. The image made him smile even as it hurt somewhere inside.

"Toby has powerful strong feelings for you." And she felt some for him as well, unless Cal was sorely mistaken.

"If I'd met him before, maybe we could have worked it out."

"Before what?"

She stared off into the distance. "Just before."

There wasn't much to be said to that. Thea had darkness in her life, and somehow those shadows stood between her and Toby as firmly as if they'd been rock solid and not just memories. Cal understood as few could. She could have been his mother sitting there.

"Will you take me back to town tomorrow?"

He studied her face before answering. No use in skirting the issue. "You're not healed enough to go back to work. I don't know about Boone, but most saloon owners don't want their women showing up bruised."

"True enough, but I need to get back soon as I can. It'll go better that way. Easier."

Something in her words stirred up some ugly memories. "How likely is Boone to use his fists?"

Thea shot him a questioning look. "How come you know so much about things like that?"

Hell, he might as well tell her. Seemed lately he was hell-bent on telling women things that even Toby didn't know. Not for sure. "My mother was in the same line of work. I saw what some of her bosses were like."

Thea nodded, as if that had answered some questions for her. "He's never hit me."

Yet.

He could hear the word even though Thea didn't actually say it out loud. Not that it mattered. He didn't want her to go back to the saloon at all, even if his own reasons weren't as clear in his mind as Toby's were.

"Like I said, you're not healed up enough."

Thea gave him a disgusted look. Refusing his help, she awkwardly rose to her feet and started the long trip back to the house. He gave her a few seconds' lead and then followed along to make sure she reached the porch safely. Not once did she acknowledge his presence.

"Thea."

She didn't look back, but she did pause in the doorway long enough to hear him out.

"Give yourself a chance." He wasn't sure exactly what he was trying to tell her. A chance to heal. A chance to be friends with Lily. A chance with Toby. All of it and none of it.

"Big talk coming from you, Mr. Preston." Thea gave him one last look over her shoulder. "You might do well to listen to your own advice."

Lily found him in the barn playing one of his innumerable games of solitaire. The soft glow of the lantern brought out the blue-black highlights in his hair and made those high cheekbones stand out in sharp relief. She wondered how many women had their heads turned by his hard-edged good looks.

"Did you come all the way out here to stare at me, or did you want something?"

She should have known that he'd been aware of her approach even before she'd reached the barn. And she wanted something all right, but she wasn't going to let the temptation dancing in his dark eyes win this time.

"You didn't come in to eat."

"Wasn't hungry." He scooped up the cards and started shuffling them over and over.

She smiled. He wasn't unaffected by her presence either. "I brought you a plate." Without waiting for him to accept her offering, she moved closer and set the food down on the board he was using as a table.

"Thanks."

So he was going to make it difficult for her. "We need to talk."

"No, we don't." The cards were sorting themselves into neat piles. His eyes remained riveted to his game.

She stuck to hers. "About the other afternoon."

He turned over the first card—the queen of hearts. Lily wasn't sure, but she thought she heard him mutter a curse under his breath.

"This isn't easy for me, Cal." She laced her fingers together to hide the tremors. "I've never . . . I mean, you know."

"Well, now you have—and damn well, I might add."

He was being deliberately outrageous. "Apologize right this minute, Cal Preston."

That did it. He stood up, knocking over his make-shift table and scattering his cards and his dinner in the hay underfoot. "For what? For bedding you good and proper, or for talking about it?" His eyes narrowed as he took a step closer to her. "It's too damn late for second thoughts, Lily."

She stood her ground while she looked around for something to hit him with. "Don't be a bigger fool than you already are. I know very well that we can't take back what happened. All I'm saying is that it can't happen again."

"I don't recall offering to repeat the experience."

She would not cry. She would not. "Fine." Trouble was, if she'd gotten what she came for, did it have to hurt so bad?

"Was there anything else? I'd like to get back to my card game."

If he was only interested in the cards, why wasn't he picking them up instead of staring at her with such fury in his eyes? What would happen if she pushed him?

"You didn't come into the house because you're afraid of me."

"Like hell!" His hands clenched into fists as he took another half step toward her.

"You want me and that scares you right to the sole of those fancy black boots of yours." She was no doubt as scared as he was, but something inside her was driv-ing her to the brink of insanity. She taunted him by kicking a couple of his precious cards. "I'll leave you to your paper ladies since they're the only ones you can handle."

The flare of heat in his eyes should have sent her running for the house, but instead she reveled in the feeling of power it gave her. She'd told herself over and over that she needed to stay clear of Cal Preston and the temptations he offered. She had yet to come to terms with the changes in Wade, not to mention the problems with the ranch and the constant threat of Upton Boone.

But right that minute, nothing mattered but easing the heated ache building inside her, a need only the man in front of her could soothe. She brought her chin up, meeting him glare for glare.

When he reached out to cup her face with his hand, his touch was so gentle that her heart almost burst with the sweetness of it. He brushed her lips with the pad of his thumb and then slid his hand around to the back of her neck, tugging her across the short distance that separated them.

This time he used his lips to caress her mouth, leaving her hungering for more. He rested his forehead against hers.

"I promised myself I wouldn't do this again, Lily."

His words hurt. She tried to step back. He refused to let her move even an inch.

"I didn't say that I didn't want to. Lord knows, I've done nothing but think about bedding you again."

With that, he leaned down and took her mouth. The gentleness was still there, but urgency was building. She allowed herself the pleasure of running her palms over the hard planes of his chest before slipping her arms around his waist.

He coaxed her lips apart, but she was the one who deepened the kiss, shyly tempting him into sharing the sweet heat of his mouth. She was vaguely aware of their surroundings, knowing the barn offered little privacy. Thea wasn't likely to wander in from the house, but either Wade or Toby could come riding in at any moment.

To be honest, she plain didn't care. Despite her best resolve, she wasn't about to miss the chance to experience Cal's lovemaking again. Nothing and no one would hold him here much longer. They both knew that. If all she was going to have was memories, well then, she wanted all the memories she could gather to keep her through the lonely months ahead.

She surprised them both by breaking off the kiss long enough to drag Cal into the nearest stall. It was her own hands that started unbuttoning the front of her dress. Cal watched, his expression enigmatic. It scared her when he didn't speak or respond. She stopped what she was doing, unsure if she'd gone too far.

Cal knew he should do something to stop this madness. He'd serve Lily far better by sending her running back to the house, in tears if necessary. But the vision of this particular woman offering herself to him, even knowing who and what he was, was more than he had the strength to resist.

"Don't stop. I'll go to hell for asking you, but I don't care." His voice, thick with the power of his need, came out more as a growl.

Lily's dark eyes studied his face. He didn't know what she was looking for, but he hoped like hell that she found it. If she walked away now, his sanity was in serious jeopardy.

But then she slipped another button free, revealing the top curve of her sweet breasts. Another button and then another gave way, freeing her shoulders from the confiñes of the dark gingham. Finally the dress pooled around her ankles, and she stepped free from it.

Plain cotton had never graced a more perfect form. He reached out to touch, but she backed away, shaking her head.

"Now you," his temptress demanded.

He was only too glad to get shed of his own clothing. His shirt and trousers joined her dress, along with his boots. The rest would have to wait a bit. In a surprise move, he slipped his arms around her, lifting her up so that her breasts were right where his mouth needed them to be. He breathed in the sweet, womanly scent of her skin as he kissed and suckled each one of them in turn. The thin cotton of her chemise proved to be no barrier at all.

She arched back in his arms as she wrapped her legs around him. Holding her close, he knelt in the hay that would serve them as well as any bed, and then sprawled on top of her. Instinctively she opened her legs, the better to cradle his need against her.

"Kiss me," he demanded as he rocked against her. If he didn't take her soon, he would simply die.

She lifted her head to meet his mouth, all the while learning the feel of him with her restless hands. He thought he would perish with the agony of his need. Easing off to one side, he tugged on the ribbons that held her chemise together. When that was done, he stripped her bare and then freed himself of the last of his own clothing.

Her skin slid against his like soft silk. He tasted every inch that he could reach. Without warning he rolled onto his back, taking her with him. Lily looked surprised and then pleased as she learned the possibilities offered by the new position. Pushing herself up on to her hands, she sat astride him, rocking gently and then with more insistence.

He reached down and lifted her, positioning himself at the entrance to her body. Slowly he slid inside, taking his time and letting her take control of the pace. She shifted to take him fully. Her eyes filled with heated pleasure as she teased him with soft thrusts.

He retaliated by cupping both her breasts and squeezing gently.

"Cal!" She all but purred his name before claiming his mouth with a kiss that threatened to burn the world down around them.

"Finish it, Lily," he pleaded, hoping to hold on to his sanity even as she went from controlled to frantic in a single instant.

He did his best to meet her demands, but he'd lost the mastery of his own body when she'd taken him. But by damn, she was a sight to see—her body glistening in the dim light offered by the lantern, her head thrown back with the dark silk of her hair cascading around her shoulders. Her eyes were closed, seeing a vision he could only imagine.

He knew the instant when her passion crested because she took him tumbling over the edge with her in a final surge of fiery pleasure.

As the tremors faded away, she melted down onto his chest with a pleasured sigh and a satisfied smile. He suspected that he had much the same look on his own face. Even though he knew the risk of their discovery increased the longer they stayed, he didn't have the heart to move her. Lily seemed no more inclined to pull away from him, so he stole another few precious minutes of her body wrapped around his.

Finally, for her sake, he had to do something. Wade had been furious before when he only suspected Lily of harboring strong feelings for Cal. There was no telling what he'd do if confronted with such blatant evidence of how far things had gone between the two of them.

"Lily, we've got to get dressed."

He nudged her with his hand. She was either ignoring him or asleep. He tried again. "Honey, as much as I like being like this, we've got to move."

Finally, she rose up, supporting herself with her arms. A smile, mischievous and wicked, lit up her face. "And if I don't want to?"

Someone had to take charge. He held on tight and reversed their positions once again. A big mistake. Their bodies were still joined, and his clearly liked it that way if the strength of its response was any indication.

Lily giggled and ran her nails up and down his shoulders before sliding them down to dig into his backside. He tried not to groan in pleasure but failed miserably.

"Lily McCord, we can't."

She knew better; there was hard evidence to the contrary. "Liar," she whispered before tugging his face-down to hers for a kiss.

He tried once more to be the single voice of reason. "We're running out of time."

"Then don't waste any more of it talking."

A man should know defeat when he's looking it right in the face. She was offering the one thing he was willing to sell his soul for. With a hard thrust, he fully took her and then did it again and again until it was no longer clear where her body ended and his began.

All too soon, he lay spent in her arms, once again trying to find the strength to let the moment end.

"So what plans have you made?"

Lily frowned at Toby but knew she was no longer going to be able to postpone the decision to take the herd to market. She might be able to facedown Wade, but the combined force of three men glaring at her was more than she could handle.

"None," she answered truthfully. It took a certain amount of determination to avoid the inevitable, but she'd done her best. "However, since the three of you obviously have some ideas on the matter, I'm willing to listen to reason."

She pulled out a chair at the table and sat down, her hands neatly folded in front of her. From the looks the men were giving her, not one of them trusted her sincerity. She didn't blame them. If she could have figured out another way to squirm off the hook once again, she wouldn't be facing them right now.

Wade rummaged around in a drawer and pulled out a piece of paper and a pen. He very deliberately laid them down in front of her. She wasn't fooled by the tactic. It was his way of telling her that she was there to take orders, not give them. Ever since the night of their fight, he'd done everything in his power to make her treat him as an equal.

Fine. She didn't like the idea of trying to mount a cattle drive when all of them lacked the necessary experience. Toby had worked cattle, as had Wade. Even Cal surprised them all by admitting to having some experience that might help.

Since her father had kept the family moving around, Lily had more than enough experience living out of a wagon. When she announced her intention to come along, all three men protested.

Once again, it was Thea who interrupted the argument. "The three of you men aren't thinking at all. If this place isn't safe with you around, how is it going to be safe for Miss Lily to be all alone while you're off chasing cattle?"

Wade mumbled something under his breath while Toby sputtered and fumed. Cal only looked resigned.

Lily flashed a triumphant smile. "That settles it. Thea and I will take care of the food and other necessities. You men will—"

"Wait a minute, here!" Thea was looking at her as if she'd grown a second head. "Who said anything about me going?"

To everyone's surprise, it was Cal who answered. "You've got a chance to put some distance between you and Boone. How often is that going to happen? Besides, Lily will need some help driving the wagon and keeping up with the cooking."

Before Thea could muster any argument, Cal kept right on talking. "Wade, can the three of us handle the herd, at least for a while? I wouldn't trust anyone we'd hire from around here, even if you could afford their salary."

Wade seemed surprised, if not pleased, that Cal was looking to him for an opinion. After considering the matter, he nodded. "If the herd was up to full strength, I'd have said no. But now," he shrugged, "it won't be easy, but I think we can handle it. We're bound to lose a few head, but that would happen anyway."

Toby had been listening to the whole discussion, but now he joined in. "How are we going to get the money for supplies? If you make a big cash withdrawal from the bank, Boone is bound to find out. He won't be pleased to find out that you're still trying to hold onto the ranch."

Lily answered him. "Actually, I have been thinking about that very thing. He won't worry too much if I take money out, because the less we have in the bank, the less likely we'll be able to make the mortgage payment. But you're right about the other. If we load up on trail supplies in town, he'll know what we're up to right away."

She drew a rough map on the paper. "If we're careful, we should have enough of everything on hand to get started, say, for a week. In that time, we should be close enough to a town to buy what we need to get the rest of the way. That way, we could be gone before Boone knows anything about it."

Thea nodded. "You don't want him sending trouble after us. I'd wait until the day after we start out to send Wade back to town to get the money. I can ride well enough to help keep the cattle moving while he's gone. He'd stand a better chance of slipping out of town before Boone knows he's there. Even if he's followed, we could be some distance from the ranch before they catch on."

"But you can't . . ." Toby started to protest.

Thea put an immediate stop to his argument. "Don't start with me, Toby. If Miss Lily wants me along on this trip, fine. But understand this: I'm going to earn my keep, same as everybody else. Even if it means cooking and chasing cattle." She stood glaring at him, hands on her hips.

Lily fought to keep from laughing. She happened to catch Cal's eye and saw that he, too, was trying not to smile. Wade looked impatient with the whole discussion. He tried to take control of the situation.

"Fine, so it's settled. Lily and Thea will see to outfitting the wagon. We'll get the herd gathered up. I say we leave in three days."

That was too soon, Lily wanted to argue. But from the way the others were acting, it was clear that she was in the minority. How was she supposed to organize the dozens of details that had to be attended to in that amount of time? Of course, she wouldn't have to do it alone. Now that Thea was feeling some better, she was pitching right in on the endless chores around the ranch.

Wade chose his own role. "I'll ride out to the valley

and start packing up the camp there. The women will need the tent on the drive. Toby, you and Preston here can see what we have and what we'll need to buy. Add it to whatever Lily has on her list so that when we're on the trail, we'll be ready. Think you can handle that?"

To Lily's mind, he was being nothing short of rude. She waited for the explosion, especially from Cal, but to her surprise both men nodded and headed out to the barn with Wade. As their voices faded in the distance, Lily watched them through the window.

"They're letting him grow up." Thea had joined her. "Even though he's young, it's his ranch, his cattle. They both know that. As long as he can handle the job, they'll let him."

"And if he gets in over his head?"

"Then they'll prod him in the right direction."

For a companionable minute, they stood shoulder to shoulder, their eyes trained on the three men. Lily was still learning to see Wade in new ways, ones that accepted him as an equal instead of a much younger brother. Even so, her eyes were drawn more to his companion.

Her lover.

She hadn't been able to walk through the barn for the past two days without blushing. When had she grown so brazen as to entice a man—practically a stranger—into making love in a pile of hay? She didn't have any regrets, not really, but her conscience was acting up. She'd been raised to believe that good women only did such things with their husbands.

"Honey, if you don't learn how to hide your thinking better than that, the whole world is going to know what you've been doing with that man." Thea's voice had threads of laughter running through the bit of advice she was offering.

"I don't know what you're talking about." Great. She knew she'd come off sounding both defensive and guilty.

Thea didn't let her get away with it. "Yes, you do. Lord knows, I'm in no position to judge, but decent women can't afford to go around laying with men like Cal Preston, not if they value their reputations."

"But no one is going to find out."

Thea was relentless. "I did. Toby suspects. Wade could, heaven forbid. But even if we all keep our mouths quiet, what happens if that man plants a baby in your belly?"

Instinctively, Lily's hand went to her waist as if to comfort and protect the child she'd always wanted and had never been able to conceive. In her mind's eye, a vision formed as clearly as if the infant were already in her arms, a smiling child with dark eyes and dark hair and his father's heart-stopping smile.

A woman would be a fool to wish for such a vision to become real, especially when it involved a man who would soon disappear from her life. But it seemed that she was indeed a fool.

Thea was still waiting for her answer. "I don't know, Thea. What do most women do when they can't resist the charms of a man like Cal?"

Her new friend, who had her own demons to fight, sighed. "We take what they offer and let the future worry about itself."

Then, to Lily's surprise, Thea slipped her arm around Lily's shoulder and gave her a quick squeeze. There was nothing more to be said as the two of them stood in silence, watching the men do whatever it is that men do.

Eleven

The dust was unbearable. Cal had followed Toby's example and tied a bandanna across his nose and mouth to keep the worst of it out. Although it helped some, his teeth still felt gritty after trailing after cattle all day. He glanced at the sun to gauge how much longer they would keep the herd moving before settling in for the night.

Another hour, maybe two.

His companions didn't look to be faring much better. Toby's duster was covered in a fine coat of dirt. Lily was handling the wagon team with an expertise that still surprised him. For such a little thing, she had amazing strength of will. Keeping the horses moving had to wear her out, but each night, she climbed down off the wagon ready to start fixing a hot meal for them all.

And then there was Thea. Damned if she didn't look as if she was enjoying herself. Her claim to ride well hadn't been an idle boast. She moved with the horse as if she'd been rounding up strays all her life.

He pulled up long enough to take a drink out of his canteen. The first mouthful served to rinse the dust and grit out of his mouth. Once he'd spit the mud out, he drank deeply. Between the hot sun and the hard work, he felt as though he'd been wrung dry. Even so, he was careful to hoard some of the precious liquid for later in case they didn't find water by nightfall.

So far they'd been lucky. They'd been following a small river for the past few days, but it had swung away from the trail they were following. Tonight might very well be the first dry camp for them. Thank goodness Lily had had the foresight to insist on carrying two barrels tied to the wagon. Each morning they filled them to the brim before moving on with the herd. It wasn't enough to help the cattle, but it would suffice for the horses and the people if they were careful.

By Toby's reckoning, they were another day, maybe two, from restocking their supplies. Cal knew Lily was starting to worry about Wade. They'd all expected him to catch up with them before now. Since they were leaving a trail that a man could follow blindfolded, it was only natural to think that something might have gone wrong.

Once they reached the outskirts of town, Cal figured on helping Toby and the women get the herd settled in and then he'd go looking for Wade if he hadn't shown up by then. Cal hoped that it wouldn't come to that. The cattle were almost more than the four of them could handle. He hated to think what could happen if Toby was left alone with only Thea and Lily to help.

The wagon was almost upon him, telling him he'd been sitting in one place for too long. After one look at Lily's weary face, he knew he wouldn't be chasing strays for a while.

"Hold up, Lily. I'm coming up." He waited for her to rein in the horses and then dismounted. He tied his sorrel's reins to the back of the wagon and then climbed up in the seat beside her.

"What are you doing?" There were dark circles under her eyes, and her sweet mouth was cracked and dried from the hot sun.

"I'm giving you a rest." He reached for the reins. The fact that she surrendered them without protest told him he'd been right to take charge.

She rubbed her eyes and blinked. A huge yawn surprised them both, making Cal chuckle. He slapped the reins sharply. The horses responded with a lurch, but then settled back into pulling the wagon along at a steady pace.

"Why don't you climb in back and stretch out? The cows can take care of themselves for an hour or so."

She yawned again. "Maybe I will. Wake me in an hour, though. Toby and Thea need your help, too." She climbed over the back of the seat and made herself as comfortable as she could on a pile of the bedding they'd been using at night. After only a few minutes, she was sound asleep.

About thirty minutes later, Toby circled by. "She finally let you spell her?"

Cal looked over his shoulder at the exhausted woman. Something like admiration and grudging respect made him shake his head.

"She's as stubborn as they come." And more beautiful than any other woman he'd ever met, but he kept that part to himself. "Have you had a chance to scout out a place for us to stop for the night?"

"That's why I came back. Thea spotted a stream about two miles ahead. It isn't much, but it'll get the herd through the night." He nodded toward Lily. "Think she can hold up that long?"

"She can and she will." Lily raised her head, holding her hand to shade the sun from her face. It took her a couple of tries, but she managed to pull herself up and climb onto the seat next to Cal.

"I'll take the reins again. Toby will need you to help get the cattle settled."

Cal wanted to protest, but he knew they had no

choice. Giving Lily an evening off was a luxury they could ill afford. Even when Wade managed to catch up with them, they would still be skirting disaster.

He handed over control of the horses and then worked his way to the back of the wagon to untie his horse. That done, he jumped to the ground without waiting for Lily to stop. He swung up in the saddle and then followed Toby back to the herd, all the time wishing he could be back on the wagon watching Lily sleep.

A long and dirty two hours later, the cattle were contentedly grazing on the lush grass along the stream. Thea and Lily were bustling around the back of the wagon, getting dinner started. Toby had taken first watch, riding slowly around the herd, doing his best to keep the cattle confined to the area surrounding the stream. Luckily, the best grass was to be found there, so most of the cows showed little interest in straying very far.

Only Cal was at loose ends. The women didn't need or want his help, and he'd get his own turn watching over the herd soon enough. He decided to go for a short walk along the stream to stretch out his legs. The ground sloped gently upward, getting rockier the farther he went.

When he climbed over one last boulder, his efforts were amply rewarded. For the length of about fifty feet, the stream pooled up, deep and slow-moving, the perfect place to wash off three days of dust and dirt. He started to unbutton his shirt but then stopped.

Cursing himself for a fool, he started down the rocky trail back to camp. The least he could do for Lily and Thea was let them use the pool first. Both of them had worked without complaint and deserved a treat.

Thea looked up at his approach. She stepped away from the stew that she'd been stirring. "Dinner won't be ready for another hour or so."

"Good, go get Lily and your saddlebags. I've got a present for the two of you."

Thea did as he asked while they both waited for Lily to come back from fetching water from the stream. When she came trudging up the slope, she looked puzzled to see the two of them watching her.

"Is something wrong?"

Cal shook his head. "Come with me and don't ask any questions."

"But dinner . . ."

"I'll handle dinner. You've got something else to do."

Before she could think of another protest, he led the way back toward the rocks. He played the gentleman and helped each of the two ladies over the rougher spots. Once they reached the final boulder, he stopped and let them go first. Their response to the sight of cool, clear water deep enough to bathe in was all he could have hoped for.

"I'll keep an eye on dinner. Take your time and enjoy yourselves." Then, despite the temptation to stay and watch the two women frolic in the water, he made himself honor his promise to see to dinner. Once they were done, he'd take his own turn and then relieve Toby early so he could wash up before it got too dark to climb the trail safely.

When he got back, he heard the sound of a rider approaching. Since it was the wrong direction for it to be Toby, he grabbed his rifle and took a position behind the wagon. Narrowing his eyes, he scanned the horizon. The rider was making a direct line for the camp with no effort to hide from view.

Lily would be greatly relieved to see Wade safe and sound. So would the rest of them—even Cal, although he'd never admit to it.

He lifted his rifle over his head and waved it back and forth, signaling to Wade that it was safe to approach. A few minutes later, the youth rode into camp. When he dismounted, he stumbled a few steps, obviously exhausted. Cal caught his arm to keep him from falling, but Wade jerked free.

"I'm all right."

"Yeah, and I'm the president of the United States." He leaned his rifle against the wagon and checked on the stew.

Wade unsaddled his horse and tethered it where it could reach both grass and water before joining Cal at the fire.

"Where is everybody?"

"Toby's on first watch. Thea and Lily are upstream enjoying the first bath they've had since we left the ranch."

Wade sat staring into the fire. "I got the money, but I'm not so sure that I wasn't followed. I've been riding in circles for two days trying to see if anyone was on my trail, but I never did see anyone."

"It doesn't matter. We've got only one way we can go, and there's no way to hide our tracks. If Boone is determined to know what we're up to, it sure wouldn't be that hard to figure out." Cal poked at the fire and added some more wood.

"I'll take second watch."

Despite his offer, Cal knew he wouldn't accept it. As tired as Wade was, he'd be a danger not only to himself but to the rest of them. His ability to react to any crisis that might arise would be seriously impaired if he didn't get some sleep and soon.

"We'll see."

The two of them lapsed into silence, more because of weariness than their normal animosity to each other. Besides, Cal had found himself feeling some affinity for the younger man. They both loved the same woman and neither of them was the right man for her. Lily would never see Wade as anything other than a beloved younger brother, no matter how much Wade wanted to change that.

And as far as Cal went, she enjoyed him as a lover, but that was a temporary infatuation at best. They both knew that he wasn't the kind of man she deserved, not for the long term. In the end, neither Wade nor Cal would have anything other than memories of Lily. Some lucky son of a bitch would take their places in her heart and in her bed.

As if his mind had conjured her out of thin air, Lily came strolling back into camp with Thea right behind her. Both women caught sight of Wade at the same time. He struggled to his feet in time to catch Lily in his arms. She hugged him close, her eyes squeezed closed as if to stop the tears that were streaming down her face.

"Wade, thank goodness. We thought . . . I was afraid . . ." she sobbed. "Oh, Lord, I was afraid that we might have lost you."

Cal couldn't blame Wade for taking advantage of the moment to hold Lily in his arms, but he'd damn well better let her go soon. He was on the verge of interfering when Lily stepped back on her own. Wiping her eyes on her sleeve, she gave Wade a shaky smile.

"You're timing was perfect. The work is done for the day, and dinner is almost ready."

Wade laughed, just as she had intended. Cal knew

he shouldn't be jealous. After all, he knew Lily in ways that Wade never would, but then she considered Wade family, a much more permanent relationship than anything Cal could hope for.

Damn, he hated feeling sorry for himself. And he knew he was starting to, but it wasn't as if his interest in Lily was a secret. She was busy filling Wade in on their progress to date, her eyes bright and smiling now that she knew that he was safe and sound.

Her hair, still damp from her bath, was curling wildly around her face. He wanted to bury his fingers in it while he kissed her senseless. Not that there was much chance of that with everyone else constantly underfoot. Amazingly, they'd had more privacy back at the house than they had on the trail.

And if he didn't get some time alone with her soon . . . He didn't let himself finish that thought. He felt someone's eyes on him. Thea's dark eyes were filled with amusement at his expense. If he was being that obvious, he might as well be sitting there with his tongue hanging out.

Fed up and frustrated with the whole situation, he decided that it was his turn to take a bath. Maybe the chill of the water would cool down both his body and his thoughts.

"I'll be upstream for a while. If Toby checks in, send him up next. I'll relieve him as soon as I get back."

"Where are you going now?" Wade asked.

Knowing he was about to get some unwanted company, he still had to answer. "There's a deep spot in the stream up above those rocks. I thought a bath would be a good idea."

Lily had to butt in. "Wade, why don't you go, too? Dinner can wait for a while."

Cal could tell from the sideways look Wade gave

him that the younger man was well aware that Cal might not appreciate his company.

"I'll wait while you get your things."

Clearly surprised, Wade hustled to gather his gear as if afraid Cal would change his mind and retract the offer. The two of them trudged up the hillside in silence. Once they reached the water, Cal sat down on a rock and started tugging off his boots.

A few minutes later both of them were floating in the water, enjoying the late evening sun. It was easy to forget the problems of the day while letting the water soak off the dirt while soothing their tired muscles.

"Well, if that ain't a sight!"

Toby was standing on shore, hands on his hips. "Here I've been working hard all damn day and what are you two doing?"

Wade responded by trying to splash Toby, who laughed and danced back out of reach. He began stripping down as fast as he could. He dove in near Cal and came up sputtering.

"Damn, that feels good. Lily says you were the one to find this place. Nice work."

"You're welcome, but if you're up here, who's watching the herd?"

"Thea." Toby frowned. "Damned woman threatened to make me sleep with the cows if I didn't take a bath like the rest of you. She's taking the rest of my watch and the first part of yours. She and Lily decided that we should relax for a while and then have dinner. As soon as you've finished eating, you can relieve her."

He knew he should feel guilty over a woman doing his work for him, but he couldn't quite muster the energy at that moment. He'd thank the women later.

Toby turned his attention to Wade. "Glad you're back, boy. We were going to start backtracking soon if you didn't show up."

"Sorry it took me longer than I expected, but I didn't want to head straight for you if someone was following."

"Did you see anybody?"

"No, but I couldn't shake off the feeling that someone was dogging my trail as soon as I left King's Creek."

"Well, not much you could do to stop them, if Boone sent someone after you."

Toby waded back to shore to get his soap and a washrag. Cal and Wade both followed suit. Having stolen a few minutes of peace, it was time to get back to camp. Dinner wouldn't hold forever, and Thea had to be exhausted. Despite her determination to pull her weight, she wasn't used to spending full days in the saddle, much less a good part of the night as well.

Cal finished up and headed back to camp by himself. He told himself that he didn't have an ulterior motive, but even so, the chance to have Lily to himself even for a few minutes was worth cutting his bath a bit short.

He found her staring off at the sunset. The sky was aflame in brilliant oranges and reds. He eased up beside her and slipped his arm around her shoulders. She sighed and leaned in against his chest.

"I miss being with you." He was surprised by the strength of the truth in the few words.

"I've been here all along," she said without looking up at him.

"So has everyone else. I'm too selfish to want to share."

This time she did tilt her face up toward his. He didn't know if she meant for him to kiss her, but just in case, he did. He plundered her mouth with deliberate thoroughness. Damn, she tasted sweet. He could have spent the rest of the night doing nothing else, but he could hear Toby saying something to Wade as they made their way down off the hill.

If he wasn't mistaken, Toby was talking louder than he needed to, probably well aware of what Cal might be up to. Reluctantly, he broke away and stepped back. He personally didn't give a damn what Wade thought about him and Lily, but Lily might feel differently.

By the time the other two men came into sight, Cal was busy saddling up his horse and Lily was stirring the stew.

"I'll find Thea and send her back."

Wade called his name just as he was about to ride out. "I'll relieve you at midnight."

Lily protested. "You need a good night's rest."

Her brother-in-law did not appreciate her concern any more than Cal did. Did she think he'd been doing nothing while Wade had been chasing down their money?

Wade looked past her to where Cal was waiting for them to make up their minds. "If I don't wake up on my own, boot me out of my blankets."

"With pleasure," Cal assured him, forcing a smile that he didn't mean. To his surprise, Wade laughed and waved him off. Cal frowned as he rode out. He wasn't sure he was ready to like the boy, but he was afraid he already did.

Riding away from the McCords when all this was over and done with might very well be the hardest thing he'd ever do.

Lily slapped the reins, hurrying the horses along while the road was still in relatively good shape. Once she had to turn off and cut across country to where the others were waiting with the herd, the going would be both rougher and slower. The gossip she'd heard had her worried. The sooner she could warn the others, the better they could prepare to defend themselves if it became necessary.

It was only by accident that she'd learned that there were some strangers in town, biding their time until a small cattle drive passed through the area. She had no doubt that it was their herd the men were watching for.

Cal had been the one who'd suggested that only Lily go into town for supplies. Considering the makeup of their small group, they wouldn't be hard to mistake if someone was looking for them. He had practically ordered her to drive the long way around the town to come in from the opposite direction. In case anyone was keeping track, she was taking the same route on her way back.

With luck, she had gotten out of town before any of Boone's men saw her. There was always the chance that they might not recognize her, since she'd rarely gone into King's Creek, but she couldn't count on it. For now, she concentrated on her driving.

About an hour later, she could see the rocky outcrop that marked their camp. If it wouldn't have endangered both herself and the horses, she would have whipped them into an all-out run. Even though she hadn't seen anything suspicious, she had an uneasy feeling that their time was running out.

The railhead was only a few days away, but it might as well be on the other side of the world if Boone knew where they were. A rider broke free of the herd and was headed straight for her. At this distance, it was impossible to pick out any details, but on some level she knew it was Cal. Some of the tension drained away, as if his presence meant safety for her.

Cal caught up with her some distance from the camp. She pulled the wagon up and waited for him to join her on the seat. As soon as he climbed up, she tried to warn him about what she'd heard in town, but he was too busy kissing her to listen. His lips lightly met hers, and for several seconds they were content with the innocence of it. Then his tongue teased its way into her mouth even as his hands relearned their way around her body.

She hated herself for trying to pull back. "Cal, they'll see us."

"Right now, I don't give a damn." He turned his attention to nibbling her ear, sending shivers dancing through her.

"But . . ."

"Shut up and kiss me," he murmured.

She did as he ordered. It took her longer this time to gather the strength to be the voice of reason. "Cal, this is scandalous in broad daylight."

"I certainly hope so." He tried to slip his hand somewhere it shouldn't be, not when they could be seen by anyone within two miles.

She slapped at his wrist. "Stop that. . . . Cal, I mean it." Maybe he would have listened if she hadn't been so breathless at the time.

Finally, he stopped. She was glad to see that she wasn't the only one short of breath and shaking with need. He gave her one more fleeting kiss on her mouth before moving farther away from her on the seat. Those few inches weren't enough for her peace of mind. She swore she could feel his heartbeat despite the slight distance between them.

"Now, what did you want to tell me?" His smile told her all too clearly that he knew that he'd done his best to scatter her thoughts to the wind.

Even so, she managed a coherent sentence. "Boone's men were in town."

Instantly, all Cal's playfulness was gone. His eyes lost all warmth, sending a chill right through her.

"How do you know?"

"I was in the general store, waiting for our order to be filled when I overheard two men talking. One of them was asking if the store owner had heard about any herds moving through." She shuddered. "He told them no, but I think he was lying. Once they left, he practically threw our supplies in my wagon as if he couldn't wait to get me out of the place."

She paused for a breath. "I took the long way back, like you said. But if they were watching, there's no telling how soon they'll figure out where we are."

"We need to move on now." He started climbing down to the ground.

"But I thought we were going to rest for the day." They all needed it badly because no one was getting a full night's sleep. She wasn't sure any of them would hold up for much longer without some relief.

"We need to put some distance between us and those men. If they think we didn't leave until after Wade visited the bank, they won't be expecting us to have gone this far. If we can move on now, they might miss us altogether."

He grabbed the reins to his horse and vaulted up in the saddle. Under other circumstances, Lily would have enjoyed a little time to admire the grace with which he moved. For now, she only wanted him to hurry back to the others and warn them that trouble could have followed her from town.

While he circled around the herd looking for Wade and Toby, Lily took the wagon back to camp. Thea was the only one there. She stood shading her eyes from the midday sun and waited for Lily to climb down out of the wagon.

"Welcome back. Hope you were able to get most of what we needed. I'm getting mighty tired of . . ."

She stopped midsentence. "What's wrong? Did something happen in town?"

Lily quickly told her the same thing she'd said to Cal. Before she was half done, Thea was already gathering up everything and repacking the wagon. Although Cal had determined Lily's route to town, it was Wade who'd suggested that they empty the wagon of everything they could. A woman picking up supplies for a nearby ranch wouldn't have all their camp gear along for the ride.

The two women were getting well-practiced in breaking camp. In the distance, they could hear the men start the slow process of moving the cattle out.

"We'll probably regret not taking the time to pack all this stuff back the way it was." Despite her words, Thea picked up another armload of bedding and tossed it up on top of the wagon.

Lily agreed, but there wasn't time. Farther along their way, they'd find some time to reorganize things. For now, though, she felt as if each second they wasted was one closer to bringing Boone and his men down on top of them.

She gave a cursory glance around the campsite. If they were leaving anything behind, they'd either have to do without or replace it at the next town. Turning her back on whatever might lie hidden in the area, she climbed up in the wagon and picked up the reins.

"Are you sure you don't want to ride in the wagon with me for a while?" She felt bad that Thea was doing a man's work, but then, most folks would consider driving the chuckwagon for a cattle drive unlikely work for a woman.

"No, I do better moving around."

Thea gave one last tug on her horse's cinch and then mounted up. She was wearing men's clothing that she'd borrowed from Wade. It was all too big on her but, it fit her closer than anything that Cal or Toby would have lent her. Lily was still wearing the dress that she'd worn to town, because there hadn't been time to change. The way the sun was pounding down on her, she knew she'd regret that decision.

Finally, all was ready. Slapping the reins on the lead horse's back, she braced herself against the initial lurch of the wagon. Thea waited until Lily had the horses moving at a steady clip before riding out to join the men. Lily noticed that Thea stood in her stirrups and stared down the trail that led back toward town.

Nothing was moving along the flat stretch that lay before them. Lily drew what little comfort she could from that. Perhaps the store owner had bought them a little time by hurrying her along on her way. Despite the heat of the day, she shivered.

"Giddyap, boys!" she called, wishing she dared urge the team into a run, but for the sake of the horses' safety, she settled instead for a slow, steady pace. She would have to be satisfied knowing that each step the horses took put that much more distance between them and possible pursuit.

Dinner was a quiet affair. Even though they weren't all riding the edge of exhaustion, the strain of wondering when and where Boone's men might catch up with them was taking its toll. Cal stretched out on his bedroll and tried to snatch a few extra minutes of rest before Lily served up dinner.

Tilting his hat forward shaded his eyes from the last of the sun but still allowed him to watch every move she made. She seemed unaware of his scrutiny. He'd yet to figure out what it was exactly that he was watching for. It didn't seem to matter. His eyes were drawn to her even when he was making a conscious effort to do otherwise.

Like now. He should be sleeping. Hell, even an extra fifteen minutes of slumber would feel like heaven. Instead, he was drinking every detail about Lily McCord that his mind could absorb, just as if he were a schoolboy suffering through his first crush.

Except schoolboys didn't know exactly how it felt to have the object of their affection underneath them in bed, naked and needy and urging them on. He stifled a groan as his body reacted to that particular image. In some ways, it would have been easier if he didn't have such intimate knowledge of the pleasures to be had sharing Lily's bed. His imagination was no match for the amazing reality of it all.

And he had to wonder if they would ever have the chance to experience it all again. Lord, he hoped so.

He suddenly realized that Lily was staring right back at him. Figuring he'd been caught, he gave up all pretense of sleeping and sat up. Instead of fussing at him, Lily blushed. Cal grinned. Evidently, she was indulging in a few memories herself.

She turned her back to him, but he only saw that as a challenge. Looking around to see where the others were, he realized that for a precious moment or two, they were alone. Never one to miss an opportunity that presented itself, he quietly got to his feet and silently walked up behind her.

He grabbed her with no warning, causing her to shriek. He muffled her cry with one hand as he used the other to turn her around. His mouth did a much better job of keeping her quiet than his hand had. She met his passion with some of her own.

Minutes passed before either of them came up for air.

"Son of a bitch! Get your hands off of her."

Cal echoed the curse, wishing like hell that it had been Toby's voice. But no, it had to be Wade. Lily froze in his arms, all vestiges of warmth gone. He held her until she met his gaze.

Pitching his voice for her ears only, he told her, "We've got nothing to apologize for, Lily. Wade keeps saying he's a big boy. It's time he acted like it."

When she nodded, he dropped his hands and let her retreat. Damn, she still looked guilty. Knowing there wasn't anything he could do to convince her otherwise with Wade breathing down his neck, he turned to face her irate brother-in-law.

He wasn't surprised to see Wade's hands clenched in fury. Without Toby to step between them, he had little doubt that this time they'd come to blows. Lily recognized the volatility of the situation at the same time and tried to ward it off.

"Wade, there's no reason for this."

Cal answered for both of them. "Sure, there is. Don't try to come between us." He pushed her back behind him again.

"I said keep your hands off of her, you bastard."

"That isn't up to you, boy." Cal knew he was taunting Wade, but he'd had it with sneaking around, and if it took pounding him into the dust to make his point, fine.

"She deserves better than you."

Wade was working himself up to charging. He circled around to the right, trying to keep Cal between him and Lily. Cal kept his eye on him, all the while making sure that Lily didn't do something stupid.

"That's up to her to decide. You have no say in the matter."

"I sure as hell do, don't I, Lily?" He looked past Cal, his eyes begging Lily to back him up.

Cal fully expected her to, but she surprised both of

them. "As far as I'm concerned, you're both acting like a pair of fools. If you want to fight, go right ahead. But get this through your thick skulls. If either of you lays a hand on the other, I'm washing my hands of you both for the rest of this cattle drive."

To emphasize her point, she turned on her heel and stalked away, leaving the two men to do what they would. Cal watched her until she disappeared behind the wagon. It wasn't the smartest thing he'd ever done, turning his back on Wade, but then he'd never claimed to be a genius.

A whisper of air movement was his only warning that Wade had decided to take advantage of his brief distraction to charge. Cal sidestepped at the last minute, but Wade was expecting the maneuver. His quick reflexes allowed him to grab Cal and take him down with him. Locked in each other's grasp, the two of them rolled in the dust, each doing his damnedest to land a telling blow.

Wade's right fist connected with Cal's jaw, jarring his teeth against each other. With a growl of pain mixed with anger, Cal shoved the younger man with all his strength, pinning him to the ground. Just as he pulled back his own fist, ready to knock Wade senseless, a woman screamed.

Both men froze.

Before they could react, the evening silence was ripped apart by a series of shots.

Cal was on his feet and running, his fight with Wade forgotten, or at least postponed.

Twelve

Cal reached the wagon in time to keep Lily from running out into the open.

"Get under the damn wagon and keep your head down!"

"But Wade . . ." she protested, struggling to pull herself free.

"Damn it, Lily, he can take care of himself. Get under that wagon now. I'll find him."

Another burst of gunfire kicked up dust and rocks in a line across their camp. Cal hit the dirt and slithered across to his saddle. Pulling out his rifle, he rolled to cover and tried to find a target both for his bullets and his temper.

He caught sight of Wade behind a low cluster of rocks to his right. The boy had picked his cover well. Neither of them was in a position to see very far.

"Can you see anything?"

Wade shook his head. "Those first shots came from behind us. That last bunch came from the other side."

The silence, not knowing if their attackers were gone or merely waiting for them to make a stupid move, was unsettling. At least Lily was finally showing good sense. Once she heard Wade's voice, she'd pulled back out of sight under the wagon. He'd been sorely afraid she'd go charging out to protect her chick.

Her earlier show of temper had been aimed equally at both Cal and Wade, but when danger threatened it was all too clear which one held her heart. Cal wondered if Wade realized the truth of the situation. She might never feel what Wade wanted from her, but his hold on her was still a powerful one.

Another burst of gunfire shattered the brief silence, but this time the shots were coming from some distance away. None of them were out of the woods yet, because Thea and Toby were unaccounted for. Boone's men were shooting either at them or the cattle or both. Either way, Toby would need Cal's help.

Figuring there wasn't time to saddle his own horse, Cal ran a zigzag pattern across the camp and grabbed the reins to Wade's mare. He ignored Wade's protest and kicked the mare in the ribs, launching her into an immediate full gallop.

A short distance out, he pulled up, trying to see through the dust raised by the milling cattle. Once again Thea screamed something, but her words were drowned out by more gunfire. In the confusion, it was impossible to tell what was going on, but her voice was coming from the far side of the herd.

He checked the ammunition in his rifle before starting forward at a more controlled pace. Wade and possibly Lily would be right behind him, so he scanned the area carefully, trying to ensure that neither of them rode into an ambush.

The cattle were definitely worked up over something. A very few were still grazing, but the others were stirring restlessly. It wouldn't take much to send the nervous animals into a deadly panic. He did his best to skirt the majority of them, not wanting to be caught in the middle of a possible stampede. Gradually he worked his way over to where he'd last heard Thea.

He caught sight of her atop a small rise, crouched

behind a cluster of boulders. Every so often, she would stand and fire off into the distance, but no one seemed to be shooting back. Although her back was toward him, she appeared to be uninjured. He allowed himself a sigh of relief, but that was before he realized that Toby lay sprawled in front of her on the ground.

And he wasn't moving.

Fear, cold and bitter, burned through Cal. Without regard for common sense, he nudged the mare into a canter. Once he was within a few yards of where Thea was huddled, he swung his leg over the saddle and hit the ground running. The mare veered away. Thea hadn't paid him the slightest heed, so he approached carefully, not wanting to startle her into firing the gun she held in her hand.

For a brief second, it occurred to him to wonder if she was the one who'd injured Toby, but he rejected the idea immediately. The two of them shot sparks, not bullets, off each other. On a gut level, he knew that neither of them would deliberately harm the other. Not physically, anyway.

"Thea, it's Cal." He pitched his voice to carry no farther than where she still huddled over Toby. If the intruders hadn't seen his approach, there was no use in announcing the fact. At first, he wondered if Thea had even heard him, but then she looked up, her face ravaged with emotion.

"They tried to stampede the herd. Toby was right in the middle of it."

He made himself ask the question, although he feared the answer. "Is he alive?"

Thea nodded. "But he's hurt bad, maybe real bad."

While she stood guard, Cal gathered the courage to approach his friend to assess the nature of Toby's injuries. His eyes were immediately drawn to Toby's left leg, which was bent at an unnatural angle. Cal gently ran his hands down Toby's other limbs, checking for additional injuries. The one leg was bad enough; it was a relief to find that everything else seemed to be intact.

At first Cal thought the blood on Toby's shirt had come from a cut on his forehead, but the small hole in the material shattered that hope. He grabbed the front of Toby's shirt and ripped it open. There was no mistaking it for anything other than a bullet wound. The cartridge had grazed Toby's rib cage, carving a jagged tear in his flesh. The wound had bled profusely. He comforted himself with the knowledge that as long as they could keep the wound from becoming infected, it was likely to be more painful than dangerous.

Neither of those injuries accounted for Toby's being unconscious.

"Do you know if he was hit on the head?" Cal asked Thea. He had to repeat the question again before she answered.

"I don't know. I heard the shots and came running. He was returning fire. He yelled for me to get down. When there was a break in the shooting, I found him like this."

"How about you? Are you all right?" Cal asked as he felt Toby's head and neck, looking for sign of another injury. He winced when he found a lump the size of an egg behind Toby's right ear. When once again Thea didn't respond, he looked up to find her still staring down at Toby's inert form.

"Thea, he's strong. With good care, he should pull through just fine. He'll need someone to look after him who's not afraid to yell back at him. He's never been one to put up with being fussed over." Cal wasn't used to offering comforting words, but evidently he'd said something right, because some of the tension went out of Thea.

"I'll tie him down if need be. He won't get past me."

Or over her any time soon either, if Cal was any judge of the strength of Toby's feelings for the woman. And no doubt she cared about Toby in return; she was just fighting against it harder. Considering Cal had his own woman problems, he wasn't about to get involved in Toby's.

"Catch my horse and fetch Wade. If the shooting starts again, I'll keep them busy while you get away. Have Lily go back for the wagon and bring it as close as possible so we can move Toby."

He waited to make sure that Thea got away. Once she was out of sight, he left Toby alone long enough to make sure that no unwanted company still lurked in the area. He climbed up the rocks to get a better look around.

Nothing stirred in the immediate area. From where he stood, he had a clear view for about a mile or so. He watched the horizon, looking for any telltale dust clouds that would reveal the presence of any riders. Again there was nothing to see.

He wasn't sure what that meant. It was difficult to figure how much time had passed since the shots had broken up the fight between Wade and him. If Boone's men—if that was indeed who they were—had only meant to hit and run, they'd had plenty of time to be well on their way back to town. No doubt they had solid alibis all set up just in case somebody asked.

Not that Cal would bother. Even if the sheriff was honest, there wasn't much the man could do. It would be their word against Boone and all the witnesses his money could buy. Without a doubt, their time would be better spent getting Toby well enough to travel.

Not to mention getting the cattle rounded up again. He looked back toward camp. He could see Lily driving the wagon toward him, but she was having to work to find a way through the rough terrain. Thea was taking a more direct route, still on Wade's mare. She had thrown the burlap bag that held their meager medical supplies over the saddle.

He took one last look around before climbing down to meet her. Other than a hawk circling overhead, there was no sign of life. Down below, Toby hadn't stirred since he'd left him—probably not a good sign at all.

"How is he?" Thea's hand strayed to Toby's face. When she realized what she was doing, she jerked it back as if she had no right.

"No change. Considering his injuries, he might be better off unconscious until we get him settled back in camp. Splinting his leg is going to hurt like hell, and I'm betting that he isn't going to like us pouring whiskey on that bullet wound any better." He forced himself to smile, hoping that his attempt at humor looked more sincere than it felt.

Thea's own response was just as strained. "You're probably right about that." Once again, she reached out to touch the unconscious man. This time, though, she allowed herself that little pleasure before she picked up her makeshift medical kit.

Lily joined them just as Thea was ready to start.

"Unless you think otherwise, I'm going to start on the bullet wound first. Until Mr. Wade gets here to help, I don't want to mess with that leg."

"That sounds right to me." Lily lifted the side of Toby's shirt and grimaced at the bloody sight.

Cal was in no hurry to mess with a broken leg either. He knew next to nothing about treating serious injuries. He was only too glad to bow to the combined wisdom of the two women. They had to know more than he did.

Thea took charge. "You two do the best you can to

keep him still. He might be quiet now, but once this whiskey hits that cut, he could wake up pretty sudden."

She was right. As soon as the alcohol poured into the open wound, Toby moaned and tried to fight them off. It took all three of them to keep him from kicking out and possibly causing further injury to his leg.

Next Thea used a piece of rag to dab whiskey onto the cut on Toby's forehead. His reaction to that was mild in comparison. There wasn't much they could do about the head injury.

Wade was the last to arrive. He pushed Cal out of the way to get to Lily. "How is Toby?"

Because his concern for Toby was obviously real, Cal ignored Wade's petty behavior. For now. Even though Wade had addressed his question to Lily, Cal answered him. "He's got a broken leg, a bullet wound, and a good-sized bump on his head. We were waiting for you to help set his leg before we try to move him."

The younger man didn't look any more excited by the prospect than Cal felt, but he gamely agreed. "Miss Thea, Lily, what do you need me to do?"

This time Cal let the proper person answer. Thea had been busy tearing a petticoat into long strips. "I need two, maybe three boards about this long." She held her hands apart. "When we have everything ready, one of you will sit on him to keep him from moving while the other one pulls on his leg until it straightens out. Miss Lily and I will bind the leg when you get it back in the right position."

Cal was grimly afraid that the procedure would not be as simple as she made it sound. However, he'd do whatever was necessary to help Toby get back the full use of his leg.

They all looked around hoping to find something suitable to use for splints.

"How about that crate I've been packing the pots

and pans in?" Lily held up her hands to show the approximate dimensions of the box in question.

Wade immediately nodded. "That would work fine. I'll ride back to camp for it."

Cal took advantage of the time Wade was gone once again to climb up and look around. He had an uneasy feeling about the whole affair. If Boone's men had been intent on stampeding the herd, why had they given up so quickly? There was little doubt in Cal's mind that they'd be back. If not today, then sometime soon.

For now, there was nothing he could do about the situation. He clambered down the rocks to rejoin Lily and Thea. A few minutes later, Wade was back with the slats he'd taken from the crate.

"Which end do you want me to take?"

"You can put those splints down beside Toby's leg; then get ready to pull on his leg when we tell you to." Turning to Cal, she continued, "We decided that since you outweigh Wade, you might have better luck holding Toby still for us."

Both men took up their assigned positions, although it was clear from the nasty look Wade gave Cal, he clearly did not appreciate being considered the weaker of the two men. Cal didn't give a damn how Wade felt as long has he did his job in helping Toby.

"What's going on?" Toby's voice was weak but clear. He'd picked a hell of time to wake up.

Lily gave him a smile that was meant to reassure. "You've been hurt. We're getting ready to set your leg."

Toby considered that. "If it's my leg, then why does my head feel like it's going to fall off and my side feels like someone set it on fire?"

No one else seemed inclined to answer, so Cal did. "Because you managed to get yourself shot and landed on your head. If that wasn't enough, you finished up by breaking your leg." He did his best to keep worry out of his voice.

"Is that all?" Toby let out a deep sigh. He rolled his eyes toward Wade. "If you're getting ready to tug on my leg, boy, give me a stick or something to bite on."

"Yes, sir."

Cal watched as Wade looked around for an appropriate twig. Finding one to his liking, he wiped the twig on the seat of his pants to clean it up some before handing it to Thea.

Before she offered it to Toby, she asked, "You want a swig of the whiskey before we get started?"

He eyed the half-empty bottle. "No, we might need it later. The stick should be enough."

They all reluctantly took up their assigned positions, determined to do their best for Toby. Cal put his knee on Toby's chest and pressed down gently. He offered his hand to Toby to hold.

Thea and Lily hovered, waiting for Wade to begin. They watched as he drew a deep breath and then another. Cal was about to lose all patience just as Wade grabbed hold of Toby's ankle and began to pull.

Sweat broke out on Toby's forehead as his color went ashen; he did his best to crush the bones in Cal's hand. Slowly, the leg started to straighten, but Wade eased off before it had come straight.

Toby spit out the stick and glared at the youngster. "Listen, son, I know you don't want to hurt me none, but leave it bent like that and I'll be a cripple for life. Now get ahold of my leg and yank on it for all your worth."

Wade tried again.

"Damn it, boy, I said pull!"

Toby's voice cracked with the effort, but evidently he'd gotten his message across. Wade gave a mighty heave, and they all heard a sickening snap as the bone popped back into place. He dug in his feet to keep the tension on the leg until Thea and Lily had the splints in place.

When Thea had tied the last knot, she gave Wade an approving nod. "You did right fine, Mr. Wade. You can let go now."

Cal slipped back on his heels, but kept his hand in Toby's until his friend released him.

Wade, obviously shaken with the experience, started to walk away. Toby called him back, "Mr. Wade, I owe you."

Embarrassed by the attention, Wade nodded and hurried away, muttering something about checking on the herd. Lily tagged after him to see to the wagon. Toby watched them go before turning his head toward Cal.

"How much of the herd did we lose?"

"I haven't checked, but not many. As far as I can tell, the bastards were only fooling around this time. Maybe trying to spook us more than the cattle."

"I didn't see any of them clearly, but I counted two, possibly three. Could be they're still waiting for reinforcements before they get serious."

"That sounds like Boone's tactics."

They'd almost forgotten that Thea was still fussing around, packing up the rest of the bandages and whiskey. She was rolling up a strip of cloth, her expression solemn.

"Then you figure he won't give up any time soon." Cal made it a statement, not a question.

Toby swore under his breath when Thea nodded. "We were barely holding this outfit together with all of us healthy."

Cal gave the matter some thought. "Lily has some money left from the supplies, but I doubt that it's enough to hire anyone to help out. Besides, who's going to want to sign on with an outfit that has this kind of trouble dogging its steps?"

Toby struggled to sit up. "Get me up. I can still ride."

"Did that bump on your head scramble your brains, Toby Thacker, or have you always been stupid?" The tartness in her words didn't do much to disguise the concern in Thea's dark eyes as she not-so-gently pushed Toby back flat on the ground.

Toby tried to knock her hands away. "Stop your fussing."

Thea didn't back off an inch. "If you were so all-fired set on doing yourself in, you should have told us before we wasted good whiskey cleaning out that hole in your side."

Cal figured the two of them could fight it out. Something in Toby's expression made him think that his friend didn't mind Thea working over him as much as he was letting on. And she seemed more relieved than angry to see Toby feeling up to fighting back.

"Cal, can you come here?"

Lily was motioning for him to join her over near the wagon. When he got there, she was trying to pry a board off the side of the wagon without any success.

"Help me get this off here. We need something to use as a stretcher, and this is all I can find." She put both hands on the top board and gave another yank; the wood creaked but didn't come free.

She obviously intended for Cal to stand beside her, but instead he slipped in behind her and put his arms along the outside of hers. He half expected her to protest, but instead she leaned back against him. The feel of her snuggled against the length of him was pure torture.

He leaned down and nuzzled the back of her neck and worked his way up to the sweet shell of her ear.

She shivered and arched her neck for more of the same. He knew damn well that they were playing with fire in more ways than one.

Even now, his body was making it very clear how much he wanted—needed—to toss Lily on her back in the wagon to finish what he'd started. What little rational thought he could muster warned him that they weren't alone. There was no telling where Wade was at that moment, and besides, Toby and Thea were waiting for the makeshift stretcher.

Frustration gave him the extra strength to rip the board off with one hard yank. It happened so quickly that it threw both Cal and Lily stumbling back. He managed to cushion her fall with his body, but the rocky jolt did little to improve his mood. Especially when Lily laughed.

He shoved her off and then struggled to his feet. After brushing the dirt and rocks off his clothes, he grudgingly offered her a hand up off the ground. She must have sensed his mood had changed for the worse, because she was doing her best to hide her smile. Her eyes, though, sparkled with merriment.

"Let's go get Toby."

"Yes, sir. Right now, sir."

Damn, she was cute, but he wasn't going to let her know that he thought so. Right up until he kissed her senseless. In a surprise move he grabbed her and hauled her right up to his chest, leaving her feet dangling in the air. Her squawk of protest died the second his lips found hers.

He liked the fact that she was the one who insisted on deepening the kiss immediately. As much as he savored her sweet taste, he hated the fact that once again his body was going to ache with the need to have her.

"Don't you two think we have more important things to do? I'm sure Toby doesn't mind lying in the dust the rest of the day just so you two can do some spooning."

It could have been worse. Thea was the one lecturing them. Wade would have come in swinging his fists. She was right; they should have been concentrating on Toby instead of stealing kisses. Since there was nothing to be said in their defense, he carefully set Lily back down on her feet and then stepped away. The two of them picked up the board and started back toward Toby, with Thea clucking after them like a mother hen.

Lily drew another pail of cool water. She started up the small rise, exhaustion causing her to stumble and spill part of the water down the side of her skirt. Deciding she still had enough to meet Toby's needs, she kept going rather than returning to the stream for more.

She and Thea had worked around the clock trying to break Toby's fever. Despite their best efforts to keep his wounds clean, he'd developed an infection that had sent his temperature soaring. They tried to spell each other, but the brief rest breaks did little to alleviate their exhaustion.

The two healthy men weren't any help either. They were willing enough, but Wade and Cal had their own work cut out for them. One of the two stood guard, watching the long stretch of land between the herd and the town. Meanwhile, the other concentrated on keeping the herd together as much as one man could. At best, they got about four hours sleep at a stretch.

The only good news was that Wade had done a quick head count and figured they'd lost no more that a handful of cattle. He'd done a sweep for a half mile or so beyond their camp and managed to round up most of the strays.

Although none of them felt comfortable lingering

in the area, they had little choice for the moment. If it had been a few of Boone's men on a shooting spree, they'd had plenty of time to send for reinforcements. Another day, two at the most, and they'd have to move on or risk starving the herd. The hungry animals had already devoured most of the available grass.

Lily stumbled into camp and set the water down near the pallet they'd made for Toby. Thea sat next to him, her hand holding his. That alone told Lily that he was asleep, because Thea rarely allowed herself the comfort of touching him when he was awake to take notice.

"How is he?"

"I think he's a mite cooler, but maybe I just want him to be."

Lily knelt down on the other side and laid her hand on his forehead. His color wasn't good, but his skin didn't feel quite as clammy as it had earlier.

"I think you might be right. Have you been able to get him to drink any more water?"

"A little, not enough." Thea reached for the ladle. "If you'll prop him up a bit, I'll try again."

Even though he'd lost weight over the past two days, Toby was still more than Lily could lift easily. She lifted on his shoulders while Thea pulled on his arms, both of them ignoring his wince of pain. Lily knew that Thea would hurt him a lot worse if it helped him get better in the long run.

Once they'd worked him into a raised position, Thea began the laborious task of spooning water into his mouth. More went down his shirtfront than down his throat, but every drop counted.

Wade had managed to shoot a couple of small rabbits earlier which Thea had put on to stew. The broth would do Toby good, even if he didn't wake enough to eat the meat. If they didn't start getting some nourishment in him soon, his condition could easily worsen.

And none of them could bear the thought of that.

She eased him back down on his pallet. Picking up a rag, she dipped it in the cool, clear water and began the arduous process of washing down Toby's chest, face, and arms. She avoided the still-seeping wound on his side, the most likely cause of the fever.

Once she settled into a rhythm, she shooed Thea off to get some rest.

"Go on, now. You can hardly sit up, much less do Toby any good right now."

"But . . ."

"I'll call you if there's any change, I promise. Now go."

It was a sign of how very tired Thea was that she didn't argue any more than that. With a quiet rustle of her dress, she rose to her feet and staggered over to where she'd laid out her own blankets. She'd tried to put her bed right next to Toby's, but Lily had made her move because Thea woke up every time he stirred.

A few minutes later, Lily glanced over to make sure that Thea had settled in. The other woman's rhythmic breathing was a clear sign that she'd fallen to sleep almost immediately.

With mind-numbing sameness, she dipped the cloth in the water, wrung it out, and washed Toby's feverish skin. Maybe her eyes were playing tricks on her, but she was almost sure that he was looking better. She paused long enough to feel his forehead again.

It definitely felt cooler. Closing her eyes, she murmured a prayer of gratitude before returning to her routine. Her mind wandered, flitting from one image to another with no sense of rhyme or reason. For a minute, Thad was there, tall and handsome and so very young-looking. How would she look to him—tired, worn out, even old?

Then his face wavered and all but disappeared, replaced by a new one. This time the features were sharp-edged, the almost-black eyes full of secrets. Where Thad's picture only made her sad, this one made her pulse skip and then race along full tilt. Feeling a little guilty, she opened her eyes, only to find the real Cal standing right in front of her.

And her pulse reacted even more strongly to the actual man. She dropped the cloth into the water, for the moment unable to do more than just stare. Despite the exhaustion etched in the lines around Cal's eyes and mouth, his dark good looks stirred her deep inside.

Cal broke the spell. "How is he?"

Grateful for the distraction, Lily picked up the cloth and started in again. "A little better, I think. We got some more water down him, and we'll try the broth as soon as Thea wakes up. He seems to be cooler, but it's too soon to tell if he'll stay that way. The fever could come and go."

Cal squatted down on Toby's other side. He seemed to want to do something to help his friend, but was at a loss as to what it could be.

"If you'll lift him up a bit, we can try the water again. The broth may not be quite ready."

She knew she'd guessed right from the way Cal immediately got behind Toby's head and oh, so carefully lifted the other man up. She knew for a fact how gentle those hands could be.

With hard-won patience, she began spooning water into Toby's mouth a few drops at a time. Suddenly, she realized that his eyes were open and trying to focus on her. The spoon slipped and spilled its contents down Toby's chin.

"You trying to drown me, Miss Lily?"

The effect of the whispered words on Cal was profound. It was as if the draining effects of the past few days were gone. In their place was a smile that lit up his face, taking years away and softening the hard edges.

"It's about time you woke up. I'm getting damn tired of doing all your work for you." Even as he complained, he gave Toby's shoulder a quick squeeze.

Lily fought the urge to laugh at the way men always had to hide their true feelings behind complaints and insults. Not that it lessened the strength of their feelings. These two men were closer than most brothers despite their differences.

She'd allow them another minute or so of privacy before waking Thea. It felt good to stand up and move around a bit. She checked on the rabbits and found the broth about ready. After ladling some into a cup, she crossed over to where Thea was still sleeping.

She shook Thea's shoulder. "Thea, Toby's awake. I thought you might want to feed him some broth while Cal's here to help hold him up for you."

Thea's reaction rivaled Cal's for intensity. She went from exhausted sleep to energized in the blink of an eye.

"Is he . . . ?"

Lily pressed the cup and spoon into Thea's shaky hands. "Go see for yourself."

Satisfied that she wasn't needed for the moment, Lily took a minute to see to her own needs. Picking up a sliver of soap and her last clean dress, she made her way down to the small stream. She allowed herself the luxury of pushing everything out of her mind except enjoying her unexpected respite from the rigors of the past few days.

In no hurry to accomplish anything, she picked a rock and sat down to enjoy the small breeze that teased the clusters of bright wildflowers that followed the path of the stream. It seemed like forever since she could afford the time to sit and watch quiet ripples slip and slide around the rocks.

She was startled out of her reverie by the sound of someone walking up behind her from the direction of camp. Thinking it was Cal, she turned to greet him with a smile, only to discover that it was Wade.

She almost, but not quite, kept her smile firmly in place. Unfortunately, Wade saw the brief falter and immediately bristled.

"Disappointed, Lily?" he sneered.

"Don't be foolish," she chided. "You surprised me, but that's only because I thought you were still out with the herd."

He clearly didn't believe her, but at least he didn't challenge her any further. Instead, he sat down next to her on the rock. She didn't know if he deliberately brushed against her side, but it made her uncomfortable on some level.

Wishing there were some way to put some space between them without being obvious, she forced herself to sit still. Things were strained enough between her and Wade already. It wouldn't take much to send things over the edge.

Out of desperation, she tried to steer the conversation toward a safe topic.

"Did you check on Toby on your way through camp? His fever broke—at least for now."

Wade grunted in response and continued to stare out into the distance. Even his silence was angry. Not wanting to be obvious, Lily peeked at him out of the corner of her eye. He had the same exhausted pallor as the rest of them. It still startled her to look at him and see a man rather than the boy she'd been bossing around for years.

It also hurt to know that she'd helped cause the anger in him. He looked as if he'd forgotten how to smile. Obviously, he'd had no clue how far-reaching the effects of that single poker game could be. He probably thought that one of the costs had been his chances of claiming Lily for his own.

Even without Cal in the picture, that would never have happened, but telling Wade that wouldn't make him any happier with her—or with Cal. If Wade's feelings for her were as strong as Thea seemed to think they were, he'd never be satisfied with the knowledge that she loved him as a brother and nothing more—but nothing less, either.

"If Toby has turned the corner, will we be moving the herd soon?"

Wade looked down at her. "We'll have to either way. The grass is about gone."

The prairie stretched out in front of her, overwhelming the small beauty of the stream. Her future seemed almost as bleak and lonely. Given that Cal would leave to pursue his own dreams and demons, she was beginning to fear that she would lose Wade as well. What good would it do her if they managed to save the ranch if she lost everything that made it meaningful?

As abruptly as he came, Wade silently stood up and walked away. The pain of watching him hurt so badly that even tears couldn't relieve it. Kneeling at the edge of the stream she cupped her hands and let the cool water fill them. With the first handful, she washed her face, hoping to soothe more than her overheated skin.

Finally, deciding that she needed a bath more than she needed her modesty, she slipped out of her filthy outer clothes and waded out into the deepest part of the stream. It barely came halfway up her calves, but it was enough to wash away the day's dust.

The thin, wet cotton of her chemise did little to keep

her warm or protect her modesty. Once she'd lathered and rinsed, she scrubbed her dirty clothes as clean as she could get them in cold water. That done, she carefully worked her way back to shore.

Cal was sitting on the same rock that she and Wade had shared.

He was in the process of pulling off his boots. Her bundle of wet clothing made a poor shield from the heat in his eyes.

"You could have told me that you were there!" she accused. Actually she wasn't all that upset, but felt that she should at least protest for modesty's sake.

"Would you have invited me in?" he drawled. His fingers were busy unbuttoning his shirt. That done, he tossed it on the ground and reached for the buttons on his pants.

She really should be doing something other than gawking at a half-naked man. Even though she already knew every inch of his body almost as well as she knew her own, she thought of herself as a lady—a proper one at that.

All her good intentions did nothing to keep Cal from shucking off his pants and everything else. When he put one foot in the water, she hurried to the shore. He let her think she was going to escape. She'd gotten about three steps when his long arms snaked around her waist and pulled her back in the water.

She squealed in protest, but he clamped his hand over her mouth.

"Unless you want Wade and Thea to come running to save your naked hide, you'd better quiet down."

When he eased up the pressure on her mouth, she whispered, but that didn't mean she was happy about it. "Put me down. I have to go."

He ignored her and continued to walk farther out into the water. She tried to kick him but failed. Luckily for her, he didn't take into account how hard it was to hold on to a woman soaked to the skin. Finally, she slipped free of his grasp, trying her hardest to be outraged.

"I've got to get back to camp." She took one cautious step away from Cal, not sure whether she hoped he'd let her go.

"I know."

"Thea will need help with Toby."

"That's true."

"Wade might come back."

"He might at that."

"So I'm going to go now."

"Fine."

She didn't trust him or the look in his eyes. He should look ridiculous standing in the middle of a shallow stream, naked as the day he was born. Instead, her eyes feasted on the sight of him, wishing she didn't have to leave him without . . . She refused to finish that thought.

He finished it for her. Once again she found herself wrapped tightly in his arms. Recognizing defeat when she saw it, she met his kiss head on, making a few demands of her own.

Cal felt raw with need, wanting to take Lily right there as they clutched each other in the creek. He couldn't—promised himself he wouldn't—finish what they were starting, but that didn't mean he'd refuse whatever Lily was willing to give him at the moment.

He loved the frustration of having a thin layer of cotton between him and what he wanted. His hands cupped her bottom, fitting her as close to the center of his own need as possible. He thrust against her, teasing them both with the reminder of how their bodies were meant to be joined. He shifted her from side to side, rubbing the sweet firmness of her breasts against his chest. He had no idea which of them enjoyed it more.

Lily made her own pleasure clear. Moaning deep in her throat, she dug into his shoulders with her nails as she squeezed her legs even more tightly around his waist. The small pain was almost lost in the host of other sensations he was experiencing.

What he wouldn't give at that moment for a bed, or even a convenient stand of trees that would offer them some small amount of privacy. But they'd played with fire long enough. If they didn't stop soon, one of two things would happen.

Either they'd get caught by Thea—or worse yet, Wade—or they'd go crazy from the frustration. Knowing he shouldn't, he slipped a hand between them and touched her honeyed heat. A few quick strokes shattered Lily's control completely. He took fierce pride in knowing that she responded with such abandon only with him, for him.

She slumped against him, her head on his shoulder as he carried her to shore. Gently, very gently, he set her down. He tipped her chin up with the side of his finger and brushed his lips over hers.

"You'd better go back to camp while I'm strong enough to let you go."

She backed away, clearly not wanting to leave. To give them both a break, he turned his back to her, letting her escape. He heard her scramble over the loose rocks, gathering her belongings. When her footsteps faded into the distance, he sank down into the shallows, the cool water a poor substitute for Lily's sweet body.

Thirteen

"Damn it, woman, leave me alone!" Toby jerked his arm away from Thea, determined to do it on his own.

Thea glared back at him, refusing to give an inch. It didn't matter that he was half a foot taller and outweighed her by better than fifty pounds. Admittedly, it was hard to intimidate anyone while lying down and unable to stand, eat, or do anything else without help.

"Who else are you going to get to help you? Wade and Cal are riding herd, and Lily is helping them. That leaves me." Thea stood over him, giving him that superior look that made him crazy. "Unless, of course, you want to risk breaking your other leg, too."

Toby closed his eyes and prayed for patience. "I can take care of myself." He spoke each word slowly, as if that would make her accept them. "I'm sure you have something else to be doing other than hovering over me."

"I could go start digging a grave for you, because that's where you're going to end up if you don't stop acting like a fool."

His mother had taught him not to curse in front of a lady, but he was about to ignore her teachings. Since Thea wouldn't walk away, he'd leave her. Using the crutches Cal had fashioned for him, he managed to push himself up from the ground. His balance wasn't

good, but damned if he'd let a woman lead him out to
the bushes to take care of private business.

Being an invalid didn't sit well with him at all. By
not doing his fair share of the work, he was holding
the others up and endangering all of their lives. Tired
men made mistakes, which could be fatal around a
herd of cattle. Add to that having Boone and his men
lurking out there somewhere, and the whole situation
was volatile.

He shuffled forward one step and then another. Thea
stood her ground, waiting for him to fall. Well, damned
if he'd give her the pleasure. Gradually he caught the
rhythm of supporting his weight with the crutches and
dragging his leg along. He made steady progress to
the edge of camp.

When he returned, Thea was waiting for him. She
was pretending to look for something in the wagon,
but he knew better. If he even wobbled an inch, she'd
be on him, insisting on supporting his weight with her
delicate shoulders. Not that he minded touching her.
No, he liked that part right fine, but he wanted to be
the one taking care of her.

And he greatly feared that the minute he was healed,
she'd go back to Boone.

He took the last few steps by sheer willpower alone.
The hard part was getting back down to the ground
without hurting either his leg or his side. At least the
dizziness from his head wound was almost gone.

He dropped one crutch and used the other for support as he eased himself back down. As soon as he
was safely sitting, Thea knelt down beside him, holding out a bowl of hot stew.

"Foolish man, what would it have hurt to let me
help you?"

The need underlying her words surprised him.
"Don't you know a man likes his woman to think he's

invincible?" He gave in to the need to touch the soft silk of her face.

For the briefest of seconds she rubbed her cheek against the palm of his hand. When she drew back, it hurt.

"I'm not your woman, Toby. I can't be."

They'd been over this before. She had yet to give a real answer. "Why the hell not? You want me; I know you do."

"I can't want you."

Which wasn't the same as not wanting him. He took some comfort in that idea. He set the stew aside and pulled her down beside him.

"What kind of hold does Boone have on you? I know you don't love him." Because she loved Toby; he wouldn't have it any other way. He gingerly raised his arm and put it around her shoulder, tucking her up against his side, nice and warm.

"I owe him more than I can say."

"That doesn't mean you have to work for him the rest of your days." He fought to keep his temper under control. She was like a wild thing he was coaxing to eat out of his hand. One false move, and she'd be off and running again.

"He gave me money." Thea stared off into the distance, seeing memories that Toby couldn't share.

Although he tried not to think about it much, he knew that a lot of men had given her money. He wasn't going to sit in judgment over her, but he wished things could have been different, for her sake.

As if she knew what he was thinking, she shook her head. "Not like the others. Boone gave me a lot of money to help me find my younger sister and help her start a new life somewhere better."

"And did you find her?"

She gave him one of her rare true smiles. "Yes, I did. She's married now with a fine husband living back east."

"Why didn't you stay with her?"

Thea rubbed her palms up and down her arms, as if overcome with a sudden chill. "She doesn't know how I live, and I don't want her to. It was already too late for me, but she has a real chance to make something of her life."

"Don't you think she'd understand?" As far as Toby was concerned, the girl wasn't worth the cost Thea had to pay to save her if she was that unforgiving.

"It doesn't matter. I can't leave Boone until I pay him back the money I borrowed, along with interest."

Toby didn't bother to ask her how much money was involved. It didn't matter. If the only way she had of making payments was with what she made working in his saloon, she'd never pay off the loan. No doubt Boone had arranged it that way, effectively purchasing the sister's freedom at the cost of Thea's. Toby wanted to kill the bastard.

And maybe he would as soon as his leg was healed. When a varmint preyed on a man's stock, he went after it with a rifle. Boone deserved the same treatment.

But for now, he'd draw what comfort he could from Thea's warm body sitting next to his. Gently, with as much patience as he could muster, he cupped her face in his hand and tilted her mouth up to meet his. He gave her every chance to escape, but to his immense satisfaction, she turned toward him, not away.

Sighing with pleasure, she parted her lips, inviting him to deepen the kiss. She tasted like his every dream come true. He loved the feel of her hands skimming over his shoulders and down onto his chest.

He returned the favor, gently learning her womanly curves. If the dazed look in her eyes was any indication, she didn't mind his explorations one bit. He undid a few buttons on the front of her dress and slipped his hand inside to find her breast.

"Toby, that's so good," she murmured, pressing herself more firmly against him. "Let me help."

She rose on her knees and straddled his lap, careful not to jar his broken leg. He thought he'd die with the sweet heat that burned wherever their bodies touched. She pulled her dress down off her shoulder, offering him better access to the dusky warmth of her skin. He nuzzled his way down to the dark peak of one breast and took it in his mouth. Suckling hard, he used his tongue and teeth to drive them both crazy.

She grasped his head and pressed him closer. "Don't stop, Lord of mercy, don't stop."

He ignored her orders and pulled away, fighting for his sanity. He wanted her so damn badly, but not this way, a desperate coupling in the dirt. She might have come to expect such treatment, but he wanted better for her. When he did take her—and he would, or die trying—it would be as his wife.

He kissed her again, carefully banking the fires, trying to convince her without words that there could be more between them than just this. Then the words slipped out of his mouth, straight from his heart.

"I love you, Thea. Marry me."

She froze. After a second, a single tear wandered down the contour of her cheek. Without a sound, she struggled to her feet, righting her clothes.

Despite her reaction, he couldn't find it in himself to regret what he'd said. It was the truth, and she deserved to hear it. Maybe if he said it often enough, he'd be able to convince her to take a chance on loving him back.

He tried again. "Marry me, Thea. Now, today, tomorrow. All you have to do is say yes."

With more dignity than any one woman should pos-

sess, she looked down at him with those huge dark
eyes and shook her head. "Don't ask me again. If you
really do care, don't do this to me."

Then she walked away without a backward glance.

Cal found her sitting by the water, staring off into
the distance. Whatever she was seeing in her mind's
eye left her looking drawn and tired beyond all endur-
ance. The still-damp tracks of tears stained her dark
beauty.

She flinched when he squatted down in front of her.
He waited until she worked up the courage to look him
in the face before speaking.

"He's worried about you."

"He should try worrying about his own self and
forget about me."

Cal shook his head. "That's not going to happen any
time soon, and we both know it."

"Tell him . . ." she drew a ragged breath. "Tell him
that he needs to work at it real hard." She clenched
her hands into fists in her lap.

Lily might have been able to come up with words of
comfort, but damned if he could. This woman was rip-
ping his best friend apart. Maybe she wasn't good
enough for Toby, but then in most ways, neither was Cal.

"He loves you." She flinched again, as if the words
tore at her skin. "I know you didn't ask him to. Hell,
I know you've done everything but take a skillet to
that thick head of his to warn him off."

One corner of her mouth twitched, as if that idea
tickled her in some small way. "It would take a mighty
big skillet."

"He told me about the money. It doesn't make any
difference to him. If you'd let him help, you'd get out
of Boone's clutches that much faster."

"It isn't only about the money."

"No, I sort of figured that it had more to do with you being a whore and all." He waited to see how she reacted to his blunt words.

She didn't deny the truth of them. "You're right. I'm a whore and he's a good man. Too good."

"I'm not about to argue that point." He stood up. "Scoot over, so I can sit down."

The change in topics confused her, but she made room for him on the rock. The gathering darkness made it easier for him to go on with what he had come to say.

"My mother was a whore, and I know for a fact that most men she dealt with weren't worth the little bit of gold dust they paid her."

He didn't bother to check to see if Thea was listening. She was, with an intensity he could feel by touching her.

"I'd like to think that if she'd ever met up with a man like Toby, she'd have grabbed hold of him with both hands and never let go." He picked a piece of grass to chew on. "She was never that lucky. You are."

He sat there another few minutes. "Lily will worry if you stay out here much longer. We need to get an early start tomorrow, so come have some dinner and get some sleep." He held out his hand.

She didn't need his help getting up, but then he was offering more than ordinary courtesy. He was offering her his support if she wanted it. When she accepted his gesture, he thought maybe, just maybe, something was finally going to turn out all right.

The sun hadn't yet cleared the horizon, and they'd already been in the saddle for more than an hour. Wade was circling around the herd from the south while Cal came at them from the north. They'd already decided that they couldn't waste any more time rounding up strays. It was far more important that they move the cattle as soon as possible.

Cal could see Wade coming around the final bunch of steers. He waved, signaling that they should head back to camp, where Lily and Thea were cooking breakfast. Except for what they were using, everything was already loaded up. Cal and Wade had harnessed the team to the wagon, and after they ate, they would help Toby up to the driver's seat.

Nobody thought he was strong enough to drive, but he'd argued long and hard for the right to try. They'd finally decided that even if someone else had to take over for him later, it would still free the rest of them up to get the herd moving.

Cal reached camp just ahead of Wade and accepted a cup of hot coffee from Thea. She and Toby had sat up late talking the night before. While neither of them had been forthcoming with the details, both of them seemed to be smiling more easily. For both their sakes, Cal hoped that their plans would work out.

Which brought his own thoughts back to Lily McCord. He took a seat where he could watch her without being too obvious about it. She was kneeling in front of the fire, checking on something. He studied her profile, liking what he saw, especially the way her hair rippled down her back. No doubt she'd braid it before riding herd, but for now the dark curls framed her face.

She chewed on her lip while she concentrated on getting their food just right, making him smile. He was willing to bet that she was unaware of her habit of doing that whenever she had something on her mind.

She happened to glance in his direction and caught him staring. He knew he should look away but couldn't muster the strength to do so. He held her gaze with his, memorizing each detail about her. All too soon their time together would end, and memories would be all he had left.

Suddenly, he wasn't hungry anymore. He tossed out the last of his coffee and walked out of camp without looking back.

Lily watched Cal storm off, wondering what she'd done to drive him away without saying a word. One minute his dark eyes had been smiling at her; then in the next, they'd turned rock hard and angry.

Her first impulse was to run after him, but pride held her back. She'd done nothing to upset him. If he wanted to be moody, fine. There was enough to do without cosseting the likes of him. He was probably missing his precious poker games or some other equally important way of wasting his life.

Doing her best to forget about Cal for the moment, she started serving up breakfast for the rest of them. She fixed two plates and carried them over to where Toby was resting by the wagon. Thea, sitting beside him, immediately jumped to her feet, looking guilty.

"You don't have to wait on me. I would have fetched my own breakfast." She held out her hands to take the plates from Lily.

"That's all right. You've been working just as hard as I have."

That left Wade and herself. She dished up a heaping plateful for her brother-in-law and looked around to see where he'd gone. She saw him sitting on a rock at the far edge of their camp. He hadn't spoken more than a few words to her since yesterday at the stream, and she'd about had it with his sulking.

However tempting it was to let his plate sit where it was until it got cold, she knew breakfast would be the last hot meal they'd have until nightfall. Picking up her own plate as well, she marched over to where he was sitting and plunked herself down on the rock beside him.

She shoved his food at him. "Eat this."

Reluctantly he took the plate from her hands and silently started eating.

"How did the herd look this morning?"

"Fine."

"Do you think we'll have trouble moving them out?"

He shrugged.

Gritting her teeth, she tried again. "Any sign of anyone else out there?"

"Just your lover," he sneered.

Her hand ached to slap some manners back into him. She blinked rapidly to hold back the tears caused by his bitterness.

"Wade McCord, you watch your mouth."

Toby was standing a few feet away, fury blazing in his eyes. "You have no call to go talking like that to any lady, much less family."

Wade tried without success to stare Toby down. "I don't hear her denying that's what he is."

"We've talked about this before, boy. What's between Miss Lily and Cal is none of your damn business. Now help me up on the wagon and get out there and do your job. We have enough problems without you acting like this."

At first Lily thought Wade was going to refuse, but in the end he shoved his half-eaten meal back at her and stalked off after Toby. Things were certainly off to a good start. Cal was mad at her for no reason she could think of, and Wade was angry because of Cal.

It was going to be one very trying day.

About sundown, Wade signaled for them to halt. Lily was only too glad to stop moving for even a few minutes. Although she often rode horses, it had been some time since she'd ridden this many hours without a rest. Her muscles had screamed their protests earlier and had now settled into a mind-numbing ache.

It had occurred to her that she might not be able to walk at all once she did get to climb down off her horse. For the moment, she stayed where she was and waited for further instructions. Wade disappeared for a few minutes. When he did reappear, he came riding straight for her.

"There's water up ahead and enough grazing for the night. Let's get the cattle settled in and then set up camp."

He didn't wait for her response but immediately headed around the herd to the other side to consult with Cal and Thea. Although Thea had spelled Toby at the reins for a couple of hours earlier, he'd managed to handle the wagon for most of the day.

About thirty minutes later, the cattle had slowed to a stop and started grazing. Lily and Thea rejoined the wagon, ready to cook the evening meal. Once Lily dismounted, she grabbed hold of the saddle to keep from collapsing to the ground. Thea, who'd been riding with the men since the outset, had no such problem.

"Do you need help getting over here to sit down?"

Pride alone made her shake her head. After drawing a couple of deep breaths, she stepped back and held her ground. Barely. Finally, she risked one step and then another, making her way over to where Thea was already unloading the wagon. She knew she should see to her horse's needs first, but until she worked some of the kinks out of her back and legs, she wouldn't be much help to anyone.

"That was a long day. Are you all right?"

Cal's concern surprised her, especially considering

how rude he'd been that morning. Did he really expect her to forgive and forget that easily?

If he noticed her snub, he gave no indication of it. "I'll take care of your horse."

Silently she handed over the reins and continued on her halting journey across the makeshift camp. Thea already had the coffee on and was slicing pieces of bacon into the beans. Lily wondered if everyone else was as tired of the monotony of their diet. Visions of fried chicken and fresh greens made her mouth water.

"I'll draw some more water, if you'd like."

Thea handed her a bucket. "I have enough for dinner in the barrels, but we'll need to refill them before the night's over."

Feeling somewhat better, Lily walked the short distance to the stream. She filled the bucket and then started back up the rocky slope. It would take more than a few such trips to restock their supply of water for the next day.

Despite the drudgery of the work, it felt better than trailing along after the cattle, breathing their dust. Cal was waiting for her at the top of the slope on her second trip.

"I'll do that." He held out his hand, but she wasn't sure if he intended to take the bucket or to help her up.

She was hot and tired and in no mood for guessing games. "Why are you being so nice to me all of a sudden? You ignored me all day long, and now you're playing quite the gentleman."

He stood there, his eyes and expression unreadable. "I'm sorry."

"For what?" she demanded, not quite ready to give up her anger.

"For whatever has you all riled up." He took the

bucket out of her hand and then pulled her the rest of the way up to where he stood.

"How many times do I have to tell you to leave her alone?" Wade had come up from behind them. He put himself firmly between Lily and Cal.

Cal set the bucket down. "The day hasn't dawned that would see me taking orders from you."

Would they never quit? Lily stamped her foot out of frustration. "Stop it, both of you. I don't appreciate being treated like some bone a couple of stray dogs are snarling over."

"I'm not a stray, but he sure as hell is." Wade sneered at Cal.

"Wade! You apologize for that remark." She tried to get around him, to force some distance between the two men.

"Like hell I will. He's admitted as much himself. He has no home, no family, and no name to call his own. His mother was a—"

He didn't get to finish his sentence for the simple reason that Cal's fist knocked him flying backward down the riverbank. Wade rolled almost to the water's edge before regaining his footing. He charged back up the slope and tore right into Cal. The two of them hit the ground with a thud.

Lily wanted to scream. If Toby were fit, maybe he could have done something to stop them, but that was out of the question. Even if he could make it over to where they were doing their best to beat each other into the dust, he would have been risking further injury to himself.

She was at a loss what to do when she saw the bucket still sitting there. Picking it up, she calmly dumped the whole thing over their heads and walked away, leaving the two of them sputtering in the dust.

"Those two at it again?" Thea looked purely disgusted with the whole affair. "If I was their mamma, I'd tan both their backsides and send them to bed without their dinner."

"Sounds like a good idea to me," Toby said, laughing softly. "Miss Lily, that was quite a sight seeing you trying to drown the pair of them."

For the first time all day, she felt like smiling herself. "I only wish I'd had two buckets with me."

Thea looked past her. "Maybe they'll finally get it out of their systems. The two of them have been wanting to have at each other since the day they met."

The two men in question definitely weren't finished with each other. The shock of being hit with cold water had done little to dampen Cal's temper, and Wade was a handy target. They separated long enough to get to their feet and began circling each other, looking for a chance to attack. Cal danced toward Wade and landed a solid punch to Wade's jaw, grunting with pain when Wade returned the favor before he got back out of reach.

In a flurry of quick jabs, Cal managed to pepper Wade's stomach and ribs with sharp hits. Enraged beyond control, Wade charged into Cal, taking them both tumbling back down on the ground. Neither paid the least attention to the rocks digging into their backs as first one and then the other managed to come out on top.

Finally, Cal's size and experience gave him the upper hand long enough to pin Wade to the ground. He drew a couple of ragged breaths before he could speak. "Now are you going to leave me and Lily alone or do I have to actually kill you to get some peace?"

Wade wiped a streak of blood off his lip with the back of his hand. "You might have to, you son of a bitch, because I can't stand to see you touch her."

Sensing all the fight had gone out of them both, he let Wade up. "I'd think that was up to her."

"You're not anywhere near good enough for her. She needs someone who's willing to stick around for good."

The boy had the right of it, but Cal didn't like him saying so. "If she's not complaining, what business is it of yours?"

Wade's eyes went from angry to bleak. "I love her, damn it." Then, as if he'd said far more than he meant to, Wade spun away and charged off through the brush.

Cal watched him go, surprised by the rush of sympathy he felt for someone who'd just done his damnedest to knock him senseless. Knowing no one would hear him, he answered Wade's confession with one of his own.

"You're not the only one."

That was one little secret that he'd keep to himself. He kicked a rock flying through the air, but it did little to improve his temper. Dinner was probably about ready, but he wasn't in the mood to face Toby, much less Thea and Lily. He stopped long enough to wash the blood off his face and rinse the bitter taste out of his mouth.

That done, he walked the long away around to the other side of the camp, where the horses were picketed. Maybe a couple of hours of riding herd would take the edge off his bad mood.

If anyone noticed what he was doing, they didn't interfere. He knew Lily was thoroughly fed up with both him and Wade. Thea probably agreed with her. Toby was too besotted with Thea to notice much of anything else.

And that hurt. The two of them had been partners for years. Even though Cal hoped that things worked out for Toby and Thea, that didn't mean that he was exactly happy about it. He'd had little enough in his life that he could count on, but Toby had been the one constant.

If his friend managed to talk Thea into marrying him, they'd no doubt settle down and build a home together. Cal wished he were a big enough man to wish them the best of luck and mean it. Truth was, he was jealous. Thea might have some problems that they'd have to work through or around, but he suspected that she'd be only too happy to have a place of her own.

He, on the other hand, had no experience in living a settled life and wasn't sure he wanted to. He glanced over toward the campfire, knowing he'd find Lily there. Somehow he couldn't see her following him from town to town, sharing the uncertain life of a gambler's wife.

To his way of thinking, there was only one choice left to him: somehow get through the rest of this cattle drive without killing Wade or hurting Lily. With that decided, he rode out to watch the cows graze. They weren't the best of company, but then they didn't complicate his life the way his two-footed companions did.

Lily lay awake, her mind tumbling with more worries than she could count. Finally, she couldn't stay still a minute longer. Doing her best not to disturb Thea, who was sleeping only a few feet away, she slipped out of her covers.

Once she was standing, she tried to decide what to do next. The sky to the east was only now starting to show the slight hint of the coming day. It would be another hour or so before anyone else would stir.

Except Cal.

He'd been standing guard for the past few hours, which probably had something to do with her restlessness. Somehow, even through the darkness, she imagined she could feel his eyes on her. Picking up her blanket to ward off the last of the night's chill, she headed straight for him.

He was leaning against a small tree at the top of a

small rise above the camp. He'd chosen his position well. From a distance his outline would blend in with the trees, making him all but invisible.

She picked her way up to where he stood watching the horizon. Even with his back to her, she knew he was aware of her approach.

His voice came out of the shadows. "I don't suppose you have a cup of coffee for me."

"Sorry, but I didn't want to wake everyone up this early."

She stopped short of where he stood, wanting more than anything for him to hold out his arm in invitation. It had been days since he'd been more than merely civil to her. On some levels, she understood why, but that didn't ease the craving she had for his company, his touch.

"Come closer," he invited. "Standing out there makes you an easy target."

She didn't need to be asked twice. His reasons for wanting her near might not be romantic, but they served the purpose. Watching her step on the rocky terrain, she moved deeper into the night shadows under the trees, grateful for their cover.

And as if he'd read her mind, he held out his hand and pulled her against his side. She slipped her arm around his waist, wrapping her blanket around them both. Content to be right where she'd wanted to be, she listened to the quiet of the night.

Not that it was silent. The earlier morning birds were already calling to each other, announcing the arrival of another day. A lonely coyote howled, calling for its mate. The grass rustled with the last of the night foragers wending their way homeward. And she could feel the slow beat of Cal's heart, its rhythm soothing her as nothing else could.

It was peaceful, all the more so because a footloose gambler was sharing the moment with her.

"I've missed you the past few days."

He drew a deep breath as his arm pulled her closer. "I thought it best to put some distance between us."

"Why? Is it because of Wade?" She'd seen the bruises on both of them, but neither of them had spoken a word about their fight or its outcome.

She felt Cal chuckle. "No, but not because he didn't try. My jaw still hurts."

He looked down at her. Although it was gradually getting lighter, she couldn't make out his expression.

"I don't know how to be a rancher, Lily. I make my living with a deck of cards."

Grateful that he couldn't see the tears in her eyes, she did her best to sound merely curious. "Have I asked you to be anything but what you are?"

"No, not in words."

She wanted to call him a liar, but he wasn't one. Despite all the times he had reminded her of what he was, she kept hoping that he'd change. In the back of her mind, she knew that what she felt for him came perilously close to love. If indeed it was love, it was because of the man he was, not who she'd like him to be.

"How long do we have?" she whispered, already knowing what the answer would be.

"Not nearly long enough."

Then, with a desperation that ached, he kissed her.

Fourteen

He savored the feel of her in his arms and the sweet taste of her on his tongue. How could something that felt so right to him on every level be so wrong for them both? In truth, he wasn't a complicated man. His needs were simple.

And he needed Lily as he'd never needed anyone else in his life.

Every time she came within touching distance, he wanted her. It wasn't just sex, although that was part of it. But there was also something special about sharing the everyday things with her: a sunset, a picnic, holding hands, all of it. Hell, he even enjoyed fighting with her, knowing she had enough spirit to take him on despite the difference in their sizes.

He let her be the one to end the kiss. She tucked her head under his chin, holding him close. The two of them stood in the fading shadows, letting the embrace linger as the sun cleared the trees.

It was then that he noticed that the birds had gone strangely quiet. The complete silence was unnerving. Abruptly pushing Lily to the side, he picked up his rifle and moved out to the edge of the trees.

"What's wrong?" Lily kept her voice low.

"Hellfire and damnation, they're coming." He looked back to where Lily was still lurking in the shadows. "Get back to camp and wake everyone. We have maybe ten minutes at the most before they're right on top of us. Help Toby find a safe place out of the line of fire and stay with him."

"What about Thea and Wade?" she asked, already hurrying back down the rise.

"I don't know. It'll depend on whether Boone's men have orders to go after us or the cattle."

He was glad to see that Lily didn't argue about leaving him. She picked up her blanket and took off at a quick run. Leaving it up to her to carry out his orders, he turned his attention back toward the approaching riders.

This time there were more than a handful. Boone, gambler that he was, had evidently decided to go for broke. Cal would give his last dollar to know what the saloon keeper was after. There was plenty of land to be had for the asking in the area around King's Creek, but there had to be a compelling reason for him to want the McCord place so badly.

Money. It had to be.

Counting at least ten heavily armed men coming straight for their camp, Cal decided that Boone's motives didn't matter for the moment. It was far more important that they manage to survive the morning.

After checking his rifle and then his revolver for ammunition, he worked his way around to highest point of ground. He settled in behind a fallen log that would allow him to move along the ridge as the riders moved beyond him. He debated whether to pick off the first rider or wait until they'd come even with his position, giving him more than one target.

Normally, he would hesitate before shooting someone who'd yet to show hostile intentions. This bunch he'd send straight to hell as fast as he could pull the trigger.

To that purpose, he took aim and waited for his chance to begin the fight.

Down below in the camp, Lily had done exactly as Cal had ordered. Toby was tucked in behind the wagon and some rocks. He had demanded both his rifle and a box of shells, determined to do his fair share of defending the women. Thea had found her own spot near him, while Wade had brought the horses in closer and tied them securely.

They could ill afford to lose any more of their herd, but the loss of the horses would be a complete disaster. Once Wade had both the wagon team and the saddle horses rounded up, he picked up his own guns and took off at a lope. Lily ran after him.

He happened to look back and saw what she was doing. "What the hell do you think you're doing? Get back there with Toby and Thea."

Ignoring his orders, she closed the distance between them. When she reached him, she threw her arms around his waist and drew him close.

"Whatever happens, I do love you, Wade. You're all the family I've got, so keep safe."

With his hands loaded with weapons, the hug he gave her was awkward but nevertheless dear. "I'll be fine. Now get back where you belong." He shoved her back in the direction of the wagon. "Keep your head down, no matter what happens."

She had to let him go, but she prayed long and hard that he come through the morning unscathed, along with Thea and Toby. Before she could add Cal's name to the list, shots ripped through the morning quiet. She screamed out his name, wishing she'd been able to stay with him. No matter what happened, she didn't want him to be alone.

Having decided where she belonged, she picked up an extra box of shells and her own rifle and started back up through the woods. She slipped from tree to tree, not being sure where Boone's men were now. At the top of the hill, she bent almost double and followed the sound of the shooting to where Cal was returning fire.

Once again he'd chosen his position well, although when she saw him pop up from behind his cover to shoot, her heart almost stopped. She waited until there was a break in the fire to warn him that she was coming up behind him.

"Cal, I'm back." She waited for him to acknowledge her presence before crossing the clearing.

From the look he gave her, she knew he wasn't pleased to have her there. He waved her forward, so she scurried across the open ground and dropped down beside him.

"What the hell are you doing here?"

She held up her rifle and bullets. "It's my fight, too. Thea is with Toby, and Wade moved out toward the other side to keep them from coming up from behind us. I figured I'd do the most good up here with you."

Another burst of gunfire put an end to their conversation. She wanted to protest when Cal took her rifle from her, handing her his empty one. Her hands were shaking so badly that she spilled about half the box of shells. After a couple of tries, she managed to reload his gun just in time to trade with him once again.

"How many of them are there?"

His smile was grim. "Not as many as there were a few minutes ago."

There were shots coming from below them now, evidence that some of the riders had got past Cal's position. Once again she asked for the safe deliverance of her friends. She sat with her back to the rocks as she and Cal fell into a rhythm of shooting and reloading.

The return fire was lighter, but she wasn't foolish enough to think that the fight was almost over. Boone would not have hired the type of men who would give up easily. No, either Cal's shots had found their mark or the enemy was regrouping to find a new plan of attack.

That was when she caught a movement out of the corner of her eye. Someone was working his way through the stand of trees off to Cal's left. Whoever it was, he evidently hadn't realized that his presence had been detected. He hardly hesitated when he broke cover, running straight at Cal's back. Without thinking, she brought Cal's rifle up and took aim.

She squeezed the trigger, just as she'd been instructed. Although her late husband had taught her well, he failed to tell her about the sick feeling that came with another human dying at her hands.

The fool was young, certainly no older than she was. She watched in horror as his steps faltered and then stopped. First came the surprise, then shock, followed by the first wave of pain. Blood blossomed in the middle of the stranger's chest and spread outward as he sank to his knees. Finally, he slumped forward, unmoving and silent.

Waves of nausea washed over her, leaving her retching in the grass as tears streamed down her face. When the worst of it had passed, Cal gently pulled her into his arms, the battle forgotten for the moment. He rocked her back and forth, letting her tears soak through his shirt.

"Have I thanked you for saving my life?" he murmured, his lips pressed to her hair.

There was some little comfort in that idea. The nameless bastard could well have killed both of them.

She knew she'd always remember his face, but given the same circumstances, she still would have pulled the trigger.

"I need to check on the others. Are you up to moving?"

She nodded, only because there really was no choice. The only shots being fired now were too far away for Cal to be of help to the others. It would take all of them to ward off this attack and save the herd.

The two of them worked their way back down the hillside, following the same general path that Lily had used. Before they left the protection of the trees, she pointed out where Toby and Thea had taken cover. Since they could hear sporadic gunfire from the other side of camp, they had good reason to hope that Wade was holding his own.

Cal checked his guns again and had Lily do the same. "Follow the tree line around to Thea and stay with her. I'll try to give Wade some help."

Before she could do as he said, he leaned down and gave her a rough kiss. "Go on. I'll watch your back until you're out of sight."

She didn't want to leave, but he couldn't do anything for Wade if he was worrying about her at the same time. No, she'd go, but she didn't have to like it at all.

Gunsmoke mixed with early-morning mist as it snaked its way along the stream. The sun was up good and proper, but it might be some time before they could do their usual morning chores. She'd been taught that hate was a sin, but at that moment she hated Upton Boone with all the strength she could muster.

How could one small ranch mean so much to him that he was willing to pay men enough to die on his behalf? Someday, maybe she'd find out the answer to that question, but for now there was a fight to finish.

She just hoped that she'd done all the killing that she'd ever have to do.

Thea was only a few feet away from Toby, the two of them holding their fire for the moment as they waited for a clear target. Lily didn't want to provide one for them.

"Thea! Toby! I'm coming in." She remained right where she was until Thea turned and waved at her.

She slid in between the other two. It took a minute or so for her to catch her breath enough to talk. Toby looked grim, with deep lines of exhaustion bracketing his mouth. She wondered how much longer he'd be able to continue.

"Are you both all right?"

"No thanks to that bunch out there. Unless something happens, they can keep us pinned down here as long as they want. Hell, even now they could be moving the cattle and we'd be helpless to stop them."

Toby wasn't telling her anything she didn't already know, but she had to hope that Wade and Cal would be able to find a way out of this mess.

"Cal is headed for Wade. Maybe they'll figure something out."

Toby started to spit, his usual way of expressing doubt, but stopped when he remembered that there were ladies present. For the first time since Boone's men had disturbed her time with Cal, she felt like smiling.

"We've made it this far, haven't we? I bet Boone thought he'd have clear title to the ranch by now. Instead, every day we hold on costs him money."

Thea smiled back. "That'll hurt him more than about anything." She tossed Lily a canteen. "Here, you look like you could use a drink."

"Depends on what's in here." She tipped her head back and drank deeply. It was only water, but it felt

good to her raw throat. They couldn't afford to be
wasteful, so she resisted the urge to wash her face and
hands.

She handed the water on to Toby. He took a few
sips and handed it back, keeping his eyes pinned on
the horizon. For the moment all was quiet, but that
wasn't necessarily a good sign.

The horses stirred restlessly. Lily tried to see what
was spooking them. A man was tugging on the reins
to Cal's horse. She brought up her rifle before she realized that it was Wade. He stopped long enough to
untie his mare as well. Using the two animals as cover,
he ran back to where she could see Cal waiting.

"Wade and Cal are up to something, Toby." She kept
her voice low, not knowing how far it would carry.
"Maybe we can keep Boone's men occupied to give
them a better chance."

Obligingly, Toby opened fire, shooting at random
targets. Thea did the same. Lily took on the job of
reloading for them as it became necessary.

When Cal and Wade had disappeared, they slowed
their shots until once again all was quiet. There was
nothing left to do but wait—and pray.

"Are you ready?"

Cal hoped like hell Wade was, because one of them
should be. Riding out from good cover into the open
had to be one of the stupidest ideas he'd ever come up
with. The fact that Wade agreed to it was a poor tes-
timony to his intelligence as well.

Together they'd decided that they had enough of
cowering behind rocks and trees while letting Boone's
men hover just out of range. Between the two of them,
they knew that the original number of raiders had been

reduced by a fair number. At most there should only be six or so left.

If the original band was all that Boone had sent after them, but Cal refused to follow that thought to its logical conclusion. Boone wasn't a man to leave things to chance. If he thought that ten men wouldn't get the job done, then he'd have sent twenty.

No, that wasn't the way of it. Boone had enough confidence in his own grand scheme of things that it would never occur to him that the five of them could fight off his hired killers. But then, he only understood money and its power; he'd never considered the strength of friendship and family.

Cal checked his cinch one more time before mounting up. Wade's mare danced in place, her normally calm manner upset by the morning's events.

"We'll ride out toward the herd. If his men have moved on, that's where they'll be."

Wade nodded. Despite his youth, he looked grimly determined to do a man's job. Under other circumstances, Cal would have been inclined to call him a friend. But when two men had a strong need for the same woman, friendship was out of the question. For the moment, they'd declare a truce, but it was temporary at best.

"Let's go." He urged his horse forward, half expecting to ride into a hail of bullets. Instead, the only shots he heard came from over near Toby and the others. He grinned. Leave it to that wily friend of his to know when to raise a ruckus to provide cover for their escape.

Keeping his head down low near the horse's neck, he rode at full charge out to the cattle. Just as he'd expected, Boone's men were there trying to scatter the herd. He drew his gun, ready to reduce the number of rustlers by as many as he could.

Wade pulled up next to him. "If we stampede the herd back at them, Boone's men will be right in the path. Either they'll have to scatter or risk being trapped in the rush."

Cal doubted that Lily would have approved of the unholy glee in Wade's expression, but he did. Without a second's hesitation, he started firing his rifle and charging directly at the cattle. In a matter of seconds, the steers were breaking into a slow run right at Boone's men.

The results were less than spectacular, but at least Boone's men were too busy saving their own hides to take much note of Cal and Wade. A couple of them were obviously experienced cowhands from the way they immediately began working to turn the small herd, changing the direction the animals were moving.

Even so, it gave Cal a chance to get off a couple of good shots. One rider swayed in his saddle. Only the quick action of his companion kept him from falling off. The two of them wheeled their horses away from the herd and rode away. For the moment, they were no longer a concern.

Wade came up on his left; he stopped long enough to get off a couple of shots at another of Boone's men. He wasn't as lucky as Cal had been, and his target returned fire. The shots were short, kicking up dust and rocks on the ground in front of them, causing Wade's mare to shy and buck.

He fought the horse back under control and immediately started shooting back. This time, one bullet found its target. The other man screamed in pain. He slumped forward in the saddle, startling his horse into a gallop.

Wade looked a little shaken by the exchange, but he didn't let it stop him from looking around for another of Boone's men to take on. Cal yelled out a warning when he caught sight of a pair of the killers riding straight for Wade, their guns spitting fire.

He charged into the fray, trying to draw their attention from Wade. One of the riders shouted something to the other and then veered off in Cal's direction. He didn't live long enough to regret his decision. Cal had the second one in his sights when Wade managed to take care of the problem himself.

There wasn't time to enjoy their deadly victory, because several others had decided to abandon their efforts with the cattle long enough to deal with Cal and Wade. They came charging across the outer edges of the herd, swerving from side to side to avoid the confused cattle. Cal took advantage of their divided attention to pick off a couple before they had time to react.

The others must have decided that Boone's money wasn't enough to make it worth their while to ride into the deadly crossfire that he and Wade were offering. Wade wanted to give chase, but Cal managed to call him back.

"Let them go. We have our own people to see to."

On their way back to camp, they stopped to check Boone's men who were down. Some were beyond needing any help, but a couple were only wounded. Wade made a show of wanting to shoot them where they lay, but his gentle handling of the two men belied his threats.

Cal was relieved. He had little enough stomach for killing. He caught a couple of horses whose riders no longer needed them and helped the wounded to mount up. Both men were barely holding on to consciousness. He only hoped Thea and Lily could tend their injuries enough to send them on their way back to wherever they came from.

There wasn't much chance of any of them reporting back to Boone. He wasn't known for tolerating failure.

They stood a better chance of living a long life if they disappeared.

"You'd better let Lily see that you're alive before doing anything about the herd."

Wade shook his head. "She's more interested in your worthless hide."

"If you think that, you're a bigger fool than I gave you credit for. She loves you."

"Like a brother." Wade's dark eyes flashed with anger.

Thoroughly disgusted with the whole mess, Cal walked away, leading his horse along with the two Boone's men were riding. Lily had loved Wade for years and would continue to do so long after Cal was only a dim memory for her. If the boy was too stupid to appreciate that, he didn't deserve her either.

She was up and running directly to him as soon as she caught sight of him. When she was close enough to be heard, she called out, "Is it over?"

Wearily he nodded. "For now, at least."

She flew into his arms, holding on for dear life as she looked behind him. "Where's Wade?"

He wished the thickheaded fool had been there to hear the barely suppressed terror in her voice when she didn't immediately see him.

"He's fine. I think he's checking on the herd."

"And Boone's men?" She looked at his injured companions with understandable wariness.

"Other than these two, they are either dead or running back to wherever they came from."

One of the men behind them groaned and then swayed in the saddle, almost losing his balance. Lily cried out and tried to support him enough to keep him in the saddle long enough to reach camp.

Once they were there, she conveniently seemed to forget that only minutes before, the two men had been doing their best to kill her and to steal her livelihood. Thea wasn't quite so forgiving, but she grudgingly helped Lily dress their wounds. Cal noticed that little of the gentleness Thea had shown Toby was evident in her treatment of the two would-be rustlers.

Once he knew the two wouldn't be any danger to Toby or the women, Cal did what he could to help by keeping the fire burning and throwing together a makeshift meal. He ached with near exhaustion, but there was too much to be done to allow himself the luxury of a few hours sleep.

Toby hobbled over to join him at the fire. "What are you going to do with the dead?"

Cal looked around to see how close Lily was. Dropping his voice, he told his friend, "If I didn't think Lily would protest, I'd leave the bastards for the coyotes and buzzards. We have enough to do without wasting hours digging graves."

"Why don't you load them up in the wagon and I'll take them back to that town and turn them over to the sheriff along with that pair?"

The idea made sense. If any more of Boone's men were lurking in the area, it wouldn't hurt for them to see what happened to those who messed with the McCords.

"See if Wade will go with you. I'd go, but right now I'm so tired that I wouldn't be much help if anything went wrong."

"Can we afford another day here?"

Cal shrugged. "You're asking the wrong man. Right now, the cattle are too stirred up to do much eating. They should be fine until morning. If you leave within the hour, you could be back by dark if you push the horses some."

"Makes sense to me." He picked up his crutches

and worked his way back to where Thea was watching Lily tie off the last bandage on her patient.

When Cal had breakfast ready, he waved the others over to join him. Wade rode up a few minutes later, in time to get his food while it was still hot. Cal left it up to Toby to get Wade's cooperation in dealing with the dead and wounded.

When the meal was over, the three men started the grim business of picking up all the dead that they could find. Since no one knew how many of Boone's men had escaped, they could only guess whether they had all of them accounted for. They'd carried down the nameless stranger that Lily had killed and laid him in the wagon with the others.

If there had been more, Boone's men had seen to them or they'd managed to get away on their own.

At last Toby snapped the reins and started the long trek to town. The small procession was a grim sight— the wagon piled with the dead and the two injured men, who were unable to stay in the saddle. Wade followed behind, his hand on his gun in case one of them made a wrong move.

As they rode out of sight, Cal prepared to leave the camp to check on the herd. Lily blocked his way.

"You need sleep more than those cattle need you watching over them."

He was in no mood to argue. "Someone needs to round them back up." Pointing out the obvious, he added, "With Toby and Wade gone for the day, that leaves me." He shoved her aside, but she'd have none of it.

"I don't care if we lose every steer out there. As tired as you are, you'd be more of a danger than a help. Now go find a nice shady spot and sleep for a while. If anything needs to be done, Thea and I will see to it."

Finally, he let her bully him into doing just what

she'd ordered. In truth, he wasn't sure how long he'd have been able to stay in the saddle now that the fighting was over.

Wearily he picked up his bedroll and laid it out in a small spot of shade near the campfire. Making sure his rifle was nearby, he was asleep almost as soon as his head hit the blanket.

Lily watched Cal sleep. Despite the horror of the morning, she had much to be grateful for. The cattle and the money they would bring at the railhead were important, but they didn't hold a candle to the people she had come to care so much about.

Wade was family, but somehow Toby and Thea had worked their way into her heart as well. And then there was Cal. She smiled as he stirred restlessly in his sleep. He'd be the first one to tell everyone how shiftless he was. At the same time, he'd stayed to fight her battles for her. She wondered if he realized how long it had been since he'd even mentioned the money Wade still owed him.

The man simply had no idea how wrong he was about himself. Admittedly, he'd gotten off to a rough start in life, but somewhere along the way he'd learned the importance of friendship. He'd lay down his life for Toby without hesitation, and he had proved that he'd do the same for her and Wade.

She felt Thea come up beside her. "How is he?"

"He's finally getting the rest he needs. The man seems to think he can do without food and sleep."

Thea shook her head. "Are you going to wake him up when he told you to?"

"Not a chance."

"He won't like that."

Lily giggled. "The worst he can do is yell, and by

then he'll already have gotten enough sleep. Besides, I'm not afraid of him. He'd never hurt me."

Thea didn't reply to that statement with words, but the look she gave Lily said very clearly what she thought. "Well, since we're not going to let him do anything about the herd, maybe I'd better go check on them myself."

Lily followed her. "We both will."

After picking up her rifle, she saddled her own horse and then helped Thea with hers. She was surprised to find how good it felt to be back in the saddle. They wouldn't do more than see how far afield the steers might have wandered, but at least they'd be doing more than hovering around the campfire waiting for the men to take care of them.

To her pleased surprise, it appeared that most of the cattle had stayed nearby. She and Thea took the time to work those that had strayed the farthest back near the main herd, but otherwise things seemed to be under control. They even managed to round up three horses that had been left behind by Boone's men. The animals weren't anything special, but they'd serve to give their other horses an occasional rest.

There had been a time that she wouldn't have even considered keeping the animals, but those days were gone. She and Wade and the others were in a struggle for their very survival. The men who no longer needed those horses had chosen to work for Boone. They'd known the risks and accepted his money for doing his dirty work without question.

Today, she and her friends had come out unscathed. It was hard to believe that their luck would continue to hold. Even Toby's injuries, bad as they were, wouldn't have lasting effects. There was a wagonload of men who hadn't been so lucky.

She signaled Thea that it was time to return to camp.

Thea called out that she'd stay awhile longer. Lily started to argue but decided that maybe it was a good idea that someone kept an eye on things. Not so reluctantly she returned to camp to see if Cal had managed to awaken on his own or if she would have to do the honors.

He was still curled up on his side, softly snoring away. Trying not to disturb him, she led her horse away and took care of its needs. When it was time to start dinner, she retrieved the necessary items from their diminishing pile of supplies.

About the time she had the fire going, she felt Cal's eyes on her. He was sitting up, looking around as if trying to figure out what time it was.

Seeing how low the sun was in the sky, his eyes narrowed in accusation. "You didn't wake me up when I told you to." He sounded like nothing more than a crabby little boy caught somewhere between sleep and wakefulness.

Since the dark circles under his eyes had all but disappeared, she didn't regret her actions, and she told him so. "No, and I'm not going to apologize for it. You needed the rest." She turned her attention back to dinner.

He joined her by the fire, sitting cross-legged at her side. "I assume that there haven't been any more problems."

"Other than needing to round up a few strays, things have been remarkably quiet." She poured him a cup of coffee. "Thea stayed with the herd, but she'll come in to eat."

For several minutes he sipped at the hot liquid and stared into the dancing flames. She wondered if he was still trying to wake up or if there was something on his mind.

"Are you all right?"

His softly spoken question startled her. There was no doubt that he was talking about when she'd saved his life at the expense of another. She'd done her best to block out the horror of being attacked, but most of all of having killed.

"I'll have to be. There's nothing I can do to change what happened."

"It was him or me."

She reached out to brush the side of his face with her fingertips. "I don't regret the outcome, only the necessity of doing it."

He caught her wrist and pulled her closer. She went willingly into his arms. His kiss was like a balm to her weary soul. This time their embrace was comforting rather than passionate, as if his touch alone was enough to heal her pain.

In the center of her being, she knew she loved this man. She let the knowledge settle inside her, but when the words slipped out of her mouth, everything changed. Cal jerked as if she'd slapped him rather than offering him her heart.

Then, with a look she couldn't begin to understand, he stood up and walked away.

Fifteen

Cal cursed for a full five minutes without slowing down or repeating himself. Hell, he didn't even know what had him so riled up. He'd known all along that Lily felt more for him than she should. If he'd been honest with himself, he would have known that she wouldn't have given herself to a man she didn't love, at least on some level.

But now he could no longer fool himself or her. As soon as she'd spoken, he'd had to bite his tongue to keep from telling herself the same damn thing. If he hadn't exerted all the restraint he could muster, the two of them would be doing more than kissing right now.

But admitting how he felt wouldn't have solved anything. The fact that the two of them loved each other didn't change what he was any more than it changed her. How could he have been fool enough to get mixed up with a good woman? And Lily—what could she be thinking of to let herself get involved with a no good son of a bitch like him?

She probably thought he'd forgotten about the money. He hadn't, but he'd also known from the first that he wouldn't take another penny from her. Sometimes he wondered if he'd have felt the same if she'd been thirty years older, or ugly, or still married. He'd like to think that he had some scruples, but playing what-if games never solved anyone's problems.

He knew he'd hurt her already by his abrupt response to her sweet declaration. Although he could tell by her expression that she hadn't meant to let the words slip out, he knew she'd still meant them.

His tirade was interrupted by the sound of a wagon approaching. Although it had to be Toby and Wade on their way back from town, he wasn't about to take any chances. He took off at a lope back to camp to grab his rifle. That was another indication of how off-balance he was. It had been only a matter of hours since they'd been under attack, and here he was, unarmed and alone.

Thea was with Lily when he reached camp. Both of them had their rifles at the ready, but neither of them seemed particularly alarmed.

"Have you seen them yet?" he asked, more to let them know he was coming up behind them than because he needed a response.

"It's Toby and Wade all right. I saw them from a distance when I was coming in for dinner."

That was one problem he no longer had to worry about. Although they'd been the ones under attack, there was always the chance that the sheriff might not respond well to a black man bringing in a load of dead and wounded white men.

He was the first to reach the wagon. Toby wearily tied off the reins and then painfully maneuvered himself to the edge of the seat. Cal held up his arm to offer Toby additional support as he slid down to the ground. He grunted in pain. After drawing a deep breath, Toby reached for his crutches.

Knowing his friend's need for independence, Cal stood back and let Toby hobble the rest of his way on his own.

"Get some dinner while I take care of the team. That way you'll only have to tell us what happened once."

"Sounds good to me," Toby agreed. "Wade will be along in a minute; he wanted to double back to make sure that we weren't being followed."

"That was good thinking on his part."

One of them would have to stand guard all night. Since it was obvious that Toby wasn't up to it, that left Cal and Wade. He'd do his share, but he was getting damn sick of being tired all the time.

Once he had the team unhitched and picketed with the other horses, he made his way back to camp. His welcome was lukewarm at best. Toby was busy trying to eat everything that Thea was shoving at him, while Lily fussed around Wade.

While Cal had always known how it felt to be on the outside of things, this made his status so clear that it hurt. Wade shot him another of his usual nasty looks, this one heightened by the knowledge that Lily hadn't immediately rushed to Cal's side.

He wouldn't give Wade the satisfaction of responding. For now, he was more interested in how soon they could get the damn cattle sold and everyone safely back to the McCord ranch. As soon as that was done, he'd be gone. And if that idea hurt, there wasn't a hell of a lot he could do about it.

He reached in his pocket and pulled out a worn deck of cards. After smoothing a place in the dirt, he dealt himself a game of solitaire. The rhythms and patterns of the cards as he went through the motions went a long way to soothing his restless irritation. It was a relief when the other two men finished their meal and Toby started talking.

"We took it slow going to town. Neither one of the injured men were much for talking, so it was quiet all the way there." He rubbed his leg for a few seconds before going on.

"Once we reached town, Wade rode ahead to find the sheriff and brought him to meet up with us. He took one look at our wagon and had himself a right big fit. Seems like Boone's men hadn't made themselves too popular in town. With the problems they'd caused there, he didn't have any trouble believing us at all."

Something in the memory made both Wade and Toby smile. It was Wade who explained.

"He was none too gentle about hauling the two wounded into his jail. He told them he'd get around to having the doctor look at them sometime. Then he slammed the cell door shut and walked out with us, leaving them sitting there."

Toby took up the tale again. "After that, he called a couple of locals to come carry off the dead. He asked if we'd be around when the judge comes through, but didn't seem too upset when we said we'd be moving on."

"I think maybe he didn't quite believe us when we denied knowing why they would have picked us to attack." Wade took a long drink of his coffee. "Leastwise, he did make sure to tell us that the rest of Boone's men had ridden through earlier. When they left, they were headed back the other way, but that doesn't mean much. We've done enough circling around ourselves lately."

Cal decided that it was time for him to get involved. The sooner they finished this fiasco, the sooner he could move on. "So what's our plan?"

Lily answered without looking at him. "We all get as much rest as we can tonight and then push on tomorrow. If we can avoid further trouble, we should reach the railhead within a few days."

No one seemed inclined to argue, but he wasn't convinced that Boone's men would give up that easily. Granted they'd lost several men to injury and worse, but these were hard cases. None of them expected to live all that long. For enough money, they'd keep coming.

He scooped up his cards. "I'll be back by morning."

Ignoring Wade's immediate protest, he headed for his horse. Setting his rifle down, he threw his saddle up on the animal's back.

"I asked where the hell you think you're going."

Of course it would be Wade who questioned him. Cal wasn't in the mood to explain himself, so he didn't. When Wade made a grab for the reins, Cal allowed himself the small pleasure of shoving the boy backward.

"I don't answer to you."

"Then tell me."

He hadn't heard Lily come up behind him. As much as he wanted to ignore her as well, he knew he couldn't.

"I'm going into town to play a few hands of cards."

Wade assumed the worst of him, just as Cal knew he would. "I'm surprised you've stuck around this long, Preston. But get this straight: if you leave now, don't be in a hurry to come back."

Cal clenched his teeth rather than his fists. He'd be leaving for good soon enough, but there was no way in hell that he'd let Wade send him on his way one minute before he was ready to leave.

Luckily for both of them, Toby came up behind them.

"You think they're coming back, don't you?"

Although he'd be only too glad to leave Wade in the dark, Toby deserved better. "Yeah, I do. I know things didn't go as they planned, but I don't see Boone hiring the type of men that give up at the first sign of blood. I can drift into town and maybe get into a poker game. If they're around, I'll find out."

"That's good thinking, Cal. Wish I could go along to watch your back."

"I'll go." Wade started toward his own horse.

"No, you won't." Before Wade's already short temper could flare, Cal gave him the only explanation that would make him stay behind. "Toby can't sit a horse. The women need an able-bodied man here if something goes wrong."

He looked to Lily and Toby for support.

Toby nodded. "Mr. Wade, I'd be a lot more at ease knowing you were nearby."

Wade accepted the inevitable even though he clearly did not want to. Toby followed him back to the campfire while Lily lingered near Cal as he finished saddling his horse.

"I'm sorry Wade always thinks the worst."

"We've gone over this before, Lily. Feeling like he does about you, he's not going to let up on me anytime soon."

"I know." She put her hand on his arm to prevent him from mounting up. "Be careful. Please."

"I'll be fine. You get some rest, and I'll be back before you know it."

"Do you really think they'll cause us more trouble?"

"There's no telling, but I'd feel a whole lot better knowing for sure. We were lucky this morning. We might not be next time if we're not careful."

She looked more resigned than afraid. "Hurry back as soon as you can."

"Yes, ma'am," he drawled with exaggerated politeness, hoping to make her smile.

It worked. She grinned briefly and then surprised

him by rising up on her toes to press a quick kiss on
his lips. Then she darted away, giggling.

He let her go, figuring the practice would do him
good.

The cigars were nothing to brag about and the whiskey was watered, but Cal didn't care. It felt damned
good to be sitting around a table with a bunch of
strangers, each one hoping Lady Luck was going to
be his companion for the night.

So far, she'd spread her favors pretty evenly around
the table. No one had lost more than he could afford
or won enough to make anyone mad. Cal had spent a
great deal of his adult life enjoying evenings like this.

"I'll take two." He waited for the cards to slide to
a stop and then added them to his hand. A pair of
jacks. Not a bad hand, but it wasn't going to make him
rich, either. With his attention divided between the
game and watching the flow of customers in and out
of the saloon, he kept his play cautious.

He didn't have all that much money to play with. If
he lost it all, he'd have no excuse to hang around the
saloon. As long as he was in the game, no one would
take particular note of his presence. He couldn't stay
all night, but it was early yet.

So far, he hadn't seen anyone who looked like the
type to work for Boone, but that didn't mean they
weren't around. Maybe the McCords had gotten lucky,
but he'd rather depend on luck at the poker table than
with his life.

The next hand was marginally better than the last.
He raised his bet and was pleased to be the one who
raked in the winnings. He'd give himself another hour
and then head back to camp. It was his turn to deal.

When he sent the first card sliding across the table,

there was a commotion at the door. Like everyone else in the saloon, he paused in mid-deal to see what was going on. Chances were it didn't concern him, but it never paid to be less than vigilant in a room full of armed men who'd been drinking.

He knew the minute the doors swung open that he'd been right all along. A group of four men came swaggering in, ready to take on anyone who was foolish enough to get in their way. While no one exactly ran out the door, Cal noticed several folks who waited until the four reached the bar and then sidled outside.

Others kept careful watch, waiting to see if it was safe to stay. Since this was the only saloon in town, they had little choice if they wanted to continue drinking or playing cards.

Cal didn't want to make himself conspicuous by bolting out the door, but he'd leave soon enough once he knew for sure that these were Boone's men. From years of practice, he managed to keep up the pretense of being fully involved in the game at hand.

Conversation at his table had been pretty sparse all evening, but he figured it was worth a try.

"Are they from around here or just passing through?"

The cowhand on his left shook his head. "Don't really know. They keep pretty much to themselves, although usually there are more of them."

The shopkeeper across the table spoke up. "They're here for a few days and then ride out again. I heard tell that two of them came back shot up today." His voice dropped to a whisper. "A couple more were dead. The sheriff wasn't too upset to have fewer of them around, I can tell you. They've been nothing but trouble."

"Why are they here?" Cal gathered the cards up and shuffled them again.

"No one knows for certain, but we hear all kinds of rumors. Some say they are bank robbers or rustlers. Others say they are waiting for someone." The cowhand muttered a curse under his breath when he picked up his cards and fanned them out. "Give me two. All I know, things are a lot quieter around here when they're gone."

After that, no one seemed inclined to keep talking, so Cal let the subject drop. Knowing he was a stranger himself, they'd think it odd that he was so curious. Besides, Boone's men weren't the type to appreciate anyone paying too much attention to their comings and goings. If he was going to get back to camp without arousing suspicion, he needed to blend into the crowd.

He continued long enough in the game to make sure no one associated his departure with the arrival of the gunslingers. He gathered up his meager winnings as he stood.

"Thank you, gentlemen. It's been interesting."

The cowhand gave him a quick smile, having just won a sizable pot. "Look me up next time you ride through. I wouldn't mind another game with you."

Cal laughed. "Since you're going to be eating off my money for the next week, that doesn't surprise me."

He glanced toward the bar. He needed to cash in his chips, but he wasn't particularly interested in getting too close to Boone's bunch. It was unlikely any of them would recognize him, but there was always that chance. He could probably take any one of them in a gunfight, but not all four.

He waited until they were all engaged in an argument about something and made his move. His luck held until the bartender handed over his cash.

The movement caught the attention of the man

standing nearest him. "Looks like you had a good night."

Years of gambling had taught Cal how to hide even the strongest of emotions. He'd hoped to get away without drawing any notice. It hadn't worked.

"Not bad. Did better than break even, anyway."

"Up for another game? I promise to be more of a challenge than they were." His smile didn't warm up the ice in his eyes at all.

"Sorry, maybe next time," Cal lied. "I'll be back tomorrow night."

The cold-eyed blond shook his head. "I won't be, not for a couple of days anyway."

"You looking for work?" Cal hoped the question sounded friendly rather than nosy.

"No, I've got a job. Pays well, too, if you're good with a gun. The boss might be looking for another hand or two."

Or more, Cal added silently.

"I do all right with a gun, but I'd rather make my way with a deck of cards."

"Suit yourself." He turned back to his companions, having lost interest in Cal.

It was all he could do not to run for the door. If Boone's men weren't planning on being in town for the next day or so, it was only logical that they'd be coming after the McCords again. He took his time walking out the door and maintained the slow pace all the way to his horse.

Once he was mounted up, he held the gelding in check until they reached the far end of town. No one seemed to be paying any attention to him, but he wanted to make sure. He rode a short distance and then led his horse off the trail to wait.

After counting off ten minutes or so, he decided that he was safe. If anybody had been intent on following him, they wouldn't have waited this long to hit the trail. He urged his horse into a fast walk. Even with the moon almost full, there wasn't enough light to risk anything faster. It was more important that he reach camp safely rather than quickly.

Sleep had been long in coming and then hadn't stayed around. Every little noise had her sitting up to see if it was Cal coming back. He'd promised to be back before morning, but she wished he'd make it earlier than that.

She rolled over on her back and stared up at the stars. For the life of her she couldn't figure out Cal Preston. On the surface, he was exactly what he appeared to be: a gambler with no roots and no ties. But if that was all there was to him, he would have given up the minute he realized that his half interest in the ranch was virtually worthless.

His behavior earlier that evening was another example of his complexity. He would have been perfectly content to let them all think the worst of him, that he'd take off to play cards and drink when they needed him. Instead, his real motives were almost noble.

"Miss Lily?"

It was Toby calling her. She scrambled to her feet and slipped over to where he was standing guard.

"What is it, Toby? Can I get you something?"

"No, ma'am. I thought you'd want to hear that Cal's back."

She didn't bother to hide her reaction from Toby's all too knowing eyes. A great sense of relief washed over her, leaving her feeling almost light-headed.

"I'll be going to bed now, if that's all right."

"Do you want me to take over?"

"No. If we were in any danger, Cal wouldn't be

walking his horse. I figure it's safe enough now for us all to get some sleep." He patted her on the shoulder. "Don't let him keep you up too long."

She could have sworn she heard him chuckling as he limped back to his own bed. Keep her up, indeed. The only reason she was going to wait up for Cal was to see if he had news for them. Otherwise, she'd already be back under her meager covers. Somehow, she doubted Toby would have believed that story any more than she did.

Cal loomed up out of the shadows. If she hadn't been expecting him, his sudden appearance would have scared her. She lit a lantern and held it up so that he could find his way into camp safely without him or his horse tripping over anything.

She closed her eyes to give them a chance to adjust to the sudden brightness. Cal was almost beside her when she opened them again.

"You're up late."

It wasn't much of a welcome, but then he'd been riding all night. She'd be less than friendly under the same circumstances.

"Toby woke me when he saw you coming."

He grunted when he swung down off the saddle. She knew tired when she saw it. She reached for the reins.

"I'll take care of the horse."

"I can take care of my own damn horse," he growled.

"Yes, but you don't have to. Now go sit down before you fall down. When I'm finished, I'll fix you something to eat if you want."

"No," he said wearily. "I'm too tired to do anything but lay down."

"Did you find out anything? Are they gone?"

"No."

He walked away before she could ask anything else, but then, she really didn't need to. If Boone's men were still in the area, there could only be one reason. Besides, their continued presence didn't change the plans for tomorrow. Even without the threat of attack, they needed to get the herd moving again.

She made quick work of unsaddling the gelding. After giving him a rubdown, she gave him feed and water and then left him to his rest. That done, she looked around for Cal.

He was already lying down, but she doubted that he was asleep. She crept closer to him in case she was mistaken.

"Go to bed, Lily."

"I will. I just wanted to thank you for what you did tonight."

"I played cards, smoked cigars, and drank whiskey." His dark eyes gleamed in the night. "Which of those are you grateful for?"

She smiled. "For risking your life to find out more about what we're up against. Now get some sleep. Morning isn't all that far off."

He turned on his side, facing away from her. She resisted the urge to settle his blankets around him. He wouldn't appreciate the fussing, and it was well past the time when she should seek her own bed.

She slipped away. His words followed after her. "Good night, Lily. Sleep well."

This time she had no trouble doing just as he ordered.

They'd had two days of relative peace along the trail. As long as he could ignore Cal, Wade almost enjoyed himself. The only real trouble had been when several steers had been startled into running by a couple of coyotes. Wade had managed to get out of the way, but barely. In the course of his escape, a branch had smacked him across the face, leaving him bloody but in one piece.

Lily had done a nice job of worrying about him, until he decided she was once again treating him like a child. Thoroughly disgusted, he knocked her hand aside and took care of wiping the last of the blood off by himself.

He knew he'd hurt her feelings, but he couldn't seem to help himself. The others kept telling him that he should be grateful for having Lily for his family. It was a sound piece of advice, but not one he could take. What he felt for her was nothing at all like what he'd felt for his brother.

No, he wanted her in the way a man wanted the woman he loved. The only reason he hadn't tried to kiss her the way he longed to was that he feared that she be repulsed. He couldn't live with that.

By tomorrow, or the next day at the latest, they should have the herd delivered to the railhead. Then it was only a matter of time before they'd see the last of Cal Preston. Maybe when he was out of sight, Lily would realize that what she felt for the man was only a passing fancy.

Wade hated that she'd kissed Cal in the exact way that he himself had dreamed about. And he strongly suspected that they'd done far more than kiss. If he weren't certain that Cal could outshoot him, he'd have called him out for that reason alone.

Every minute that he was forced to spend in Cal's company chafed. The only thing that was getting him through the endless days was knowing that each mile they walked took them closer to the time when Cal would leave forever.

Wade took advantage of the quiet to ride back to

the wagon and refill his canteen. Toby saw him coming and slowed the team to a stop. The injured man was doing a fine job driving the wagon, freeing the two women to help with the cattle.

"I'm out of water."

"We've got plenty in the barrels. Take what you need."

Wade hesitated only briefly before taking his hat off and dumping a full ladle of water over his head. He shook the excess from his hair, laughing when he managed to spray Toby with the flying droplets.

"That felt good. Want some?" He held up a ladle full of water.

Toby grinned as he reached for it. "Don't mind if I do."

When he was done, Wade treated himself to another cupful. The water cascaded off his head and soaked his shirt. The damp fabric clung to his skin, but it felt like heaven. Enough was enough, though, so he filled his canteen and mounted up.

"Keep a close eye on the horizon, Mr. Wade. Those men haven't got much longer if they're going to try to stop us from delivering the cattle."

"You don't think Boone's given up?" He didn't either, but they could always hope.

"Not a man like him. You've got something he wants bad enough to risk killing for it. That kind of greed doesn't fade away."

"You have your own rifle handy?"

Toby picked it up to show him. "I'll be fine. You and the others are the ones in danger. Even if you manage to dodge bullets, them damn steers are a skittish lot. They'll be as much of a danger as Boone's men if things get stirred up too much."

The sound of another horse approaching caught

Toby's attention. Wade knew without looking that it was Cal.

"You two decide to take a bath in the middle of the day?"

Before Wade could think of something rude to say, Toby spoke up. "Better now than never, don't you think? Wouldn't hurt you none to try it yourself."

"Maybe later. Actually, I was looking for Wade."

How dare the bastard check up on him. "Afraid I'm not doing my fair share?"

Cal ignored that. "I think it's too quiet."

Toby frowned. "You complaining about that?"

"No, but I don't trust it. I thought Wade might want to ride along with me while I do some checking on Boone's men."

That caught him by surprise. "You want me to back you up?"

Cal dismounted and reached for the ladle. Despite his earlier comment, he proceeded to dump some water over his own head. "You have a problem with that?"

"I don't know. Up till now, you haven't wanted me to ride with you. Why now?"

"Because I'm damn sick and tired of waiting for them to make the first move. We've been lucky so far, but if we let them pick the time and place, it isn't going to be where we can get the women to safety. I'm of a mind to do a little attacking on our own."

For the first time since Wade had met Cal, he felt like smiling. "When do we go?"

"Tonight. We'll stop early. It looks like we're coming up on some rocky places that could provide good cover for Toby and the others. After they're settled in, we'll do some hunting."

Cal's grin was wicked, and Toby's matched it.

"Sounds good to me. Don't tell Lily, though. She

won't want either of us to go if she knows what we're up to. Thea, too."

Toby shook his head. "You'll have a hard time fooling either of them. Even if you manage it, they'll be right angry when they find out the truth."

Cal swung back up on his horse. "Then they'll have to be mad. Something's got to be done, and soon."

"I'd better get back."

Wade rode away, leaving the two friends alone. Although he'd been about to wait for Cal to get a better idea of what he had in mind, he thought better of it. If he and Cal were suddenly to act friendly to each other, Lily would be immediately suspicious. Besides, it was only a temporary truce, anyway. Despite the common ground they shared, there was a division between them that couldn't be bridged.

Not as long as Lily stood right between them.

Even so, he looked forward to sundown. Like Cal, he was damn tired of being herded like the damn cattle. Tonight it would stop.

Sixteen

"Where are you going?"

Cal ignored the question, knowing that if he answered it truthfully the ensuing arguments would only slow him down. He picked up his rifle and saddle while Wade followed suit.

"Cal . . . Wade? I asked where you two are going? Thea's already out with the herd."

The two men looked at each other and then bowed to the inevitable.

"We're going hunting."

Lily put her hands on her hips, a sure sign that she wasn't buying what they were selling. She included Toby in the dirty looks she was handing out. "For what?"

The other two turned away, suddenly busy with nothing, leaving Cal to face her. "We're going to track down Boone's men."

That did it. "Of all the fool things! Toby, I can believe these two would try something like this, but you? Don't we have enough problems without looking for more? We haven't seen any sign of them for days."

"And that's what's got us worried. I think they're letting us do all the work of getting the cattle to the railhead. Now that we're no more than a day away, they'll come sweeping in to finish the job. Then they've only got a few hours of eating trail dust before they can sell the cattle themselves."

Before she could marshal any more arguments, Cal started saddling his horse. Wade did the same. It wasn't more than a minute before she started in on them again.

"Even if that's true, what can two of you do against all of them?"

"Maybe nothing. We won't know until we find them."

Lily took the stack of plates she'd been about to put away and threw them to the ground. Evidently that did little to vent her frustration, because she took to kicking them next.

Cal knew that if she caught any of them even smiling at her little fit of temper all hell would break loose, but he couldn't help himself. Wade made the mistake of laughing out loud. She turned on him.

"Don't you laugh at me, you oaf. The three of you made all these grand plans without bothering to discuss them with me or Thea. Have you thought about what will happen to us if you two manage to get yourselves shot up or even killed? Even if we can get the herd the rest of the way, what good will the ranch be to me without you?"

Oh, hell, the tears were starting. He fought the urge to give in and hold her. Instead, he and Wade exchanged looks and knew what they had to do. Seconds later they rode out of camp, leaving Lily behind.

"Cocky bunch, aren't they?"

"You'd think they'd at least have one of them standing guard."

Cal wasn't about to question their good luck. They'd managed to trail one of Boone's men right to where they'd set up camp. The two of them had hung back, not wanting to blunder into any traps.

They tethered their horses nearby, keeping them close enough to reach if things went wrong. It took longer than expected to work their way to where they could overlook the makeshift camp without turning themselves into targets. What they saw had them both shaking their heads because no one was standing guard.

"Boone probably never asked them if they could think. He was more interested in whether they could shoot. That doesn't take much in the way of brains."

Wade chuckled softly. "Any ideas?"

"Give me a minute." Cal continued to study the scenario. A couple of men were playing cards while three slept. A few others were busy cooking a meal, cleaning their guns, or doing nothing much at all.

The horses were all picketed together. His eyes started to move on but were drawn back. A glimmer of an idea started to form. Before he could put it all together, Wade tugged on his sleeve.

The younger man looked grim. "Can we take out that many men before they get to us?"

"Probably not," Cal told him. "But how far do you think they'll get without horses?" He pointed across the camp. "If I can work my way around to that side, I can drive them off."

Wade was looking decidedly cheerier. "It's a long walk back to town."

"You'll need to distract them for me." He handed Wade his rifle. He'd need his hands free to take care of the horses, and Wade would be safer if he could keep shooting. Between the two rifles and his revolver, he should be able to give Cal enough time.

"Keep an eye on that big tree to the left of the horses. When I get there, I'll wave my bandanna. Count to thirty and then start shooting."

"Do I shoot to kill?"

"You'd be better off keeping the whole bunch pinned

down as long as you can. Start picking them off and that'll just make the others more desperate."

Cal thought he saw relief flash across Wade's face. He figured that no matter what answer he'd given, Wade would have done his damnedest to do what was required of him.

"Unless you've got questions, I'll start out now. I'm going to go back to our horses and take mine with me. I don't want to be caught on foot once I run off their horses." Cal eased back down from their lookout point. "Good luck. If we get separated, wait for me at that small stream about a mile back. You'll recognize me right off—I'll be the one riding like hell for camp."

Wade managed a weak grin at Cal's remark and then turned back to watch the camp below. It dawned on Cal that somewhere along the line the two of them had reached an uneasy truce, at least for the night. He even trusted Wade to do a credible job of drawing fire from Boone's men long enough for him to free up the horses and get clear.

No doubt as soon they reached their own beds for the night, they'd be back to snarling at each other. It wasn't as if the biggest stumbling block to their friendship was going to go away anytime soon. No, as soon as either of them saw Lily, he'd remember how much he hated the relationship the other had with her.

Now wasn't the time to be worrying about that. Even though Boone's men appeared to be pretty lax about posting guards, that didn't mean stupid bad luck couldn't intervene. If he happened to cross paths with someone out for a stroll, all hell could break loose at the wrong time.

He made a wide circle around the camp in order to come in from the other direction. He led his horse, doing his best to slip through the gathering shadows undetected. Other than a couple of determined mosquitoes, he didn't run into anyone on the way.

When he was in position, he pulled his bandanna out of a hip pocket and waved it through the air. He hoped that Wade caught the brief motion, because he didn't dare wait until the gunshots started to approach the horses.

He securely tied his own horse's reins on a low branch. If he managed to get the others moving, he didn't want to have his taking off with them. When he reached the first of the horses, he grinned.

All of the animals were tied to a single rope. If he cut both ends, he could lead the entire bunch away at the same time. Once he put some distance between them and the camp, he and Wade could divide the animals between them. Since he had no desire to be caught and tried for being a horse thief, he intended on taking them back to the sheriff they'd met.

While the lawman might not believe that Cal had stumbled over the animals, he probably wouldn't ask too many questions. If Boone's men managed to walk back that far, he could easily return the horses, saying someone had found them wandering loose.

After cutting one end of the rope, Cal kept his head down and worked his way down the line, checking each set of reins. He reached the other end seconds before the first gunshots rang out. The horses stirred restlessly, but none of them panicked.

Cal started back through the woods with the horses trailing behind him. He heard a shout behind him and broke into a run. Although he hadn't thought about it in advance, being surrounded by a bunch of horses made for good cover. Even when Boone's men realized what was happening, they couldn't risk shooting at him for fear of killing their own horses.

He was glad that he'd tied his own mount because

it shied nervously when it saw the others coming straight toward it. He could have ridden one of the others, but none of them were saddled.

A shot shattered the branch over his head, causing him to duck down, not the safest thing to do directly in the path of the horses. He managed to keep his feet and tried for his horse again. The next shot hit the tree trunk a few inches from his head.

It was obvious that Wade had managed to hold the attention of most of Boone's men, but at least one had realized that they were being attacked on two fronts. Deciding he had no choice if he was going to get out of there unscathed, Cal yanked his horse free and vaulted into the saddle. Doing his best to keep low, he urged his animal into a run, dragging the others along behind.

His attacker yelled out for help. Cal couldn't make out the exact words, but there was no doubt in his mind that Boone's men were about to turn their full attention to stopping him. Wade's distraction had served its purpose, but now Cal was on his own. He only hoped that the boy had the good sense to backtrack pretty damned fast and get the hell out of there.

Lily would never forgive him if something happened to her brother-in-law.

He figured if he made it another few yards, he was in the clear. Evidently, his attackers thought the same thing, because suddenly the air was filled with bullets. That bad luck he'd been worried about earlier finally reared its ugly head. He felt a sharp sting in his right arm and then it went numb.

Unfortunately, that lasted only a few seconds. Burning pain exploded in its place, making it hard to hold onto the lead rope for the horses. If he dropped it, then all of their efforts would have been for nothing. Once they had their horses back, Boone's men would come after them with a vengeance.

Doing his best to ignore the pain, he wrapped another loop around his hand to make the rope more secure and kept going. Once he reached Wade, he could give in to the need to bind his wound. For now, he concentrated on staying in the saddle.

There was no need for secrecy on the way back to the rendezvous point, so he took the most direct route. He could feel blood running down his arm, accounting for the dizziness that had him reeling in the saddle. He sincerely hoped that the growing darkness was due to the sun's going down and not to his blood loss.

Finally, he caught sight of the creek. When Wade came riding straight for him, he offered up a prayer of thanks to whoever was up there looking out for him. He pulled back on the reins and hoped that the horses following close on his heels would slow up at the same time.

"Did you see those guys scrambling for cover when I opened fire? They looked like a bunch of jackrabbits looking for their holes." Wade was grinning like a fool, but the smile faded quickly when he got a good look at Cal.

"Damn, I was hoping we'd get away with it." He circled around Cal to take the lead rope from him. "Do you need me to take a look at that?"

Cal shook his head. Without the horses to worry about, he could concentrate on hanging on until they were a safe distance away. "Later. Right now, let's get the hell out of here. We got all the horses they had in camp, but we don't know if all of Boone's men were there."

For once Wade was willing to accept Cal's orders. Now that he had control of the string of horses, they could make better time. Once they hit the main road, the going was considerably easier considering how dark it was. When they caught sight of the lights in town, Cal stopped.

"We don't want to parade this bunch down the

street. I was going to take them to the sheriff, but now I don't think so. There's that corral out behind the stable at this end of town. Turn them loose in there."

The pain had settled into a dull throb, but it was getting worse again. He was beginning to have his doubts about being able to make it back to camp, figuring Wade might have to tie him in the saddle.

"Will you be all right for half an hour or so while I get rid of the horses?" Wade sounded worried.

"I'll have to be." He edged his horse off the road and into a small stand of trees. "I'll be fine until you get back."

Wade hesitated only a few seconds before turning away. The sound of the horses gradually faded into the distance while Cal concentrated on staying upright. He hoped like hell that everything would go well, because he wasn't going to be much good to anyone for a while.

It crossed his mind that he wouldn't mind Lily fussing over his injury like Thea had fussed over Toby. Of course, the chances of that happening were pretty remote considering how mad she was when he and Wade had left—but a man could always dream.

He filled the time counting the fireflies that flickered among the trees. Finally, the silence that surrounded him was disturbed by the sound of a solitary rider coming straight for him. In all likelihood, it was Wade, but Cal didn't take any chances. He remained back in the deepest shadows until he heard Wade calling his name.

"Cal? Cal? You ready to go back to camp?" Wade kept his voice to a rough whisper, no more anxious to reveal their presence than Cal had been.

He urged his horse forward. "I'm ready. Since I didn't hear all hell break loose, I assume things went as planned."

Wade chuckled. "I'd just finished turning the last

horse loose in the corral when the stable owner came out to see what was going on. I told him I was acting under orders from the sheriff. I left before he could check my story out."

"Nice thinking."

"I thought so," Wade agreed, clearly proud of himself. "Now let's get out of here before he finds the sheriff."

Wade circled closer and took charge of Cal's reins. "You work on hanging on. I'll get us back to camp."

Cal was only too glad to let his companion lead the way. He focused his full attention, as much as he was able, on gripping the saddle as hard as he could with one hand. He was fairly sure his wound had quit bleeding for the moment, but any sudden jolts could start it up again. He cradled his arm against his chest and prayed for time to pass swiftly.

Something was wrong.

Although both Thea and Toby had told her that she was worrying too much, she knew better. They thought she was fretting over nothing, but she was convinced that all had not gone well for Cal and Wade.

She had tried to get some sleep, figuring she might need all her strength when they finally got back. After dozing fitfully for a couple of hours, her eyes refused to stay shut any longer. When even lying down became too much, she'd crawled out of her blankets and taken a seat near the dying embers of the fire. She was beginning to wonder if she would ever sleep through the night again.

A few minutes later Thea joined her.

"I'm sorry if I woke you up."

Thea waved off her concern. "I figured you might like some company while you worry."

Lily picked up a handful of kindling and carefully

laid it on the fire. If both of them were awake, they might as well be warm.

The dry tinder caught fire quickly, providing a small circle of light in the darkness. For the moment, the flames were too few to cast much warmth, but Lily felt better already.

"You must think I'm acting crazy."

"No, you're acting like a woman in love."

Lily wrapped her arms around her waist. "Think so?"

"A body would have to be blind not to see it whenever you look at Cal." Thea gave her a knowing glance. "Of course, he feels the same way about you."

The quick surge of hope Thea's words caused died a quick death. It didn't matter how either of them felt if they faced a future apart. Try as she might, she could not picture Cal settling down any more than her father had been able to. The only difference between the two men was that her father gambled that the next place down the road would hold him, dragging a wife and family along with him.

Cal, at least, was honest enough to admit what he was. She couldn't fault him for that. He hadn't asked her to fall in love with him. In fact, he'd argued long and hard against it.

She picked up a bigger piece of wood and added it to the fire, thinking that her hopes for the future were as likely to survive the next few weeks as the log in the fire. Before her thoughts had time to sink any lower, she noticed that something beyond the yellow glow of the firelight had caught Thea's attention.

Her heart skipped and danced, hoping that the shadows would pull back to reveal Wade and Cal.

She got her wish, but her relief was short-lived. Wade came into view first. Some part of her mind took note of the fact that he was all in one piece and that other than looking tired, he was fine.

Her heart caught in her throat the instant she got a clear view of Cal. She was up and running for him before she even realized what she was doing.

"Cal, you're hurt!"

He managed a shaky smile. "But Wade isn't. That's the important thing."

"Don't be stupid." Did he think she didn't care what happened to him every bit as much?

When he suddenly slumped forward, she held up her hands to steady him in the saddle until Wade pushed her to the side.

"Cal, can you take your foot out of the stirrups? Good, now lean toward me and I'll catch you."

Wade staggered under Cal's dead weight landing on him, but with Lily's help they kept the wounded man from hitting the ground. Between the two of them, they half dragged him to a blanket that Thea had spread by the fire. She already had a kettle of water on to boil.

Lily dropped to her knees beside Cal and began working to get his shirt off. While her shaky fingers worked at the buttons, she quizzed Wade about their evening's activities.

"What did you two idiots do—take on the whole bunch of them by yourselves?"

"Not exactly."

Wade made a move toward the horses, no doubt trying to avoid telling her any more.

"And what does that mean? Did you have help from someone?"

He sighed and gave up. "No. We followed their trail to their camp. When we found the place, Cal saw that they had all their horses tied together. I kept Boone's men pinned down while Cal, uh, freed up their horses."

"Freed them?" She rounded on her hapless brother-in-law. "You mean that you two took up horse-thieving? Do you want to get hanged?"

"Oh, come on, Lily. We didn't exactly steal them. We gave them to the sheriff."

She prayed for deliverance. "And didn't he question this sudden bounty?"

"Don't know. I didn't stick around to find out. Besides, I needed to get Cal back here."

"Lily, don't take it out on Wade." Cal's eyes were open. "He did what I told him to. If you need to take a strip of hide off someone, it should be me."

She took one look at his bare arm and shook her head. "I don't have to. Someone else got to you before I had a chance." She reached for the clean rags that Thea had set beside her.

"Wade, you go see to the horses."

She waited until he thought he'd got away and called after him, "I'll deal with you later."

Cal's moan drew her attention back to his wound. "How bad is it?"

After lifting his arm into her lap, she wiped the blood away, careful not to start the bleeding again. "The bullet went straight through. It's hard to tell, but nothing seems broken. How does it feel?"

He managed a small smile. "You'll be happy to know that it hurts like hell."

She wasn't ready to let go of her anger, which had been fueled by fear and worry. "I'm glad. That'll teach you to be more careful."

She spent the next few minutes dressing the wound, making sure that it was both clean and dry. That done, she moved away from her patient.

"Don't go." His voice was barely a whisper. He reached out for her hand with his.

She shifted slightly, making herself comfortable. As long as he needed her, she'd stay. "Do you want something to eat?"

"Not yet. Right now what I need is some sleep. Lay down by me." He offered her his good arm.

The comfort of his touch was too much temptation to resist. She knew Wade might be upset, but at that moment she didn't care. Even though Cal's injury wasn't all that serious except for the loss of blood, if the bullet had been a few inches the other way, it could have easily killed him.

Without her ever reminding him how much he meant to her.

Another jolt like that last one and he'd give up and walk. He'd tried to tell Lily that he could ride herd for at least part of the day, but she was having none of it. Instead, he was stuck sitting next to Toby in the wagon. At least on horseback, he could have gone around the roughest part of the ground.

Not so with the wagon. And if he didn't know better, he'd swear that Toby was going out of his way to hit a few of the bigger holes. It would be just like him to show his displeasure with Cal even if the ride hurt his leg, too.

"Damn it, Toby, I thought you at least would understand that we had to do something."

His friend looked at him out of the corner of his eye. He flicked the reins to speed the horses up a bit before he answered. He also took the time to spit over the side of the wagon. "You weren't the one who had to stay behind and listen to the women wanting to wring your necks. I kept thinking they'd turn on me if you two didn't get back when you did. I acted real tired and went to bed early, figuring they'd take pity on me that way."

For the first time all day, Cal felt like laughing. "So she was worried about me?"

"Don't let it go to your head none. Remember, without you two, she wouldn't have anyone to finish taking the cattle to market."

As tired as he was of looking at the backsides of cattle all day, in some ways he dreaded the end of the trip. Once they'd sold the herd, it wouldn't take them long at all to return to the ranch. Once there, Cal would have no reason to stay.

And he wanted to. Maybe.

It was time to ask some tough questions, ones he wasn't sure he wanted to know the answers to. Most of them were for Lily, but a few only Toby could answer.

"Once your leg is healed, what are you going to do about Thea?"

Toby's eyes instinctively sought out the woman in question. She was trailing along behind the herd, looking as if she'd been doing that very thing for years instead of a matter of days.

"I want to marry up with her."

Even though his words came as no surprise, they still hurt. For so long, he and Toby had been closer than brothers. Now, that was going to change for good. But then, he always had been the outsider.

"What does she have to say about that?"

"I think I've about talked her into it. The problem is, she owes Boone money, more than the two of us can scrape together right now." Toby's expression turned fierce. "And I sure as hell ain't going to let her go back to working for him in that damn saloon of his."

"Then we'll have to convince him to take payments."

"Or else kill the bastard. Either one works for me." With that, Toby snapped the reins again, hurrying them all on their way to the end of the trail.

Trouble was, Cal was the only one who was in no rush to get there.

Seventeen

The view out the window made her sick, not that it had changed dramatically since she had first made the ranch her home. But now, it meant she was back home and that Cal would be riding out, if not tomorrow then the day after.

Blinking rapidly, trying to hold back the tears, she turned back to face Thea's sympathetic eyes.

"Talk to him. Tell him how you feel."

Thea had been saying the same thing to her for the past week. She wouldn't accept any of Lily's arguments to the contrary. If Cal didn't already know how she felt, then telling him again wouldn't make any difference.

"He'll still leave."

"You don't know that. Maybe you can give him a stronger reason to stay than he has for going."

"But he wasn't cut out to stay in one spot. My father was the same way. I won't raise a family with no place to put down roots."

Now Thea looked thoroughly disgusted with her. "He's never been wanted badly enough by anyone to keep those feet of his from wandering, so you don't know what he's capable of. Neither does he."

Her friend's eyes slid past her to look at the two men standing out by the barn. "I don't know anything about being a wife, but Toby seems to think that he can teach me. Your Cal was the one to give me the courage to try. If you weren't such a coward, you'd do the same for him."

The words stung, but Lily was through arguing. It didn't matter what she wanted if the man himself wasn't interested. Other than the few hours he'd held her close the night he'd been shot, he'd been avoiding her whenever possible.

Unable to resist the temptation, she joined Thea at the window. She cared deeply about all three of the men out there, but in different ways. Toby was a friend, and Wade was like a brother. He even seemed to have come to terms with that. She didn't know what had changed things for him, but she was glad that the strain between them had eased.

That left Cal. She'd done her best to memorize every detail about him: the exact shade of his hair and the way that it curled over his collar; the power and grace in the way he moved; the way his hands fascinated her. She had to wonder if he would always stand out so clearly in her memories, or if he'd fade until he was a vague image that made her smile.

"What are those three up to now?"

Lily leaned forward, trying to see what had Thea frowning. At first she didn't notice anything, but then she realized that Wade was counting out a pile of money into Cal's outstretched hand.

That was when all hope died. She thought he'd forgotten about the money Wade owed him, or at least was willing to forgive the debt. In her dreams, she'd even hoped that owning a half interest in the ranch would keep him there with her.

But then, even with the money they'd gotten for the herd, they didn't have enough to make the mortgage. They'd done well selling the cattle—better than expected—but they were still short. If Wade gave Cal the full payment owed him, the ranch was as good as gone.

She went charging out of the house with Thea right on her heels. Wade caught sight of her before the other two, but all three men were clearly unhappy to see them coming.

Lily didn't wait for any explanations and didn't ask for any. Eyeing the money still in Cal's hand, she said, "So you got what you came for, I see."

Neither of them took much note of Thea trying to shoo Toby and Wade away, leaving Cal and Lily to glare at each other. Wade pushed in between them.

"It's not like that, Lily. Listen to what he has to say before you get all huffy."

She frowned at the two equally. "Fine. If there's a better explanation for what I saw, I'd like to hear it."

Cal's expression was stony. "We know that Boone has been behind all your problems, but we can't exactly prove it. Even if we could, we'd need a U.S. marshal to deal with him. You know the sheriff isn't going to listen, and since Boone owns the bank, you're not going to get any sympathy there."

"I know all that."

Toby waded into the fray this time. "So the only way we can fight Boone on equal ground is at the poker table. The man is a gambler at heart. He'll have to accept a challenge or lose face with everyone around him. Cal has a better than equal chance because nobody plays any better than he does."

Lily didn't know which one of the idiots to yell at first. She'd almost come to terms with losing her home. Somehow, someday she might get over losing Cal. But taking what money they had and risking it on the turn of a card was more than she could deal with.

"No."

Wade threw his hands up in the air. "What do you mean by that?"

"I mean no. I'm not going to turn over my money for someone to gamble it away."

"Why the hell not?"

She kept waiting for Cal to explain himself, but he continued to let Wade do his arguing for him. Why would any of them even think this was a sensible idea?

Then Thea sided with the men.

"I hate to say it, Miss Lily," she said, falling back on her more formal manners, "but I think they are right. The worst that could happen is that Cal will lose the money and the ranch. You've practically lost the ranch already, so why not give it a try. Boone won't cheat at cards. His pride won't let him."

Lily wanted to scream. It was evidence how crazy they all were that their arguments were starting to make sense to her. But the real problem was that no matter how the poker game turned out, Cal would leave once it was over.

She'd hoped he'd stay as long as things were unsettled.

With the four of them ganging up on her, she didn't stand a chance of convincing them that they were wrong. The taste of defeat was bitter, and not a little frightening.

She met the gaze of each one of them, conveying her displeasure without words. Holding her hand out to Wade, she said, "Give me the money and then leave me and Cal alone."

Her brother-in-law reluctantly did as she ordered. Thea and Toby went with him. She waited until they were some distance away before speaking. Cal surprised her by standing quietly beside her until the others were out of hearing.

"I know you don't like the idea, Lily, but someone's

got to do something. You stand to lose everything, and none of us want that to happen. Short of robbing the bank or shooting Boone dead, we're about out of options here."

She knew all of that. But none of them seemed to realize what seemed obvious to her. Cal was doing exactly what she feared the most. He was walking away from the ranch to take up his life as a gambler again. Once he did that, her time with him was over. Forever.

There was nothing left to say. If Wade wanted to let Cal gamble with their money—actually, their lives— she wouldn't stand in their way. All she had left was her pride, and it was her pride that spoke next.

"Do what you want. If you win, fine. If you lose, fine. But don't come back here again." She thrust the stack of bills into his hand and walked away.

Damn Lily, anyway. He'd known all along that there would come a time when he'd have to leave, but he hadn't been expecting it to be so soon. He'd been sure he could keep finding excuses to stay on, but now that was out of the question. Delaying his departure wouldn't change things in the long run, but he'd hoped . . . Hell, it didn't matter what he'd hoped. Now wasn't the time to think about Lily, especially about the feel of her in his arms, in his bed.

Every step of the way to town, Lily's image hovered defiantly in his mind. He'd always thought her so strong. But when she'd handed him her last dollar, she'd seemed so brittle that the slightest breeze would have caused her to shatter.

How in the hell could she think that he'd been taking Wade's money again? The first time, he'd won the money fair and square. But now, he wouldn't have dreamed of accepting another dime of money from the McCords—either of them.

Despite her anger, he was going to do his damnedest to save Lily's home for her, even if she didn't approve of his methods. Once again, he did his best to shove ruthlessly away all thoughts of Lily, with those big dark eyes of hers.

Three hours later, Cal walked into the Silver Slipper. It had taken him almost that long to find the calm he needed in order to face Boone. After weeks on the trail, even his black suit felt stiff and strange. Comfort was important, but he also believed in dressing well for the game. A man couldn't hope to entice Lady Luck to his side in a game if he didn't take such things seriously.

The first glimmer of luck was with him. The man in question was standing at the bar talking to James, the bartender. Cal slowed his steps. If he went charging up to Boone like some knight on a crusade, his enemy would sense danger.

No, the game had to be Boone's idea, so Cal would have to tread carefully until the other man issued the challenge. There would be time to go for the man's throat after they'd played a few hands. Rather than pasting an insincere smile on his face, Cal did his best to look bored.

Boone took note of him almost immediately. Cal could feel the man's eyes on him as he made his way through the cluster of tables to the left of the bar. He kept his stance casual as he watched one game for a bit before moving on to the next.

About the time he was moving toward the third table, he felt Boone come up on his right side.

"Can't find a game that interests you?"

Cal shrugged. "Not sure I want to play tonight."

"Why not? Aren't any of these gentlemen," he said, waving his hand in an arc, "up to your standards."

Not wanting to insult an entire saloon full of men who'd been drinking all evening, Cal shook his head. "It's not that at all. I'm just used to playing for higher stakes."

Boone's smile had all the warmth of a wolf on the trail of a wounded deer. "Really? Why, we can't have you leaving without having at least a little fun. How about you and I sit down to a friendly game? I think I can afford it." He glanced at his watch. "Shall we begin in, say, twenty minutes?"

Cal studied his opponent for a moment before accepting the challenge. Finally, still maintaining his bored air, he nodded. "Why not?"

Boone looked over his shoulder to the bartender. "Bring fresh decks, a bottle of the good stuff, and a couple of glasses."

Cal took up a position at the bar to watch the preparations. Boone walked upstairs, leaving it to his employee to clear a table for the two of them. The displaced customers were waved away, their complaints ignored. Grumbling, they moved on to other games or else left the Slipper altogether. The man's power evidently knew no bounds within his kingdom.

In short order, the table was set. From somewhere, Boone had even found a couple more players, evidently also given to high-stakes play. Cal didn't complain. The more money in the game the better. The mortgage payment to Lily's ranch wasn't all that he was after.

He sipped his drink, waiting for Boone's return. Everything they did was a show of power. Each move strategic. Cal wouldn't sit down until just before the saloon owner did, so as not to appear too anxious. To delay his move without being obvious about what he was waiting for, he asked the replacement bartender to show him a selection of cigars.

A man could spend a surprising amount of time in choosing what to smoke. He'd picked out several by the time Boone reappeared. The other man slapped Cal on the shoulder as he walked by.

"Looks like you've got everything you need now. Let's not keep the others waiting any longer." As he led the way to the table, he offered perfunctory introductions.

"Jim Blakely, Jacob Daily, and Davis Black, may I present Cal Preston. I thought we might show him the kind of game that he's used to in the bigger towns."

Cal nodded to each in turn. "Gentlemen, shall we get started?"

Each man handed over a pile of bills to James, who was serving as dealer. As soon as everyone had a stack of multicolored chips in front of him, James tore the cover off the first deck of cards and expertly shuffled them. Then, with a deft flick of his wrist, the cards went sliding across the table to stop in a neat pile in front of each man.

Cal smiled at his opponents and reached for his hand. Spreading them out into a neat fan, he arranged them by value. Apologizing to the deuce at the end, he tossed it back on the table and waited for its replacement to come.

Meanwhile, he did a quick study of the others at the table. Only Boone had the cold-eyed demeanor of a man used to making his living by courting the lady. The others had other, more traditional professions, leaving them vulnerable to the few men who were willing to win or lose their fortune by the turn of a card.

They wouldn't prove to be any real competition over the length of the game, because they'd never be willing to gamble more than they could afford. Once the stakes became uncomfortable for them, they'd back out, leaving only Cal and Boone to face each other.

Cal couldn't wait.

Two hours later, the crowd in the saloon had thinned out considerably. Most of the remaining clientele had taken positions around the last remaining card game. Cal was only vaguely aware of their presence. On the other hand, he was acutely sensitive to every small detail about his two remaining opponents.

Of the original three besides Boone, only Jacob Daily remained, and he wouldn't be here for long. Most of his money was pretty evenly divided between Cal and Boone. The other two had left a fair portion of their chips behind when they'd walked away as well.

Cal was pretty sure that he and Boone had scared them off. If they'd had any illusions that they were skillful with cards, those ideas had been pretty well destroyed. Some men had killer instincts when it came to poker. Most didn't.

"I'll raise."

Boone threw in a couple of chips. Cal followed his example, but Jacob threw in his cards.

"That's too much for me. If you'll excuse me, gentlemen," he said as he stood. He walked away with his pride and very little else.

"Shall we take a short break?" Boone asked as he checked the time on his watch. "Say, fifteen minutes?"

Cal nodded. Trusting James to keep an eye on things, he walked out the front door of the saloon. He could use a breath of fresh air before the real game began. He'd done fairly well so far, but the real play had yet to begin.

A few minutes later, James came outside and took

up a position a few feet away. After checking to see that Cal was alone, he whispered, "How is Thea?"

Cal was careful not to look at his companion, in case someone was watching. "She's fine. I don't think she plans on coming back."

"Boone's still looking for her. If he finds out where she is, he'll send his men after her."

That came as no surprise. After a minute, Cal felt the need to ask, "So, where are his men, anyway? I didn't see many of the hired guns around tonight."

James shot him a questioning look. "Seems like they were delayed during their efforts to disrupt the McCords' drive to get their cattle to market. Something about their horses being stolen by another gang."

A slight smile was Cal's only reaction to that bit of news. Of course, they'd known all along that it was Boone behind the attacks. The only question left unanswered was why. It was worth a shot to ask James.

"I hear the McCords are a bit puzzled about someone's interest in their ranch." He kept his tone conversational.

Before James could answer, a group of rowdy cowboys tore down the street in a race, sending a few latenight pedestrians scrambling for safety. When things quieted down a bit, Cal tossed the last of his cigar down in the dirt and ground it into the dust with his heel. He pulled out his watch to check the time. His fifteen minutes were about over.

As Cal walked past, the bartender caught his arm. "It's a shame that the McCords had to go such a long way to sell their cattle. Next time they won't have to go to the railroad, since it's coming to them."

Cal chalked up yet another sin against Boone. The price for any land near where the railroad planned its right of way would skyrocket. He wondered how much of the land Boone had already managed to steal or buy.

It wouldn't do to sit back down at the table with his emotions ruled by anger. To play the game with skill took cold concentration, not hot temper. Once inside, he took a leisurely route through the tables to where Boone was already waiting. Cal didn't risk looking back to see if James was coming in right behind him.

He was relieved when he caught sight of him coming in the door that led to the back alley. The man had good survival instincts. Boone wouldn't hesitate to eliminate anyone who was disloyal.

James was the first one to sit down. He picked up yet another new deck of cards. As soon as Cal and Boone were seated, he had the cards flying across the table. Both men waited until the last card stopped sliding before reaching for their hands.

While they studied their cards, James laid out the rules for them. "Mr. Boone, Mr. Preston, the stakes have doubled. Nothing is wild. Play is limited to the money on the table or on your person. No IOU's. Do you both agree to the terms?"

Boone nodded, as did Cal. Though there had been a certain amount of tension in the earlier play, it had been nowhere near the level there was now.

Cal mentally counted his money. He was still a thousand short of what he needed to consider the evening successful. There was three times that on the table. He closed his eyes briefly and then opened them to see what the lady had sent him.

Two queens and an ace. He tossed the two others facedown on the table, asking for two replacements. Boone took one. That done, it was time to see which of them was the strongest.

At the beginning, the game was strangely silent. Even the other late-night customers respected their need for concentration. For some, it might have been the first time that they got to watch high-stakes play up close.

Boone finally broke the silence. "It's been some time since we talked about getting up a game. I thought maybe you'd left the area."

Cal met his gaze over his cards as he tossed a handful of chips into the center of the able. "I was helping friends."

Boone arched an eyebrow as he mentally calculated the bet and then matched it, adding a few more. "Anyone I know?" he asked as he waited for Cal to make his play.

It was time to make the game interesting. He tossed in some more chips even as he tossed out his answer. "I'm sure you do. It's a small town after all. I know for a fact that the McCords know all about you."

Boone's hand faltered only slightly as he reached for his chips. "Really. You don't look like a cowhand."

"And you don't look like a thieving bastard, but then appearances can be deceiving. I call." He spread out his full house, aces high.

It was hard to tell whether Boone was madder about losing the hand, or the fact that he'd been deliberately drawn into a game that could cost him more than the cash on the table. It didn't matter to Cal. Anger meant carelessness.

More of the crowd disappeared. It seemed as though no one wanted to be around when Boone's temper was uncertain. Even so, there was no way the man could back out of the game without losing considerable face in his own town. A gambler at heart, there was no way he'd leave, anyway. He'd been winning so long in everything he did that it would take an all-out disaster to convince him that Lady Luck had sided with someone else.

Boone made a brief recovery, taking a few hands,

and with them Cal's money. But that didn't last long. Not when Cal drew another full house to Boone's pair of kings. Now even James was looking nervous, no doubt wanting to be as far away as possible if Boone lost control.

"I hear another gang stole some horses from your men. That's too bad."

"And I suppose you know something about that as well." Boone's face had taken on an unattractive flush.

Cal ignored his comment as he waited for James to finish dealing the next hand. Before he picked them up, he leaned back in his chair.

"It's getting late. Do you want to make this the last hand?"

Boone tried to sound gracious; he didn't come close. "You're the guest here, but I'd like a chance to earn back some of my losses."

Cal had him and he knew it. "Fine by me. One hand for everything you've got left."

Even as he waited for Boone's decision, he was glad that neither Toby nor Lily was anywhere around. He'd already won enough to make the payment on the mortgage, and even enough for that other little matter. But the law would never punish Upton Boone for all the trouble he and his greed had caused. That left it up to Cal.

Boone glanced around the room to see how many were left watching, not that it mattered. The story would get around regardless of how few saw it first-hand.

"Fine." He reached for his cards.

Cal hoped that the lady hadn't proved fickle. He waited for Boone to see his hand before calmly picking up his own. One by one, he spread out his cards. The ladies were back. Three of them. He kept his emotions in check. Boone, too, looked pleased with his luck.

Cal only threw down one card, keeping the queens and a jack. James waited for Boone to decide and then dealt out the cards the two men had requested. This time Cal's hand was a little shaky. He hoped the others would forgive him if it was his ego, and not luck, that had driven him to risk the McCords' stake as well as his own substantial winnings.

But there was more riding on this game than just money. It was as if, should he convince Lady Luck that he was worthy, then maybe he could do the same with Lily.

The men around the table stirred restlessly, waiting for the two players to show their hands. After all, how many chances in one man's lifetime did he get to see a fortune change hands on the turn of a card?

Cal spread out his hand and carefully laid it down. One way or another, his life was about to change. Boone met his gaze with a smile and played the five cards that he'd been dealt. The crowd pushed forward to see which man would walk out empty-handed.

Like the gentleman gambler he was, Cal pushed his chair back, stood up, and offered his hand to his opponent.

To put it bluntly, Lily felt like hell. As soon as Cal rode out, she locked herself in her room and cried herself into an exhausted sleep. Now it was the middle of the night, and she and the coyotes up on the hillside were the only ones awake.

Not only that, everyone else had deserted her. Pride, which was all she had left, kept her from wandering out to the barn to seek the company of her brother-in-law and her friends. If they were still her friends. She was pretty sure that even Wade had disapproved of her actions, especially in telling Cal not to come back.

Of course, she hadn't really meant what she said, but it was too late to recall her hasty words. It wasn't that she didn't want Cal; she wanted him all right, but the way he'd been on the cattle drive. The stranger in the black suit was the gambler who'd turned her life upside down. She'd already lost half her ranch to a poker game.

This time, she stood to lose far more. If he took up his gambling ways again, then she would end up alone. She couldn't bear the thought.

What in the world could she do at this hour of the night? Morning was hours away, so cooking was out of the question. She'd already straightened up the house and swept the floors, twice for good measure.

Unable to stand being trapped inside the same four walls, she threw open the door to let in the night air. The coyotes were still complaining about their lot in life, and she could hear the sound of tiny feet scurrying under the porch. As company went, it wasn't much.

The slight breeze felt good on her skin. She turned her eyes skyward, trying to find some peace in the beauty of the stars splashed across the heavens. When she looked down, he was there.

He was still some distance away, but even in the dim light of the moon, she knew it was Cal headed straight for her. Her heart fluttered in her throat as she waited for her life's direction to unfold.

Despite her need to take back all that she'd said, the words wouldn't come. Instead, she watched helplessly as he headed for the corral. It took an eternity for him to unsaddle his horse and turn it loose. In the dark shadows of the barn, she lost sight of him, scaring her into thinking he'd gone inside.

But then, he stepped into a patch of moonlight. He'd taken off that hateful black coat, so his white shirt gleamed in contrast to the night shadows.

"I'm back."

"Yes," was all she could choke out. She had to grab the porch rail for support because her knees were shaking so badly.

"I know you didn't want me to gamble."

Now was her chance to apologize. "I shouldn't have said what I did. At the very least, I should have known that you wouldn't have taken our money this time."

He stepped up on the porch. She could feel the heat of his body across the inches that separated them.

"Yes, you should have." He took off his hat and ran his fingers through his hair. "I played poker with Boone."

She could only nod. He was in a funny mood, one that she couldn't read. "Did you . . . I mean . . . who . . . ?" Her words trailed off as she realized that it didn't matter who won or who lost. What was important was that Cal was back.

He moved a little closer. "Lily, I've been a gambler my whole life. I've told you enough about my background, and Toby's probably told you more."

This time, she was the one who moved. "None of that matters to me, Cal. I've told you that."

"Money has always been a way to pay for a night's lodging or my next meal. That's all. So when it came to gambling, I was never really risking much that mattered to me."

She reached out to touch his arm, hoping he'd accept that little bit of comfort from her. He rewarded her gesture by putting his hand on top of hers.

"Tonight I gambled with far more than I could afford to lose."

So he'd lost. As frightening as that was, she found it didn't scare her as much as it could have.

"We'll figure something out. After all, we built this

place from nothing. I expect we can do it again, especially with some help from friends."

There, she'd extended the invitation. She held her breath to see if he'd accept it.

He turned to face her head-on. With the crook of his finger, he lifted her face up to look him straight in the eyes. The small patch of light that came through the open door etched his face in stark relief.

"I wasn't talking about money, Lily. I'm talking about you, or maybe I really mean us. I don't want to leave, but you have to want me to stay."

Hope flickered to life. "I've thought all along that you could learn to be a rancher."

"Not unless I can be a husband, too."

She was in his arms before either of them could draw another breath. When his lips found hers, she felt as if both of them had finally come home.

"Shall we tell the others?" she asked breathlessly when he finally gave her two seconds to think.

He grinned at her, all the day's worries gone from his face. "Not now. There'll be plenty of time tomorrow. We've got better things to do tonight."

With that, he swept her up in his arms and carried her inside, kicking the door shut behind them.

"What do you think it means?"

Thea seemed reluctant to approach the house. As soon as they'd seen Cal's horse in the corral, they'd known something was up.

Toby spit on the ground and shook his head. "I'd guess they finally figured out what we've been telling them all along."

He looked over at Wade, who studied the house with a troubled expression on his face. "You going to be all right with this, boy?"

Wade looked more resigned than angry this time. "Don't have any choice. He'd better be good to her, though, or he'll answer to me."

Toby patted Wade, no longer a boy at all, on the shoulder. "He'll answer to both of us."

Cal and Lily took the problem of whether or not to approach the house out of their hands. The two of them came outside arm in arm.

"Morning, Cal; morning, Miss Lily."

Cal nodded at Toby. "Good morning, Thea. Wade."

The last name was a softly spoken challenge.

Wade ended the tension. "Morning, Cal, Lily. We were just wondering how last night went."

When Toby saw how guilty both Cal and Lily looked, he shook his head. "He meant the poker game, Miss Lily."

Her embarrassment worsened. "I forgot to ask."

Toby burst out laughing at the two on the porch. Thea quickly joined in. Even Wade grinned and threw his hands up in the air. "She forgot to ask."

Cal took on a solemn expression that Toby didn't quite trust. After all, the man had learned to school his features into a mask years ago.

"You did play."

Cal nodded. "I did at that."

"And?"

With a loud whoop and holler, he grabbed Lily and swung her around. "I won enough to pay the mortgage and to restock the herd, if that's what you all want to do."

When he finished swinging her, he charged over to Thea and pulled a tattered piece of paper out of his pocket. She took it from his hands and slowly unfolded it.

"This is my note with Boone."

"Yes, ma'am, that's what it is, all right."

"But he marked it paid in full."

"That's because it is."

"But . . ."

He didn't give her a chance to finish her thought. Instead, he twirled her around just as he'd done Lily. When he set her down, she buried her face in Toby's shoulder, tears streaming down her face.

Toby held onto her with every ounce of strength he could muster. He figured it would be another fifty years or so before he'd have to let go.

Cal and Lily slipped away, leaving Toby to tend to Thea, and Wade to himself.

Lily waited until they were alone and then gave Cal a taste of what she had in mind for him later. He accepted her gift with great pleasure.

Finally, he tucked her head against his chest, memorizing the feel of her body's fit against his. As he did so, he thought about that other lady in his life and was grateful for the last lady she'd sent him: the queen of hearts.